---------- ★ ----------

The duffel's fat zipper sticks at first and he has to work it down little by little. Strands of red hair, caught in the teeth, trail out onto the sand like man-o'-war stingers.

He works the zipper all the way down and gently separates the two sides. Inside, Jackie is folded in half, nose to knees. Her arms stretch toward her feet like a diver in mid-jackknife. Her skin glows the waxy white of plants kept too long from the sun. The jumble of jagged rocks weighting the duffel have gouged and torn soft flesh. Seawater has turned her strawberry silk dress the brownish red of dead leaves. Tiny crabs skitter all around.

Kolby reaches in, moving the head to one side so we can see. Particles of sand stick in odd places. Her eyes, partially open, stare vacantly. Her mouth forms an O as if surprised.

"Is this Jackie?" he asks.

---------- ★ ----------

"...brisk and breezy...the heroine is a sparkling ball of energy..."

—Harriet Klausner Internet review

Previously published Worldwide Mystery title by
SUSAN SUSSMAN with SARAJANE AVIDON

AUDITION FOR MURDER

CRUISING
FOR
MURDER

Susan Sussman
with Sarajane Avidon

WORLDWIDE.

TORONTO • NEW YORK • LONDON
AMSTERDAM • PARIS • SYDNEY • HAMBURG
STOCKHOLM • ATHENS • TOKYO • MILAN
MADRID • WARSAW • BUDAPEST • AUCKLAND

For my brother, Art Rissman, at peace in the trout stream
—S.S.

For Dick Simpson, August Donley, Kate Donley
and O.D. (wherever you are)
—S.A.

CRUISING FOR MURDER

A Worldwide Mystery/June 2002

First published by St. Martin's Press, Incorporated.

ISBN 0-373-26424-0

Printed in U.S.A.

Acknowledgments

Thanks to actors Kat Hart and Iris Lieberman; musician Elaine Burke, entertainer Renee Peterson, cabin stewards Bettina Whiteford and Brian Thompson, Roland Boudreau, guest relations manager, American Hawaii Cruises; Actors' Equity Central Regional Director Kathryn Lamkey and old friend and troubleshooter Carol Black; David Stanley, vice-president, Royal Caribbean Cruise Line; Scot Hill; Mary Lyons; Belle Lyman; Michael Weir; cruise mavens Jonnie Ballis, Carolyn Shear, JoAnn and Kenneth Rifkind, Sandee and Al Burger; herpetologist Corey Blanc; Kathy Bloch and the Asher Library; agents Jane Jordan Browne and Annette Green, and our wonderful editors on both sides of the ocean, Kelley Ragland and Gillian Green.

Authors' disclaimer: Our profound thanks to all who took time to answer our questions, share their expertise and take us on tours of ships. We received, as always, the best possible attention and information. And, as usual, we beg understanding from one and all for those places where it has been necessary to bend truth to create fiction.

DAY ONE

PROLOGUE

SHE SWAYS DOWN the deserted passageway. This is the worst night yet. Seasick on top of morning sick. All the saltines and apple slices in the world can't calm this nausea. Won't someone please turn off the motion machine?

The ship rocks violently bouncing her wall-to-wall—a pinball in a machine gone mad. Why didn't someone warn her about the constant demands of working a cruise? It's exhausting being "on" all the time. At least back home her offstage life was private. Not here. Not in this floating city where she's expected to be a "Little Ambassador of Goodwill" to two thousand passengers twenty-four hours a day, seven days a week, six months straight. Hard enough in the best of times, impossible now when all she longs for is to lie down and not move until the nausea passes. Which it never does.

The ship heaves again, slams her against the handrail. Two young Filipino crew stride past, laughing, talking, gaits as steady as if walking on land. The sharp bite of bile burns her throat. She is not cut out for this.

She slows outside the bicycle hold, slips inside. The metal door clangs shut behind her. Dim safety lights glint off hundreds of handlebars, thousands of spokes of the ragtag junkers crew members bargained for a few dollars at island flea markets. Her eyes strain against the dark. He's not here. No one is here. Then where. . .

Something skitters past, brushes her leg. She jumps. Screams.

Nothing. It's nothing. Get a grip.

Her nerves are rubbed raw—sleepless nights, exhausting days. If only she had someone to talk to. Four thousand humans on this ship, and she's never felt more alone. Water, water everywhere. . .

Where is he? He wasn't in the cabin. She was so sure she'd find him here at one of those all-night craps games she'd heard whispered about. Reggie denies they exist. He denies a lot of things. It's what liars do. What made her believe that a man who cheats on his wife would be truthful to his lover?

She leans back against the cool wall. "Not 'wall,'" Reggie would snap, "bulkhead. On a ship it's called a bulkhead!" He's tried to make a sailor of her. What's the point? As soon as her contract's up she's out of here.

Time is running out. Should she keep the baby or—

A rustling in the corner. She holds her breath, listens hard. Nothing.

Should she keep the baby? She should have decided weeks ago. But she'd prayed the problem would take care of itself. Hadn't college friends who thought they were pregnant gotten their periods? Hadn't her own mother had two miscarriages? She kept waiting, hoping.

"Time's up," she says. The cold air swallows her voice.

She's heard of a doctor on Nassau. Cheap, fast, "cheap" being the operative word. But she doubts it's possible to abort in the morning and perform the "French Follies" high-kicking cancan number at night.

And if she decides to keep the baby?

And do what with it? Raise it like her mother raised her and her twin brother, supporting them by waitressing for snotty college kids in campus diners, fishing tips from under overturned water glasses? No thank you. And you can forget office skills. What she is good at, very, very good at, is musical theater. Yeah, right, she and a thousand others all fighting for the same few parts. Only a handful of the shoreside performers she knows make a living at it. None of them has children.

Something crashes nearby. She listens against the darkness for other sounds. Footsteps. Voices. Nothing. Only the steady thrum of the engines pulsing like a heart.

She could carry the baby to term, give it up for adoption. But how will she survive the next seven months? Where will she live? What will she do? Her meager savings won't stretch that far. She's heard about attorneys who pay all expenses if you sign the baby over to their clients. Where do you find someone like that? Her head throbs. Adoption is too complicated to even try to figure out.

Scratching noises. Rats? Panic whispers along her nerves. The ship pitches again.

What other options does she have? She's not ready to raise a child on her own. And forget any help from Reggie. They'd been clear from the beginning theirs was a shipboard romance. No. "romance" is too strong a word. "Accommodation" is more like it. She's lively, good company, available. He has an officer's stateroom with a view and a real bathtub.

He also has a wife and four kids in San Diego.

Another sound. Sometimes, in rough seas, bikes fall over, toppling one into the next like dominoes.

Her brother senses her unhappiness, has been reading the darkness between the lines of her cheery postcards home. He wants her to come home. She will, she promised, as soon as her contract's up. She honors contracts, not like the father who walked out on them and never looked back. The ship pitches. A wave of dizziness and nausea spins the room at a crazy angle. Maybe if she stays very still she won't feel so sick.

Two crewmen burst through a small doorway next to her. Their arms are linked through those of a drunken friend they're dragging between them.

They startle when they see her, eyes wide with fear. Crew caught drunk on duty are fired on the spot, put off-ship at the next port. She has enough problems, doesn't need theirs. She'd tell them if she spoke Spanish. They drag their buddy past her without a word, disappearing through a door in back.

They must have come from the craps game. She'd got it wrong, the craps game isn't in the bicycle hold, it's next to it. That's where Reggie is.

She pushes against the door, has to lean her full weight to get it open. It's time Reggie knew. She doesn't have to go it alone.

IF...

IF MY ROLE in "Rent" had been less physically grueling like, say, running a marathon backward...

If Chicago weren't being battered by its most brutal winter since the ice age...

If I weren't struggling to get through this final day of an exhausting eight-month run...

If a rabid fan hadn't broken through my comfort zone, leaving notes, flowers, and poems outside my apartment door...

And, most of all, if I weren't becoming nervous about my relationship with one homicide Detective Roblings...

If all these elements hadn't converged at the exact moment of Kathy's call, I never would have accepted her offer. Never.

"If, if, if," as Grandma Belle says. "If cows had wings they could fly."

But all these things did converge. And I accepted Kathy's offer. Plea, really. If only I'd taken a moment to think things through.

If.

Let me explain something. Working a megahit like "Rent" is a Jekyll-Hyde experience. Kind of a cross between being featured on the cover of *People* the same time you're trying to survive the Bataan Death March.

Okay. That may be a little extreme. But just a little.

Heading into the last week of the sold-out run, when the physical/mental/emotional exhaustion wouldn't go away, when I'd gaze out my apartment window at Chicago's latest blizzard and dread the long shlep to the theater, when I had to drain every reservoir of strength to get "up" for a performance, I made a list to remind me how blessed I was.

The upside of an eight-month run:

1. "Rent" lets me pay my rent on time.
2. I supplement my usual meals of discount tuna and Ramen soup with real food. The kind you need teeth to chew.

3. I've been able to stash a few thousand shekels for the inevitable hard times ahead.

4. My body—too long away from the rigors of dance rehearsal and performance—has, once again, grown lean and mean. (Grandma Ruth complains I'm too thin. It's a sure sign I'm looking buff.)

5. I score points with family and friends who fight over my meager allotment of free tickets. In the downtimes between jobs, I'll trade these points for meals. Figure an eight-month run, two free tickets a week, that's a lot of good eating. (My brother Paul, renowned city snob and social cynic, claims our Highland Park cousins scalp their tickets, use the money to support their Starbucks latte habit. Fine by me. My cousins can whittle those tickets into toothpicks for all I care, as long as they feed me.)

6. For the past eight months, I haven't had to say those dreaded three-and-a-half little words: "I'm between jobs."

So, I was truly grateful for eight months of regular work. At the same time, I was relieved the run was nearly over. The show and most of our cast were moving on to Seattle. If I were smart, I'd go, too. But I can't stand long runs. Repeating the same lines, dance routines, and songs drives me to the brink. I figured out a long time ago that my particular personality craves variety more than security.

This is probably why my career has more erratic jumps than a North Avenue Beach checker game. In the last five years I've worked legitimate theater in three states, appeared in two feature films, taped Italian-French-Spanish-and Bronx-accented voice-overs, played a young wife, corporate attorney, and loving daughter in assorted commercials, recorded one Book on Tape, and danced my way through three convention trade shows.

"A Jill of All Trades," Dad says.

"Restless," says Mom.

"Attention Deficit Disorder," says my sister Sylvia, the Czarina of pop-psychology.

"I just bore easily," I say.

Which helps explain why I'm still single, and why I'm jittery since the relationship between Chicago homicide Detective J. Roblings and moi broke the one-year barrier. This is a new World Commitment

Record for me, folks, and I'm having a real hard time dealing with it. But I digress.

My tendency to become bored might also help explain why I'm so frequently "between jobs." I rarely know if my next paycheck is days, weeks, or months away. It can be downright scary, staring into a fridge that's empty except for my last two tins of tuna. Somehow, during the past eight months of regular paychecks, I'd forgotten. But it all comes back to me during "Rent's" final week. Little nervous tremors twist my stomach. I begin phoning Flossie "agent to the stars" Feingold, who, as far as I can tell, isn't breaking her neck lining up my next job.

"You really should consider the Seattle thing," she says. "Stay with the show. You already know the part." She puffs one of her perpetual cigarettes, blows smoke into the receiver. I hear remnants of a New York accent, which is strange since Flossie hails from Munster, Indiana. "You know, Morgan, there's nothing wrong with earning a steady income." Puff, puff. "It's not like anyone's beating down my door for your glossy and bio."

Really? I hadn't noticed.

My friend Kathy Bloch's call came the last Saturday of "Rent's" run. I'd finished the matinee and slogged home through freezing sleet and gale-force winds to rest before the evening's performance. By the time I trudged three flights of stairs to my apartment, all I wanted was to crawl under my cozy quilt and never climb out again.

The telltale corner of a blue envelope stuck out from under my door. Another love poem hand-delivered by my anonymous fan. It's one thing when fans leave missives at the theater. There is a romantic history of Stage Door Johnnies waiting hats and roses in hand. But this is creepy. I'm spooked that he can get into the building, deposit notes and poems and flowers at my door.

For a long time, I didn't mention this to Roblings. I hate sounding like one of those helpless females who can't handle her own stuff. On the other hand, what if the guy isn't so harmless? I finally told him.

"You have a stalker," said Roblings.

The word sent shivers. "I don't think it's anything that serious."

"Are the notes lewd, threatening, crazy-sounding?"

"Actually, they're poems, mostly. Very sweet."

"So, you don't have a feeling he's dangerous?"

"Not really."

"Except he's getting into your building."

"Right."

"Think about it." I did. The thoughts weren't comforting. "I'll look into it," he said.

I tossed this new envelope, unopened, on a stack of similar envelopes. I might read it later. Might not. Normally, I am dangerously curious. It gets me into all sorts of trouble. But just then I wanted out of my wet clothes.

I dialed up my voice mail and listened to messages while I unwrapped sodden layers.

"Hi, Morgan! It's Kathy!" Her raspy voice fires words like bullets. "I'm calling from the ship. Look. I know this is last-minute. But I need you. I mean, I really *need* you! This is an emergency! One of my girls broke a leg in Puerto Rico, Jet-Skiing with some ding-a-ling passenger. Another gal...um, left us. So I called the production agency and they found one replacement. Said they can't scrape up more until after New Year's. Which means I'm still one short. Basically, I'm doing a 'Best of Broadway' show tune medley, 'French Follies,' and a Latin night. The kinds of things we used to do. I can teach you all you need in about two seconds. The other nights you just help out with Passenger Talent Night, Country Western Theme Night, that kind of thing.

"Think palm trees," she says. "Think working two shows a night and having the rest of the time to lounge around the pools or go on land excursions, or roam secluded romantic islands or crawl into your bed and sleep. Whatever. You've done this. I don't need to tell you it's the best job on the planet."

You have to understand that, as she's giving her spiel, snow is dripping off my clothes and puddling on the floor. My frozen feet, blissfully numb until now, begin to thaw, pulsing sharp pains up the toes. All feeling is gone from my cheeks and I am positive my left earlobe is frostbitten. So I am listening to Kathy's monologue with particular interest.

"I know you hate long commitments. You'll be taking over Angela Parker's contract. It has three more weeks. Then you're free to do whatever. You'll get her full salary plus round-trip airfare and transportation to and from the ship. Please, please, please! Call me as soon as you get this."

Timing, as They say, is everything.

I dial. Seaman something or other answers, takes my message, repeats it exactly word-for-word, and assures me it will be delivered to

Kathy's cabin. I haven't said yes, but I haven't said no, either. I'll wait until after tonight's performance when my head is clear and I know more of what Kathy has in mind.

Around one o'clock in the morning, I roll in from the cast party. It's only a few hours since the play ended but I already feel the dark weight of letdown that follows every final performance. I try shaking it off but it is, in its own way, the end of the world—my world these last months. Monday I go back to work sorting through other people's treasures at Junque and Stuffe and nudging Flossie to line up auditions so the whole crazy process can begin all over again.

Kathy has left a phone message, answered all my questions, and left my flight information.

Within an hour I've

- packed
- left messages at police headquarters and home for Roblings telling him where I'll be, giving him the ship's number
- left a message for Flossie telling my agent what I'm up to and how to reach me in case Spielberg calls
- slipped a note into Mr. Diego's mailbox, warning my building's super that I'll be away three weeks and he or his nephew-in-training should check my apartment at least once a day for frozen pipes
- left an effusively apologetic message for poor Harold who was counting on me to train the other actors he hired to staff Junque and Stuffe through the Christmas rush
- called my friend Beth's answering service asking her to collect my mail, pay urgent bills, water my plants, take any perishable foods she can use from my fridge.

It's too late to call my folks. If their phone rings after ten o'clock at night, they think someone died. I'll call tomorrow from Miami.

It's not until I'm flying thirty thousand feet above the Earth that all the reasons I vowed never to work cruise ships again begin trickling back.

Too late. I'm committed.

I should be.

MONSTERS

MONSTERS. BEHEMOTHS. Leviathans.

Terrifying constructions loom in the port of Miami. Blinding white edifices soar twelve stories into the sky. I stand dwarfed on the dock staring straight up. The ships tilt toward me. Falling, falling.

Evidently, a couple of things have changed since last I worked cruise ships. Size for one. Size for another.

I look away, take deep breaths against a sudden foreboding. These are nothing like the ships Kathy suckered me into working on after college. The *Constitution* and the *Independence,* twin sisters sailing endless loops around the Hawaiian islands, had V-shaped hulls, reasonable proportions. You could point to them and say, "These are ships."

But these…these… I risk looking again. High-polished brass fittings glint in the Florida sun. Kathy's ship, the *Island Star,* floats among five other giants the size of hotels—very large, elegant hotels. Only their titanic smokestacks and the ropes tethering them to land give them away.

I can't move, stand grounded like a rock in a creek as people flow around me, up the gangplanks. My heart's jitterbugging. I'll be fine. I just need a little time to get used to the amazing size, screw my courage on straight before I board.

Two officers, striking in their crisp dress whites, stand at the base of the gangplank acting as official greeters. When I worked the Hawaiian cruise, officers were the prime targets for female passengers on the prowl. The first night at sea was like a feeding frenzy, the survival of the fittest at its most vicious. Many a boredom-filled night down in the crew's quarters, Kathy and I were subjected to woeful tales told by frustrated musicians, waiters, and stewards waiting further down the pecking order. It might be worse this trip, more passengers vying for each officer. Or better, more passengers available for the second tier. Like anything in life, it all depends on your point of view.

A bank of pay phones stretches between the *Island Star* and me, reminding me I need to call my folks. They think I'm home in Chicago sleeping off the cast party. I join the long line of crew and passengers waiting to make calls.

The sudden whine of a construction crane startles a flock of seagulls. They fly up complaining, settle further down the dock. The crane lifts a red container car out of the ship's hold and sets it gently on the bustling dock. Similar cranes work the ships up and down the pier, unloading empty supply containers, loading the new. Crew swarm the area. They have only a few hours to restock supplies for several thousand people.

The phone line moves quickly. Five more to go. Men in blue uniforms prowl the cargo area with dogs. Sniffing for drugs, I reckon. The dogs seem friendly but disinterested. A gaggle of kibitzers stand hands clasped behind their backs, rocking on their heels, overseeing the cargo loading operation. Retired gents, I'd judge from their gym shoes and gray hair and keen delight in watching other people work.

The phone line moves up. I'm next. Yesterday, standing in the blizzard, I thought I'd never thaw. Today I'm melting. My turtleneck's strangling me and my black slacks are a sun magnet. How come the other women in line knew to wear sundresses, shorts, halter tops? A willowy redhead near the cargo area wears an aqua cotton dress with big bold butterflies that would look knockout on me. I'd love to ask where she bought it but it doesn't seem a good time to interrupt. She's arguing with her boyfriend. I assume boyfriend because they're in mid-jilt from the looks of it. I assume they're arguing because, even though their voices are low, their body language speaks volumes...all of it angry.

I study how they stand, mimic the hunch of their shoulders, the tight crossing of their arms. I start to feel the anger, my heart rate climbing, neck muscles tightening. Suddenly, she jabs his chest a few times with her finger, then stomps off toward the ship. He comes storming past me, his features distorted by rage. Mashed nose. Heavy brow. Scarred lip. Basic boxer or Cro-Magnon type. My face hardens as I track him, my brows draw together, lips lift in a slight snarl. I feel his anger, yeah, I'm inside it now. Good. Got it. An elderly woman in line behind me stares wide-eyed, backing away as I turn my rage face toward her. Sometimes I forget there are civilians around. My species should be required to wear signs: *Danger, Actor at Work.*

The phone booth nearest the water's edge opens and I take it before

I realize my phone card is back home on my dresser and I have no change. A change booth taunts me from the far end of the phone bank. *Now* I see it. Why didn't I notice it when I was standing in line? I'm not about to give up my spot. I turn toward the glass partition separating me from the next booth. The woman on the phone faces me, her eyes concealed behind immense dark glasses. A yellow sun hat droops over her head like a wilted flower. I tap on the partition.

"Excuse me," I mouth, holding up a five-dollar bill, "do you have change?" No response. I wave the bill to catch her attention. "Change?" Nothing. She's not looking at me but *past* me toward the gangway where the two drop-dead gorgeous officers welcome people aboard. Methinks the lady's scoping for a romantic adventure.

So, I have no coins and I don't want to give up my phone. And, at four million dollars a minute, it's for sure I don't want to make calls from the ship. There's only one other option. I call collect.

"You're where?" my father's voice blares over the phone.

"Port of Miami."

"Quart of what?"

No, folks, Skokie Sam the Shoe Shop Man's hearing isn't fading. It's the rest of the world that's not speaking up. Mom, he tells me, is out investigating a story at the Skokie Lagoon where a man walking his dog found the remains of a human leg. I'm hoarse by the time I communicate all the information: name of ship, dates I'll be gone, ship's emergency phone number. It's a crapshoot how any of this will translate to Mom.

Roblings should be home now. I start to dial, then hang up. Dial again, all but the last number. Hang up. My detective is too savvy. No matter what I tell him, he'll know that part of this cruise gig is my running away from the "us" we are becoming. What if he asks questions? Of course he'll ask questions. And, at this particular moment, I don't have answers.

"You through, lady?" An anxious crewman hovers clutching a fistful of coins.

"It's all yours." I gather my bags and get out of his way.

The sunflower hat woman hasn't moved. She's still staring at the officers, her lips pressed in a hard line, the phone's receiver motionless against her ear. It's a prop, pure and simple.

BUSES CLOG THE DOCK, disgorging passengers. Everywhere I look I see people I think I know. Five inches shorter and that man waddling past could be my penguin-shaped high school drama coach. A couple of studly guys mugging for photos in front of the ship are doubles for chorus I worked with in "Les Miz." My usually crumpled Uncle Leo passes a few feet from me, except this one is forty pounds thinner and wears a dapper blazer and crisp pressed slacks. Everyone is a half-step off, too tall, too thin, too fat.

Happy people rush past me. Excited, bubbling, cheerful people. Great hordes and mobs and crowds of people. I force my feet toward the *Island Star.* A never-ending line of taxis drops off more people in ones, twos, and threes. A minibus unloads an odd assortment, no commonality of dress, age, look. They follow a lanky man with a prodigious Adam's apple—Ichabod Crane incarnate—to the ship.

The river of people flowing around me swells to a flood. Their excitement charges the air as they climb the gangway to the ship. Laughing generations of the Bud Rosin Cousins' Club hurry along in bright red T-shirts. The Pied Piper comes to mind. All those happy children disappearing into the mountain, never to be seen again.

"Morgan! Morgan! Up here!"

I scan up the ship, following the voice, squinting against the sun. Kathy waves both arms from a nosebleed-high railing. Fear drums nervous fingers along my spine.

"Don't move!" she yells. "I'm coming down."

She disappears.

A woman pauses at my side, her gaze following mine up to where Kathy had been. "Grand, isn't she?" she says.

At first I think she's talking about Kathy, then I understand she means the ship. She assumes I've stopped to admire it, doesn't see the nervousness in my eyes.

"Grand," I say.

"Yes." She seems in no hurry to board.

Late thirties, early forties, she exudes the timeless elegance of moneyed society. Her type always makes me feel rumpled. While the humidity crimps my hair into raucous kinks, her blond strands gather demurely into a tortoiseshell clip at her nape. A single row of pearls rests against her peach linen dress, which remains crisp and unwrinkled.

"I love to watch them sail out each week," she says.

"You live here?"

"Yes. Most Sundays I like to sip a glass of wine outside Smith and

Wollensky and watch the line of ships leaving port. They come so close you feel you can reach out and touch them. It's really quite magical, thousands of lights sailing past against the darkening sky, passengers shouting and waving, throwing streamers. It's occurred to me that the life of at least one person must change forever, for better or for worse, during a cruise. It would be interesting to participate in that, don't you think?''

Unlike the hordes brushing past us dragging wheeled suitcases and huge shoulder bags, my sidekick carries the latest Susan Isaacs hardcover and an alligator handbag barely large enough to hold a pack of tissues and a stick of gum. Where does she keep her tickets? Her makeup? Her brush and comb and pick and hairspray and hand lotion and address book and calendar and bottled water and high school yearbook and all the other necessities of life? My own ever-present audition bag, crammed to the hilt with last-minute panic packing, leans affectionately against my leg.

"Well," she says, sighing, offering a small smile, "I think we should be in for an interesting voyage." She floats away trailing expensive perfume. A goodly number of male heads snap as she passes. She seems oblivious.

The blazing sun slips around the ship, casting me in its terrifying shadow. I can still leave. It's not too late.

"Morgan!"

Too late.

Kathy runs up, hugs me so hard I can't breathe. She looks at me and laughs.

"I can't believe you're here!"

"I was," I say, "just thinking the same thing."

A FITTING MOMENT

FIFTEEN MINUTES LATER I stand nearly naked in the Entertainment Department's Wardrobe Room. Rosa—a sepia-toned crone, wrinkled as a dried apple—tosses me one costume after another. "Try this. No, maybe the other skirt." A pair of razor-sharp scissors swings dangerously from a ribbon around her neck. Numbers on her ancient tape measure are barely visible. A wrist pincushion backs up the supply of pins held in her mouth. Chipped teeth are a costumer's badge of honor. "Tha's better," says Rosa. "Stand straight." My voice-over ear catalogues her accent, Puerto Rico by way of New York. My friend Mitzi could nail the borough. I'm not that good, yet.

It's hard not to fidget. I study the metal racks crammed with glittering costumes that fill every available space. "We have three major productions each week," Kathy told me on the way down, "each with multiple costume changes. Our passengers expect Broadway and we give it to them." When you add in the outfits worn for other events like Country Western Theme Night, you're talking a few hundred costumes to keep clean and repaired. Staggering. Especially to someone like me, who has—and I'm not proud of this—worn scarves to conceal missing buttons and Scotch-taped hems that needed restitching.

The floor sparkles with broken sequins. Wisps of boa feathers waltz on air currents. Peg-board walls are covered with spools of thread, tape measures, shelves of plastic boxes filled with fabric scraps, shoulder pads, bangles/baubles and beads, and enough sewing notions to rival Vogue Fabrics. Three industrial sewing machines and a serger fight for space on a long table.

Ensemble members dash in and out checking tonight's costumes, making sure the inevitable performance rips and tears have been mended. Rosa grows eight more hands, tends to us all at once. The redhead I'd seen arguing with her boyfriend onshore floats in. Her dress is even more wonderful close up, bright butterflies fluttering on an aqua field, the simple spaghetti strap bodice flowing into an A-line skirt. I would look so unbelievably knockout in it. Gone is her snarling anger, replaced by the sunniest of smiles. I return the smile. "Hi," I say.

She seems startled, hadn't noticed me. Her smile cools to a Queen Motherly "how lovely you're here, please don't bother me," then returns full force for Rosa.

"Rosa," she says, "I've bought this wonderful skirt but the waist is miles too big." She holds out a succulent silk the color of mangos and limes. I salivate. After my black-on-black Chicago winter, I am hungry for color. "Be a dear," she says, "and take it in for me."

"What? Now?"

"Why, yes."

Rosa waves her away. "Impossible," she says. "Maybe tomorrow. The nes' day."

The redhead pouts prettily, makes a small purring sound. I know that look, watched all three of my otherwise bright brothers become dithering idiots for women who mastered it. Okay, I admit I've practiced The Pout in the mirror—strictly as an acting exercise, you understand—sort of like firing a gun on a practice range. And, yes, I'm good, could hit a target square in the heart...or points south. So far I've never been forced to use it.

The pouter rests her hands on Rosa's shoulders. "Pretty please?" she says, adding a "you're so gifted and I'm so helpless" head-tilt. She's good. My brothers would have turned to butter by now.

Rosa sighs, examines the waistband, sighs again, and nods. In a flash, the gal shrugs off her dress and pulls on the skirt.

I've seen underwear—excuse me, lingerie—like hers featured in *Elle* and *Vogue*, hand-cut little nothings the models are almost wearing. I've never known a real person who could afford the stuff. Certainly none of the hundreds of actresses with whom I've shared dressing rooms. Once, when I had a residual check for a Gap TV commercial burning a hole in my pocket, I strolled Oak Street and priced a pair of undies crafted from a whisper of silk. The price tag, which covered a larger area than the panties, said two hundred dollars. I couldn't do it. If I bought the panties I'd keep them "for good" in my drawer, where, over time, they'd grow brittle and decompose, the price tag still attached. I are what I are.

My bladder complains, reminding me it's been a while since the plane ride. "Bathroom?" I ask. Rosa nods to a door behind one of the costume racks. By the time I come back out, the redhead is gone, her mango/lime skirt pinned and laid out on a sewing machine.

"Now," says Rosa, helping me into a cancan costume, sculpting fabric into pleats and folds to make it fit. The Amazon who had this part before me is longer-waisted, four inches taller, and two bra-sizes bigger. Rosa frowns at the excess fabric hanging around my breasts. "You'll have to tape and pad," she says, pulling pins from her mouth, marking, adjusting.

I'd forgotten taping. It's been ages since I wrapped thick bands of silver duct tape under my breasts to create cleavage. "I can't tape," I say. "Not if I have to sing."

"You sure?"

"Positive. Can't draw full breath. You can pad me as much as you like, but I can't tape."

"Just like poor Angela."

"Who's that?"

Rosa quickly crosses herself. "Such a sweet girl. Tape gave her hives. Big ugly red bumps. It took two months before the last one disappeared. Such a shame."

"So, she just pads?"

"Did." She crosses herself again. "She is dead."

"Dead?"

She nods. "Last week. She is the one you are replacing."

My costume—*Angela's* costume—zaps electric, stings, itches, *crawls*. What had Kathy told me about the entertainers she needed to replace? One gal broke a leg Jet-Skiing. And the other—what had she said?—ah, one "left us." Kathy conveniently avoided using the "D" word.

"Hold still," says Rosa.

I can't. The costume prickles my skin like fiberglass insulation. "What happened to Angela?" I ask.

Rosa is about to answer when Kathy bounds in, "You're going to love this show!," plugs in the tape player, "All the old favorites," pops in a tape, "The cast is fantastic!," hits a variety of buttons, "You won't believe the talent!," searches the right sheet music to go with the songs, "Tonight we're doing 'The Best of Broadway.'"

Rosa kneels on a foam pad, pinning my hem. Kathy turns up the volume, dancing around the room to the medley of show tunes: "I Hope I Get It" from *Chorus Line*, "Hernando's Hideaway," "Anything Goes."

Kathy is perpetual motion on speed, has been since we met as freshmen at Northwestern University. Age hasn't slowed her and divorce hasn't soured her. The only time I've ever seen her "down" was eight months ago when her wonderful mom died suddenly of a heart attack. Except for the cigarette rasp growing deeper, and her hair color shifting from brunette to blond, Kathy hasn't changed.

She clicks off the tape and hands me the sheet music.

"How many numbers do I have?" I ask.

"Angela was the lead singer."

My stomach twists. "Lead?"

"Oops. Didn't I mention?"

"I think I would have remembered." I flip through the sheets. "I'm going to need time to learn the routines, to rehearse—"

"Not to worry. Dancing wasn't Angela's strong suit so I kept her out of the big numbers. But she had a fabulous voice."

"Beautiful," says Rosa.

"I mostly leaned her against the piano while the chorus did the leg work. You can do this part blindfolded. Trust me."

"Trust you? This," I tell Rosa, "is the same woman who swore the wire never breaks when Peter Pan flies."

Kathy winces. "That was a totally freak accident."

"Look." I separate strands of hair over my left ear, show Rosa the curving line formed by sixteen stitches.

"That scar gives you character," Kathy says. "Besides, you dated that doctor for a year." She opens the door. "How much longer?" she asks Rosa.

"Five, ten minutes."

"Great. I'll go set up in the theater. Meet me there when Rosa finishes and I'll take you through the show. I'm cutting out your dance numbers tonight—"

"You said Angela didn't dance."

"Nothing major. A couple of entrances, some easy soft-shoe. You don't have to worry about anything but the songs for tonight's performance. We'll rehearse the next show tomorrow morning."

"What happened to the part where I get to lounge around the pool, soak up the sun?"

"Did I say that?"

"Sounded like you."

A crewman passing behind her freezes at the sight of me aglitter in sequins and padded bra. In the theater, everyone walks around in various states of undress. His leer reminds me this is not the theater. I give him a hard look, which he misses because he's not focused on my face.

"Do you mind?" I say.

"Scat!" Kathy shoos him off, and follows with laughter.

Rosa works quietly a few moments. I put on the next costume, a gypsy blouse with bangles and ruffles. She is arranging the elastic top slightly off the shoulder when something about the costume gives her pause. Two large tears run down her cheeks.

"Rosa?" I say. "Are you all right?"

She pulls a handkerchief from her apron, wipes eyes and nose. "Fine, fine," she says. Then, even though we're alone, she glances around, lowers her voice. "They *say* Angela, she fell and hit her head." She gives me a look.

"I don't understand."

"They *say* her death, it was an accident."

"You mean it wasn't?" No answer. A sudden shiver shoots through me that has nothing to do with my standing near naked. "What do you say?"

"Me?" She heaves a sigh. "I'm just a poor seamstress. What could I know?"

Rosa is dying to talk. I, too, glance around, lower my voice. "If you ask me," I say, "it's people who work behind the scenes, people like you, who know the real truth about what goes on."

"Exactly!" She grips my arm, pulls me close. "No one knew. But I knew."

"Knew?"

"Angela, such an angel, came to me last week. She put on this very costume. 'Oh, Rosa,' she say in that sweet voice of hers, like a bird, like a bird—" Rosa's voice catches. "'Oh, Rosa,' she say, 'could you let the waistban' out a teeny bit? My costumes they feel snug. I have been eating too much.' Ha! As if I do not know when it is eating and when it is baby."

"Angela was pregnant?"

An elfin woman bustles in and heads straight for the sewing machines. With a wiry frizz of gray-black hair atop a Yoda body, she is the spitting image of my Tante Leah, the Mah-Jongg champion and undisputed (almost) kugel queen of West Rogers Park (if you like raisins in your kugel, which I do).

"You're late," says Rosa.

"I am, to the second, on time." I hear German Jew by way of New York with perhaps just a soupçon of something British.

"You knew," says Rosa, "today was busy."

The elf looks at me swimming in Angela's costume. "So now it's my fault people die? You are?"

"Morgan," I say.

"Rhea. Welcome. You're from New York?"

"Chicago."

"Never been. Rosa and I are refugees from the garment district. Escaped four years ago. If I never see snow again it will be too soon."

She hunkers down at one of the sewing machines and begins working on my alterations. Rosa says something to her in rapid-fire Spanish.

"I thought you were in such a hurry for Angela's costumes," says Rhea. "Now you want I should work on her royal highness' skirt?" Even as she complains, she switches my costume for the mango/lime skirt. "I hope this time she's paying something, or am I once again supposed to kvel from the great honor of working on her clothes?"

"What about those diamond chip earrings she gave you?"

"You mean those dime store rejects? I got a backache from hanging a magnifying glass around my neck looking for the stones. Of which, for your information, there weren't any."

Rosa yanks the waistband of my skirt, Angela's skirt, adjusting the excess, sticking pins around in neat pleats.

"Do you really think Angela's death wasn't an accident?" I ask.

Rhea tisks. "Rosa, Rosa, Rosa. Why are you filling this girl's head with stories? Did you also maybe share your brilliant pregnancy theory?"

"I know what I know," says Rosa.

Rhea peers over the tops of her glasses. "You know what you make up. You see conspiracy behind every palm tree."

"And you wouldn't know pregnant if you caught the baby coming out."

"Aiiiiii," says Rhea.

"Aiiiiii," says Rosa.

It has the sound of a comfortable war between friends.

I'm about to ask Rosa more about Angela's death but she hoists a warning eyebrow. A cue if ever I saw one.

I try not to squiggle while Rosa finishes pinning. I need to call Flossie, tell her I'm headlining. The ship's photographer can take publicity stills of me in the different shows. It'll give Flossie agent-ammo. Maybe she'll line up something interesting. A job that pays, for instance. Who knows? This cruise gig might turn out to have career perks, after all.

I skim through the lead sheets and am trying to figure out if I can hit a Yma Sumacian three-octave run when Rosa says, "That should do it."

"Thanks," I say, giving her a hug.

"Maybe it's better you don't say nothing about what we were talking," she whispers, shooting a glance at Rhea. "Not everyone can handle the truth."

"Right."

Rhea sighs mightily at her machine.

I stuff the music and tape player into my bag and walk out more curious than ever about the angel-voiced Angela. It's hard enough when an old person dies, someone who has had a chance to live a full life. But it's altogether different when death comes to call too early— like, say, for someone my age. I head for the theater, trying to shake off thoughts of Angela zipped into a cold plastic bag, her young dancer's body—pregnant dancer's body—off-loaded from ship to ambulance like a piece of cargo. I head for the theater. Kathy will be able to tell me more.

LOST AT SEA

DOWN AT THE Twilight Zone of the cruise ship, there are no clear markings telling me where I am, where I've been, where I might be going. Every turn leads me into a crew-filled passageway identical to the one I just left. I'm like Groucho Marx in "A Night at the Opera," becoming totally lost in one door-filled hallway after another. I used to think it was funny.

Ships should take a page from hospitals, where directionally challenged people like me are able to follow colorful lines painted on the floors. "X-ray Department? Yes, ma'am. Follow that bright yellow line to the red line, red line to the blue line, blue line to the end." The crew I ask for help either don't speak English or haven't a clue where the theater might be. These are the Clay People, living their lives underground. (BRING UP FLASH GORDON THEME. FADE OUT.)

Let me explain something. There are people, like my brother Art, who have an innate sense of direction. Who, if set in the center of a foreign city and told to find some obscure esoteric ruin—say the Cave of the Disenfranchised Sheepshearers—will go directly to it without so much as a single wrong turn.

Then there are those like me for whom one direction is pretty much the same as another. North, south, east, west, left, right all meld into one glorious blob. Only up and down retain any degree of clarity.

"You were born with a broken compass," says Grandma Belle, who never demeaned me, never thought me stupid or unwilling to pay attention. She'd draw cute little maps of my neighborhood, complete with dogs peeing on hydrants, to help me get to school, the grocery, etc. A Grandma Belle map sure would help on this ship. I should call and see if she and her latest beau would like to come cruising.

I mention all this by way of excuse. Five minutes later, I am once again standing in front of the Wardrobe Room. This is shaping up as one long cruise. And we're still in port. I start out again, this time following a couple of crew pushing bicycles. With any luck, I'll spot a staircase along the way. The bikes take a hard right and I follow, right into a massive bike hold. Hundreds of bikes rest in long metal racks. There's not a theater in sight.

I step back into the hall trying to get my bearings. Left looks the same as right. Neither staircase nor elevator. Maybe if I just stand here, help will find me. There's no place like home, there's no place like home. In seconds, an ancient mariner, his torso bent on a slant, limps toward me. His blue scrubs are crisply pressed. A Greek sailor's cap tilts at a jaunty angle. His weathered face sits atop a wiry body. I move aside to let him pass. He doesn't.

"You look a mite lost," he says in a lilting Irish brogue.

"Actually," I say, "I'm a whole lot lost."

"Ah." Deep lines crinkle around his eyes. "And where do you want to go?"

"The theater?"

He brightens. "You're a little early. The shows won't be startin' 'til after supper."

"I want to be sure I get a good seat."

He laughs, thrusts out a welcoming hand. Thick veins twist like cables up his arms. His grip is cold steel. "Sean O'Brian," he says. "Supply Chief."

"Morgan Taylor," I say. "Entertainer."

Sadness flickers. "Have ya come to replace our poor Angela, then?"

"Yes."

"Well, you're welcome on board, though I'm sorry enough for the reason." He blows out a puff of air. "So, now, the theater is it? Don't want you wanderin' off to who knows where. Follow me, then."

We wend our way through the crew's quarters, mess, exercise room. I keep stubbing my toes, forgetting to lift them over the metal thresholds. Good thing I don't have to dance tonight.

"Do you fancy the lift or the stairs?" he asks.

I never take elevators when I can climb. It helps keep my hips and thighs from spreading into the next time zone. But, since my guide is the one with the limp, I figure I'll leave it to him. "Your call," I say.

"Stairs, then. That's how I keep my girlish figger."

Ours is a long and convoluted route. It would take a Stanley to find Dr. Livingston on board. I presume. Even with the aid of one of Grandma Belle's hand-drawn maps, I could never do this on my own.

A couple of decks up from steerage, bare floor gives way to carpeting. Every time I think we've arrived, Sean leads me to more stairs. We head down a hallway housing a sundry shop and the Purser's Office. Sharp voices pour out.

Angry woman: "Our cabin is a joke."

Angry man: "Totally unacceptable!"

Soothing man: "Mr. and Mrs. Granger, please. I've explained. That's the room your travel agent booked for you."

Angry woman: "That's not the cabin in this brochure."

Soothing man: "You're right. That's a suite. Here, look. It says 'Suite' below the photo."

Angry man: "Don't pull this bait and switch on us. That's the cabin we want. And at the same rate. We're stockholders, y'know."

Soothing man: "I would love to accommodate you. Believe me. But we're one hundred percent booked. There are no other cabins."

Angry man: "That's bullshit! I know for a fact you people always save one of the best cabins in case a VIP comes on board."

Someone closes the door as we pass, muffling the voices.

"Poor Richard," says Sean. "The abuse people heap on him. I wouldn't take his job for all the tea."

"Are we really a hundred percent booked?"

"More. They've tucked a few college lads in the crew's quarters to accommodate an overbooking. Folded the poor sods into cabins so small they have to step outside to change their minds."

I groan. "That's a very old joke."

"I'm a very old salt. Besides, you look too young to know it."

"It's my father's fault," I say. "He never met a bad joke he didn't like—or repeat—often."

"Sounds a fine fella."

We climb up out of the darkness into the light where the paying guests live. A food theme emerges. Cold buffets, coffee stations, biscotti and bagels, soft-serve yogurt machines. We haven't even set sail and already passengers stand in line filling their plates.

"Is food being served on every deck?"

"Fore and aft. It's part of the cruise experience." The phrase trills off his tongue.

I give the brogue a try. "The crrrrrruise experrrrrience?"

He slows. "Were you wanting to stop for a bite?"

"I were but I won't. You're not the only one who needs to keep a girlish figger."

He resumes speed and I have to hustle to keep up. "And what exactly does the Chief of Supply do?" I ask, hoping to slow him a little. Bad move. He shifts into a higher gear.

"A little of this, a little of that. Mostly make sure we stock enough of the essentials. Wouldn't do to run out of martini olives mid-ocean. We'd have a mutiny on our hands for sure."

We pass the deli stand. A crowd of people circle the gourmet spread, bantering good-naturedly while constructing architectural wonders of sliced ham, beef, turkey, chicken, corned beef, pastrami, salami, cheeses, tomatoes, cucumbers, lettuce, pickles, olives.

Many of the wrought-iron café tables in the area are occupied by passengers snacking on piles of food that would be a full meal for me. Several people hunker over their plates, eating with ferocious urgency as if afraid of not getting their share. Maybe that's it. The food is paid for. As much as they want. Any time, night or day. To undereat is to not get their money's worth.

Food smells work on me. Hunger pokes its bony finger in my gut. This is rough. As long as I don't see food, I'm fine. At home, I dare not leave food out where I can see it, don't go to the grocery until absolutely necessary, don't have Oreo cookie refrigerator magnets or bowls of wax fruit or dishes of little glass candies. Except for the first year after I stopped smoking—when I pretty much ate nonstop—I've always been able to go a long time without eating. But let me smell, see, hear about food and my digestive system revs into high gear. I go from not thinking about food to thinking of nothing else. Which is what is happening now. I need to eat something. Immediately.

"Shortcut," Sean says, pushing through a door to the outer deck. Blinding sun. Furnace heat. Sean leads me around rows of chaises, past a swimming pool filled with splashing teens, toward the far end where a long line snakes out from the frozen yogurt machine. "Excuse us," Sean says, "coming through."

I slow as we pass the Tropical Fruit Fiesta carousel. The Ichabod Crane I'd seen getting off the tourist bus is stuffing a paper grocery bag with bananas and grapes. He sees me looking, turns away. As if I care he's taking food to his cabin. Honestly. The things people think to go on about. I manage to swipe a tropical shish kebab as we swing past, chunks of pineapple, banana, orange, and watermelon impaled on a long wood skewer.

It's tricky to eat while jogging up yet another flight of stairs. Good thing I'm in shape or Sean would leave me in his dust. Whatever bent his body—birth defect, illness, or accident—didn't affect his mobility. Back inside, we cut through a tiny casino deserted except for a sullen man sitting at a blackjack table.

"Not much action," I say.

"It's the law, isn't it?" says Sean. "No gambling on ships in port. Do you like games of chance?"

"Me? I never have enough cash to find out. I did once work a Las Vegas show, which was once too often. All I remember is the stink of booze, cigarette smoke burning my eyes and throat, and drunks shouting over my singing."

"You've not seen a casino like this, I wager," he says. "Each of these stools is hand-tooled leather. The gaming tables are teak." Sean stops suddenly, bends down. "Come have a look."

A four-by-eight-foot piece of casino floor has been cut out, the deep opening fashioned into a fantasy scene festooned with pirate treasure: pieces of eight, strings of pearls, pewter goblets, silver plates. The diorama is covered with a thick piece of glass. Everyone entering or leaving the room walks over it.

"There's an Elvis livin' somewhere in here," Sean says.

"Elvis?"

"Yes."

I scan the treasure trove. It takes a hard search to finally find the King almost totally obscured by a treasure trunk. He appears to be enjoying the embrace of a mermaid. "Pretty risqué," I say.

"Just a bit of a chuckle." Sean taps a finger to the side of his nose. "Thousands of people pass over it without noticing."

He takes off and I run after, popping the last piece of pineapple in my mouth. We mount the stairs to the main lobby. Sean slows at the top, waits while I take it all in. Powerful bronze and steel sculptures anchor the elegant space. Giant weavings undulate around pillars. A black marble monolith soars three stories up through the ship's central atrium, a wall of water flowing so smoothly down its sides only the glisten of light gives it away.

"She's something, isn't she?" Sean's voice is so loving, he could be talking about a woman.

"Yes," I say, "she certainly is. I've been in museums with less art."

"Less good art, I'll wager." We cross the lobby. Paintings warm alcoves and pillars. Sean points out a Rembrandt-style portrait. "Angela loved this one.'' That sadness again. ''She was a bit of an artist herself. Sketched me once, she did. Made me look almost handsome.''

Rosa thinks there's something suspicious about her death. I wonder. ''How did she die?'' I ask.

''Accident,'' he says quickly. ''We were in rough seas. She fell and hit her head. A terrible waste. Terrible. Sweetest girl you'd ever want to meet.'' His eyes tear up. I've picked a scab off something trying to heal. Me and my big mouth.

The lobby is crowded with people crossing from one side to the other, couples strolling hand in hand. Four toddlers chase each other around a ten-foot-high fish tank. Several older passengers relax in plush chairs enjoying the nonstop parade. Sean pulls open the massive theater door. We're hit by a burst of frigid air.

''Here you go, then.''

''Thanks,'' I say. ''You're a saint.''

''Careful,'' he tips his cap as he leaves, ''you'll be ruinin' my reputation.''

A CHANCE FOR GHOSTS

VAGUE FORMS TAKE SHAPE in the darkened theater. A sea of red velvet seats stretches out before me, tiered in graceful semicircles down toward the stage. Be still my heart. This stage is massive enough for Siegfreid, Roy, and assorted Bengal tigers. An entourage of elephants and a 747 jet would not be out of the question.

Like a pilgrim to Lourdes, I approach with awe and reverence. What maniac/visionary/genius built a theater like this in the middle of a ship? Every person in the audience enjoys a luxurious seat and unobstructed view. Of me. The thought sends shivers.

Kathy's voice, rasping someplace offstage, plays like a distant undercurrent. Stagehands' voices travel clear and sharp from the stage to the back of the theater. Banks of overhead lights suddenly blaze bright, then slowly fade to black as they're put through their computerized paces.

"It's so thrilling."

The tiny voice startles me. I search the shadows, find a white-haired woman dwarfed in an aisle seat.

"What's thrilling?" I ask.

"This. All of this." She gestures toward the stage. "I adore theater. It transports me."

I follow her gaze. What I see are grizzled stagehands in torn jeans, stained Grateful Dead T-shirts, and scruffy biker boots. World-class beer bellies hang over a goodly number of biker belts. I glance back at the woman, at the look of supreme beatitude on her face. You'd think she was watching Baryshnikov at the Bolshoi.

"I expect the actual shows will be a little more exciting," I say.

"Oh, I don't know. Just being here in the theater is special. Don't you think?"

She's too perfect. Central casting sent her to play the prototypical Little Old Grandmother. Better make that Great-grandmother. My mom's a grandmother who gave up her beloved Harley and unfiltered cigarettes five years ago, the day her first grandchild was born. Mom also spends her days tracking murderers, felons, petty thieves, and other unsavory characters for her column in the *Chicago Globe*.

But this lady is pure spun sugar, melts me with one sweet smile. I am touched by her childlike delight in watching preparations for tonight's performance. How does a person make it this far through a long life without losing that sense of wonder? How does the sheer effort of day-to-day existence not harden you?

"I especially love the curtains." She gestures toward the stage. "You don't see them so much anymore."

The stage is framed by floor-to-ceiling curtains. No sham, these. No skimpy bits of fabric cleverly folded and nailed in place to create the *illusion* of full stage curtains. These are the kind that actually open and close. I adore curtains. In most of today's legitimate theaters, I'm forced to run on- and offstage in full view of the audience. I miss the mystique of a curtained stage, the elegance of final bows taken as yards of velvet sweep open.

Two stagehands roll a baby grand piano onstage. "Hey," one yells to us, "theater's closed. We have rehearsal starting."

The woman pushes up out of her seat, fumbles with her cane.

"Stay," I tell her. "They won't kick you out."

"Oh, dear, no. I'm quite certain I shouldn't be here. I'd best go." She walks slowly up the aisle. I go along to help open the door. "See you tonight?" I say.

She brightens. "Do you have first seating?"

It takes me a second to understand she's talking about dinner. "I mean I'll see you at tonight's show."

"Ah. I'm, ah, I'm not certain. It has been a rather long travel day."

My Ego elbows its way into the conversation. "Actually," It says, "I'm in the show."

"You are?"

"Yep. I sing, I dance, I act." I do a Ginger Rogers swirl up the aisle, belting out:

"In old-en days a glimpse of stocking
Was looked on as something shocking
Now heaven knows, anything goes."

She claps her hands, delighted. "I adore Cole Porter. Such a dear man."

"You knew him?"

"Oh, my, yes. I was quite the hoofer in my day. And you, my dear, are wonderful. I can tell you love what you do."

"Actually, I'm just filling in for one of the cast, so if I miss a few cues tonight you'll understand. I'm Morgan Taylor," I say.

"Ida Mills." She smiles as I pull open the door, then pauses a moment, looking back into the theater. "There is something else here, I think. Do you feel it?" She pulls her sweater tighter around her. "Almost like a note off-key. I've felt it in many an old theater, particularly in Europe, but then, they have such long histories, don't they? A chance for ghosts, as it were. Strange to feel it here. Ah, well," she smiles, "the ramblings of an old lady. Thank you, my dear, best of luck tonight. Break a leg." She enters the parade of passengers strolling the lobby.

When I get to my cabin—if I ever get to my cabin—I will dig out one of my head shots and autograph it to her after tonight's show. It's fun to know I've already made my first fan and I haven't even performed yet.

ALL THE STAGE A WORLD

THE THEATER air conditioning ices my neck, tightens my muscles. I roll my head in slow circles as I follow the rasp of Kathy's voice onto the stage toward the wings.

Kathy: "I'm not saying you're wrong."

Angry man: "She's never been on time. Not once."

Kathy: "I'll talk to her."

Angry man: "You've talked to her."

Kathy: "I'll talk to her again."

A magician's paraphernalia litters the wings: lacquered Chinese boxes, tables with hidden compartments, false-bottomed pitchers, a large Vanish Box, knotted chains of colorful scarves, a top hat, and other tools of the trade. I recognize the assortment from my misspent youth as my brother Paul's assistant. We worked every kid's birthday party from Evanston to Highland Park.

"Ladies and gentlemen and children of all ages, allow me to present myself, Margenon the Magnificent, and my beautiful assistant Wanda."

While my friends were out jumping rope and sneaking first kisses, I, "Wanda," was folded like a pretzel into any number of "tricked" boxes. Nothing like this one, though. This Vanish Box is extraordinarily beautiful, high lacquer paint, ornate brass fittings. I run my hand along the Chinese pastoral scene painted on the side.

"Hey!" a voice barks from the wings. "Don't touch that."

A man strides toward me. Tall, powerfully built, dressed in black, he moves with the forceful grace of an Andalusian gypsy. Flamenco genes dance in his blood. I straighten my shoulders, suck in my tummy. Just because I prefer my men craggier around the edges doesn't mean I don't find this man sexy. A boa constrictor drapes his shoulders like a shawl.

"Sorry," I say. The snake raises its head at me and smiles. I smile back.

The gypsy eyes me with interest. "You don't mind snakes?"

"Some of my best friends are."

"No, seriously."

The boa loses interest, looks away. I reach out and trail the back of my hand over its cool skin. "I grew up with three brothers," I say. "Snakes are a long way up the food chain from a lot of the critters they dragged home."

Kathy emerges from the wings, arms loaded with sheet music. "I see you've met."

"We're working on it," says the gypsy.

"Morgan, this is Dominic, our magician in residence. Dominic, this is Morgan Taylor, Angela's replacement."

"Temporary," I say.

"Temporary replacement. Unless, of course, I can talk her into staying."

"Staying?" I say. "You never once mentioned—"

The redhead, still wearing the butterfly dress I covet, emerges from backstage. The smile she showered on Rosa has given way to a look of abject boredom.

"And this," says Kathy, "is Dominic's assistant, Jackie."

"My very *late* assistant," says Dominic.

Kathy sets the music on the piano and begins arranging sheets.

I smile at Jackie. "We met in Wardrobe. Sort of."

Jackie's eyes narrow like a lioness regarding prey. I swear I hear her growl. "So," she says, "you're the one."

"The one?"

"Angela's replacement." It sounds like a curse. "I should have her part."

"Cut it out," says Kathy.

"It's true. *I* am already here. I can do the routines in my sleep."

"Give it a rest. You know you don't have the voice to carry the show."

"Oh, please." Jackie's voice drips disdain. "I've appeared on Broadway. I'm *certainly* good enough to sing here."

"Jackie," says Kathy, "I'm not going to get into it with you now. You volunteered to help Dominic until his assistant's leg is out of the cast."

"But that was before Angela died."

"This isn't musical chairs. You can't keep jumping to the juicier parts."

"Give Dominic one of the other girls. Karen, or Patti, or Susie. What about your friend Morgan here?"

"You're working with Dominic. Period." Kathy hits a few chords for emphasis.

Jackie's stare bores through me. "It's all about who you know in this world, isn't it? People like you have it so easy."

"What do you mean, people like m—"

"The rest of us have to make our own luck."

"I hate to break up this love-fest," Dominic tells her, "but you and I need to rehearse."

"I'll rehearse when I'm ready." Jackie's heels click offstage. The theater grows eerily quiet.

"I guess," I say, "not everyone's happy I'm here."

"Luckily," says Kathy, "you caught her in one of her good moods."

"That's scary."

"Oh, I don't know, Ollie." She Stan Laurels the top of her head with her fingertips. "I'd say what's more scary is, you're rooming with her."

"Any more good news you'd like to spring on me before I start?"

"Don't take it personally," says Dominic. He lifts the boa constrictor off his shoulders and eases it into a black silk bag. "Jackie's just high-strung. You know how it is."

"Don't talk to him," says Kathy, "or you'll wind up folded into a box with a saw through your belly."

"Kinky," I say.

"Come on, Sport." She starts playing "Another Opening, Another Show." "We've got until eight o'clock to make you a star."

IT FEELS LIKE old times, Kathy sitting at the piano pounding out tunes while I stand behind, reading music over her shoulder. After singing the arrangements three times through, I've nailed all the little twists and turns. I never forget a lyric or a dance step. Which is why my brothers never believed I could get lost on the way to school.

We all have our little quirks.

A Tommy Tune clone, all gangly-legged and smiling, comes onstage, welcoming hand outstretched. "Keith Thompson," he says, "your dance partner."

"Dance?" I panic. "I thought I was just singing tonight."

"Right," says Kathy. "But we do need to move you on- and off-stage."

"Ah."

She heads for the wings, "Something like...," enters upstage left, sweeps gracefully across, finishes with a couple of swirls at the piano. "Got it?"

"Check." Keith and I walk to the wings. He slips an arm around my waist, fingers pressing firmly under my ribs.

Kathy strikes the chords on the piano, nodding directions with her head. "And five, six, seven, eight—"

We enter stage left, dancing on a diagonal toward the piano. Keith, six-feet-four of unbridled exuberance, hurtles along at breakneck speed. I lunge to keep step. Kathy stares openmouthed until—wrong-footed and off-tempo—we reach the piano. She breaks into whoops of laughter.

"So," I say, "I guess you're saying that looked as bad as it felt."

"Worse," tears running down her cheeks. "Remember our audition for 'Cats'?"

"Nothing could be that bad."

"Trust me."

"It was my fault," says Keith, pale cheeks red with embarrassment. The poor guy's supersensitive and Kathy's hysteria isn't helping any. "It's just...I'm used to...was used to dancing with Angela. She's...she was much taller than you. I'll tone it down."

"You tone it down and I'll pick it up," I say. "We'll be fine."

We work hard for the next hour, adjusting to each other's styles until we master the simplified movements Kathy designed for tonight's performance.

"That should do it," she says, closing the piano, tucking her music in her bag. "Tomorrow morning, nine-thirty," she tells Keith. "We'll rehearse the 'French Follies.'"

"Right," says Keith. "See you bright and early."

"I should warn you," I say. "Morning's not my best side."

He leaves, undaunted. Dominic begins arranging his equipment on-stage. Jackie has not returned. Evidently Magician's Assistant is not her dream job.

"C'mon." Kathy slips a cigarette from her bag. "We'll go over the sequence of tonight's costume changes out on deck." She leads me through a backstage doorway, down a narrow corridor, and out into the world.

FREE AT LAST

TROPICAL AIR SLAPS my air-conditioned body like a steamy towel. We weave through the maze of sunbathers lounging in deck chairs. These are the seasoned cruisers who pack a small case with a bathing suit and cover-up so they can get out and enjoy the sun instead of waiting cooped up in their cabin for their luggage to arrive.

A scattering of men—pant legs rolled, shirts stripped off—lie supine on chaises like bloated sacrifices, offering up hairy expanses of winter-white skin to the broiling sun.

One bejeweled woman in a flowing caftan has commandeered a prime poolside area, arranging a circle of eight chaise longues with their feet together like spokes in a wheel. She pulls old *People* magazines from a large bag and tosses them onto the chaises to make them look occupied.

"You can't save chairs," says another woman, pulling away two of the chaises.

The first woman yanks them back. "I'm not saving. My friends will be right back."

Kathy and I exchange looks. The woman's friends, *if* they've arrived at the ship, are most likely in the Spa line waiting to make all their appointments before the ship sails. A week's worth of late-afternoon massages, manicures, and hair appointments are snapped up in the first few minutes. On the last cruise I worked, some women had their hair done every night.

We lean against the railing overlooking the dock as Kathy goes through the list of costume changes. Most are done on the fly. What did performers do before Velcro? I'll tuck the list into my bra tonight. A little extra padding never hurts. The harsh sunlight catches the bags under Kathy's eyes, lines around her mouth.

"You look beat," I say.

"These last couple of weeks have been a nightmare." She lights up, pulls smoke deep into her lungs. I inhale, too, hoping for a hint of secondhand smoke. Old habits die hard.

"I swear," she says, "if I ever catch any of my performers Jet-Skiing again I'll personally break their legs. Luckily that ding-a-ling was Dominic's assistant. Jackie volunteered to replace her and I was able to get another dancer from the production company that designs our shows. But then Angela...I lost Angela."

"Rosa told me she died."

Kathy shakes her head. "It was such a rotten break. You would have liked her. She was a strong performer, real energetic."

"What happened?"

"Freak accident. A violent storm blew up. I mean, it was so bad even I felt sick. One of the crew found her body in the bike hold."

"Trying to ride out the storm?"

Kathy groans. "I thought you were giving up puns."

"Tried. It didn't take. So what do they think happened?"

"It looks like the ship pitched, threw her off-balance. They're guessing she rammed her head against something."

"When Rosa was fitting my costumes, she said something about Angela's death not being an accident."

"Rosa can't accept that Angela could have died like that. For no reason."

We're quiet for a while. "How old was she?" I ask.

"Twenty-two."

I shudder. I've already had seven more years of life than Angela will ever have. I tease my dad about reading the obits, but I can see it's sobering to measure one's own mortality.

Kathy tilts her face to the sun, closes her eyes. "Anyway, last week Angela dies. I call the production company again for a replacement and they tell me I'll have to get in line. Some of their other ships have also lost performers and now they can't find enough people who want to work the holiday season. They'll have all the replacements I want *after* New Year's. A lot of good that does me now. I can pinch-hit for a few performances, but it's hard to do that and take care of all the other responsibilities I have."

"That'll teach you to be efficient," I say. "If you were less orga-nized, like me, you'd still be on the boards."

"I don't know, since Mom died, little things that never bothered me before seem more than I can handle." We take another drag of her cigarette. "I mean, one minute I think I'm okay and then I'm not.

You know I'm not a crier. But lately...if you hadn't come to help me out..."

A couple of forty-something men sidle up sucking cigars the size of broom handles. They smile. We smile.

Men: "Buy you gals a drink?"

Us: "Thanks, no. It's a little early for us."

Men: "Maybe later."

Us: "Sounds good."

They tip their cigars—

Men: "Long ashes."

—in some fraternal cigar smoker's salutation. MEN exit deck right, trolling for a couple of friendly women to help pass the time.

"It's the Looooooove Boat," says Kathy.

"Oh, really?" I waggle my brows. "Is there someone special I should know about?"

"I wish. I'm ready."

I feign horror. "Not you! You're my ideal. The happy bachelorette."

"It's time. I've sown enough wild oats to feed the third world. Maybe it's Mom's death, maybe it's Angela dying so young and me looking thirty in the face. Whatever. But lately I'm feeling this powerful urge to settle down, have kids. Doesn't that ever happen to you?"

"Mostly when I'm not working. Downtime is dangerous. But your job has no downtime. You're always working."

"Ain't that the truth."

I look out over the activity on the dock. The earlier flood of arriving passengers has thinned to a trickle. A convoy of service and supply trucks moves along the wharf. The cranes are silent now, new supplies loaded on the ships, lines of trucks hauling away empty container cars.

Blaaaaaaahhhhhhhhhhhhhhhaaaaahhhhhhh!

A deafening blast explodes overhead. I press my hands over my ears until the ship's horn stops. It's followed by an announcement for all visitors to leave the ship. I feel sudden panic as time races toward my first performance. Lack of sleep mixes with the thick sea air. I've been running on fumes and it catches up with me. A three-thousand-pound exhaustion sets in.

"The ship's rocking," I say.

Kathy gives me a look. "We're still docked."

"Maybe I should take a seasick pill."

"Relax. You'll be fine."

"This heat's getting to me," I say.

She hooks her arm in mine. "What you need, my landlubber friend, is to get out of your winter clothes and put your feet up awhile. Come on, I'll get you settled in."

IT'S NO PLACE LIKE HOME

OUR WINDING CONFUSION of passageways and stairs ends in a windowless interior cabin barely big enough for two beds, a four-drawer dresser built into the wall between them, and a desktop bolted to the wall. Kathy watches me take it in. "A little different from our last ship?"

"This is like a suite at the Ritz," I say, "although I sort of liked the old concrete bunk beds and eau de mold."

A puffy silk comforter drapes one bed, whose mattress is twice the thickness of the other. Lacy sheets peek out from under. A mountain of feather pillows languish in hand-stitched shams. The other bed, the one with the tic-infested straw mattress, is encased in a battleship gray blanket woven from diseased lamb's wool and old Brillo pads. The sackcloth pillowcase appears to be harboring a rough-cut board. "Let me guess which bed is mine," I say.

Kathy laughs. "Jackie likes her comforts." She pats the Brillo blanket. "Angela used to make her bed up real cute but we shipped all her things back to her family. If you want, I'll see if I can dig up some scarves and stuffed animals, try and cozy this up for you."

"I'm only here a few weeks," I say. "It'll be fine."

She pulls a sealed envelope out of her bag. "Your contract," she says. "Look it over when you have time. And these," she digs out a few videocassettes, "are our shows. It's just stuff I shot for myself, but they'll help give you a sense of pacing." She flicks on a small TV.

"Every room has television?"

"Mostly for the video player. People rent tapes, and the ship broadcasts some stuff. TV's been out of my life so long, I don't even think about it." She slips in a tape. "Although, I've seen passengers go through TV withdrawal." Music blares. She adjusts the volume. "One man threw a tantrum when he found out he couldn't get his favorite sports programs. He stormed off the ship before we ever sailed. Left his wife and luggage on board."

"You're kidding."

"His wife stayed, had a ball." Kathy fast-forwards to the overture for tonight's show. "This ought to catch you up pretty well. I'll be down the hall in my cabin if you need anything. Enjoy."

I hum along as I throw on a T-shirt and shorts and unpack my clothes, which takes all of three minutes. For someone like me, who hates making clothing decisions, cruising is a real no-brainer. In the evening I'll wear costumes, followed by slacks and a blouse. Daytime clothing is shorts and tops. I packed one black dress with two different silk jackets, which I can dress up or down with assorted scarves and jewelry. One pair each of running shoes, sandals, heels for the black dress, three pair of character shoes—black, brown, and neutral—to dance in, silver and black tap shoes, and I'm ready to go.

In the tiny bathroom, I set my toiletries in the sink and open the medicine cabinet. The top shelf is crammed with expensive face and body lotions. Extremely expensive. One of my three million temp jobs was pushing a French cosmetics line at Neiman Marcus. My Parisian French accent helped sell a ton of Parfum de $$$$$$. I know for a fact that these jars of face creams start at a hundred bucks a pop. The next shelf down is filled with contact lens supplies and a pharmacopoeia including sleeping pills, birth control pills, allergy medications, and exotic concoctions I've never heard of.

The two bottom shelves, Angela's shelves, are empty save for a small spill of body powder. Little warning shivers goose bump down my arms. It's not that I believe in bad luck/mojo/vibes, but the girl who last used this shelf is dead. Until this moment, she was an abstract idea. The powder makes her real flesh and blood. I press my finger against it, bring it to my nose. Yves St. Laurent's Opium. My flavor, when I can afford it. I wet a tissue to wipe it from the shelf. Something stops me. I can't be the one to erase this last little bit of Angela. Let her stay awhile, keep me company. *A chance for ghosts.* I set my toiletries on the shelves under Jackie's. Move over, Neiman Marcus, Wal-Mart is moving in.

In the next room, the overture ends and the cabin fills with the first strains of my first number. I rush in and flop on Angela's—on my—bed, mesmerized as the red velvet curtains open. *THE BEST OF BROADWAY* flashes on a huge marquees. The troupe bounds onto the stage, dancing across the small television screen. There I am, or at least there I will be, swirling alongside the towering Keith Thompson.

But this is Angela with Keith, a stunning brunette with Cyd Charisse legs and the kind of playful smile that invites everyone in the audience to be her best friend. She had wonderful stage presence and a maturity that made her look older than twenty-two.

I rewind, watch her enter again. And again. How can someone this vital and energetic be dead? The ghost of an old sadness rises unbidden. In high school, my best friend was killed in a car crash. A cross-country trucker, driving too many hours and popping too many uppers, lost control. It took years for my anger to fade, for the pain to find a quieter place in my heart.

I rewind again. My best friend's family was devastated by her death. I wonder how Angela's family and friends are coping. How can they bear having this joyful creature ripped from their lives? Rosa said Angela needed her costumes altered because she was putting on weight. Pregnant, said Rosa. She made it sound as if Angela was trying to keep it secret. Does Angela's family know? If there were an autopsy, a pregnancy would be found out. But if the death were accidental, would they do an autopsy? I hoped not. Death is tough enough on a family without adding complications.

This time I let the tape play through. "The Best of Broadway" is solid musical theater. The caliber of production numbers and performers has cranked up a bunch of notches since the old days. Angela was a competent but self-conscious dancer, her movements studied and deliberate. I can almost hear her counting the tempo clicks as she moves across the stage. It's nothing civilians would notice, only we dancers can hear the metronomelike sounds that keep us on tempo. Angela's gift was knowing how to play to the audience, involve them. And her voice is knockout. In fact, I'm going to borrow some things she does—did—with timing and shading. I spread out my sheet music, making notes as I watch, begin singing over Angela's voice.

Half an hour later, I drift into the music, float toward sleep. I must be beyond exhaustion, because the ship's rocking, which I feel no matter what Kathy says, soothes instead of sickens. An hour later, curled into a ball, my face buried deep in the pillow, I wake to the creepy sensation of something crawling up my spine. I jump up, yelling.

A startled crewman leaps from the edge of my bed. "Dio!," stumbles over his duffel, and rams into the desk.

"What the *hell* are you doing?" I say.

"W...where is Angela?"

"Angela?" I shake the cobwebs. "Angela...Angela..." He's a pimply kid, barely five feet tall, eyes wide with fear. "Angela's...gone," I say. "I'm her replacement."

"I...I did not know. I am sorry. I have been away. I just came to say... Angela, she is my friend. I'm Paco. She will tell you. I thought you were, she was—ho boy..."

"Okay," I say, rubbing my eyes, trying to wake up.

"Please." He's trembling. "I don't mean nothing."

"Paco, it's okay."

He picks up his duffel. "Angela, she teach me singing, I teach her Spanish. I thought you was her."

"Really. I believe you. It's all right."

"Oh, jeez," he says. "Please."

"I promise. It's all right. You didn't know."

"Thank you. I did not mean...I would never...thank you."

He backs out of the room with short bows, dragging his duffel. This time I lock the door.

I could have told him about Angela's death but that's rough news to hear from a stranger. His shipmates will tell him soon enough. I have a feeling the poor kid's going to take it hard. I stretch tall, reaching my fingers toward the ceiling, lifting up on my toes, then flop over, loose as a rag doll, letting my arms dangle. It's a good thing he woke me. I forgot to set an alarm. Wouldn't do to sleep through my first show.

A LONG SHOWER revives me. I hold my face up to pinpricks of scalding water. A nervous thought weaves through the steam. How could Paco have mistaken me for the statuesque Angela? But he'd been so scared. Maybe the way I was scrunched up on the bed made it hard for him to tell the difference. Especially since he wasn't expecting me *not* to be Angela.

I try to convince myself the incident is nothing more sinister than a case of mistaken identity. Still, I must make absolutely sure to lock my door at all times. I'm bad about that, am usually running so late I fly out of my house forgetting little details like locking doors, turning off lights, shutting off the oven. And I don't even want to discuss the times I've left water running in the bathroom and kitchen sinks. I'm sure one day I'll run out while the bathtub is filling, sending water cascading into the apartments below. My tendency to run late drives the always prompt Detective Roblings absolutely crazy. Roblings. Thinking about him calms me right down. Paco's was an honest mistake. Nothing more to it than that.

I work my voice up and down the scales, bouncing it off the metal walls. I feel Angela's spirit in this place, running scales, oiling her chords. Tonight, I'll try to "sell" the songs with the same pizzazz and energy she put into them. My voice still sounds a little furry. I go through the tunes again, honing the edges. Should be all right by show time.

Reluctantly, I leave the shower to dress. There are signs that Jackie has come and gone: shoes placed neatly next to her bed, the butterfly dress airing on a padded hanger hooked over the closet door. She must have heard me in the shower, known I was in the room, but didn't bother poking her head in to say hi. Looks like being "best friends" is not in our future. I just hope she doesn't turn into a roommate from hell.

The sealed envelope with the contract has been opened. Evidently Jackie is more curious than me about my salary. I check it out. A few hundred dollars a week, plus travel expenses and an allowance for incidentals I may need. Considering my room and board are free, Kathy has given me a generous cruise contract. Jackie may be right. It does help to have friends in high places. I rummage through my drawers trying to remember where I've unpacked all my stuff. By the time I dress and head for the theater, I'm feeling like a new woman. It is during one of several wrong turns that I glimpse Uncle Leo's hair-combed-over-the-bald-spot wedged into the back of a crowded elevator. The doors slide shut. It can't be him. I didn't see Aunt Bertha's hive of white-blond hair next to him and the two of them have been joined at the hip over forty years.

Well, if it is Bertha and Leo I'll find out soon enough. My mother's big sister isn't exactly the shy retiring type. If Aunt Bertha is on this cruise and spots me onstage, she'll let out a shriek to shame the Sirens. After all, it's her fault I'm an actress. She's the one who shlepped the three-year-old me on two trains to see the "Nutcracker." She's the one who informed my parents, "...this child has more talent in her little pinky than all those kids onstage combined!" She's the one who for years dragged me to every voice/dance/acting lesson and audition in Chicago, transported me to and from rehearsals.

If she had had children of her own to push onto the stage, my life would have turned out differently. I might have grown up to become an attorney or doctor or joined Dad in the shoe repair business, or married a nice guy and raised a gaggle of kids in some suburban cul-de-sac community.

Mom's never forgiven her.

SHOW TIME!

IT HAS, OF COURSE, taken me several wrong turns to find the theater and then to follow a stagehand's mumbled directions. I work my way backstage climbing over Dominic's magician's gear and assorted show props, around a pile of light cans and cables, and down a short, steep staircase. It's bad form to be late, especially on my first day. I hope my fellow performers don't misinterpret it as arrogance.

I open the door on total chaos. There are bodies in motion everywhere, pulling on costumes, putting on makeup, fixing hair. Yes, Virginia, there is an honest-to-goodness dressing room. On board this floating city, designed by space misers who dole out square centimeters with demitasse spoons, someone somehow wrangled a state-of-the-art place for performers to change.

This is a high-energy group, everyone laughing and talking at once. Keith waves a lanky arm from across the room. The ambiance is welcoming, yet I am keenly aware of being an outsider. This is a new production for me, a new space, all new people. It's tough enough to understudy a show you've lived with awhile, let alone come in cold like this. Every night is opening night. All Sisyphus had to do was roll the world back up the hill.

Four racks of costumes press against one wall. Rosa and Rhea, a colorful array of pre-threaded needles stuck in their collars, help dress. People toss clothing and accessories across the room, stretch legs and torsos against tables and walls, walk their voices up and down scales. Tonight's show has eight couples in the chorus plus me and Keith plus Dominic and Jackie plus assorted musicians and, it seems at the moment, the entire Ringling Brothers circus. The walls close in. My familiar pre-show nausea starts, a pure adrenaline boost laced with nerves, shortness of breath, shaking hands, quivering knees. It's like seasickness with attitude.

A sheet draped over a rope bisects the room. If it's supposed to create a men's and women's changing area, it doesn't. Everyone undresses in front of everyone. Actors' shoreside unions may spell out exact requirements regarding dressing rooms, hours, number of performances, and a million other hard-fought rights, but none applies here in this union-free zone. If a performer doesn't like something, tough. There's a long line of people waiting to work cruise ships who won't complain about less than perfect conditions. Besides, modesty is a luxury of time and space. After months of living and working together on a ship, you get to be family.

Kathy spots me and bangs an old bongo drum for attention. "Listen up," she calls. "This is my friend Morgan Taylor, who has come to help us out for a few weeks. Morgan, this is everyone."

I wave to the throngs. Welcoming shouts come from all sides. Rosa and Rhea have my outfit and accessories pulled and waiting. I am dressed in seconds. Rosa pulls a threaded needle from her lapel and takes in an extra tuck under my left breast. "Good," she says, turning me around once, "Good," then moves on to the next victim.

A blond pixie waves me over to take the dressing table space next to her. "Hi," she says. "I'm Elaine Burke."

"Hi."

She pushes her makeup box over to make more room for mine. "Sorry it's so cramped."

"You kidding? This is pure luxury." I set out my stuff. "I worked a ship where we changed costumes in a small library off the entertainment space. You wouldn't believe the number of gents suddenly overcome with a need to read during performances. Some of them even managed to hold their books right side up."

She flashes a great smile. I sent an orthodontist's children through college trying to make my teeth look like hers. I apply my makeup quickly. After eight months of "Rent" I can do this in my sleep. Have done a few times.

Elaine brushes on eyeliner. "I'm the dancer closest to you onstage," she says. "Kathy told me to keep an eye on, sneak you cues if you get lost, grab you if you head in the wrong direction."

"I hope you're getting combat pay."

She laughs. "Kathy says you're the world's quickest study."

"Just your basic savant."

"It should happen to me." She adds mascara. "It takes me forever to learn routines. Angela and I used to prac...used to practice..." Tears mound on her lower lashes. "Darn," she says, blotting them with tissue before the mascara can run. "Sorry. Seem to do that a lot lately."

"You and Angela were close?"

"The closest."

"Places," calls Kathy.

"That's us." Elaine blows her nose, dabs her eyes, clicks her makeup case closed. "Break a leg."

"You, too."

Costumed bodies flow out the door. I hang back, take one last look in the mirror. Theatrical makeup works wonders, lightening dark eye circles and deblotching skin. I lean forward, stare into my eyes. *You can do this. You're a professional. Piece of cake.*

Jackie passes behind me, adjusting the strap of her Magician's Assistant costume. I smile at her in the mirror. In this harsh light, her pigeon-blood lips and intense scowl create an eerie vampiresque effect.

She pauses on her way out. "Why don't you go back to your Broadway play?" she says.

"It wasn't Broadw—"

"Give someone else a chance." She leaves me smiling like an idiot into the mirror. Oh, Lord, please don't let the rest of the ensemble feel that way, that I think I'm some big-shot star. I don't. I'm not. They'd seemed friendly enough. Or was that wishful thinking?

Show time!

I join the cast waiting nervous and expectant, in the wings. Kathy stands close to the stage. "All set?" she whispers.

"Set." I nod toward Jackie. "She's really not happy I'm here."

Kathy rolls her eyes. "She's not happy, period. Steer clear. She's trouble."

"Which is why you made us roommates?"

"Believe me, if I had an extra bed, anywhere, I'd have put you in it."

Jackie moves next to Keith, whispers something in his ear while pointing at me. My affable partner's face shifts from happy to perplexed. Jackie keeps talking. I wonder what little tales she's telling him about me. A little arsenic with your old lace, dearie? She's a danger, this Jackie. Have to remember not to turn my back.

The audience begins clapping in time to the overture. Kathy winks at me. "There's nothing like a cruise ship audience." She eases the corner of the curtain aside so I can see. I look out into the sea of expectant faces. I'd forgotten what a joyful group they are. And why not? Passengers roll out of the dining room and into the show room—no slogging through snow and sleet, no fighting for parking spaces, no driving baby-sitters home or getting up early the next day for work.

Their excitement is infectious. Energy crackles through our ensemble. I stick my trembling hands under my armpits. Erratic heartbeats cha-cha in my chest. I suck in long deep breaths but there's not enough air backstage. And then, the curtains sweep open.

The dancers burst onto the stage as Keith slides his arm around my waist. "Ready?" he asks.

"Ready."

"Great. It's going to be fun." His fingers keep time on my waist as we count down the clicks to our entrance.

And away we go! We sweep onto the stage, our bodies light as air, swirling, twirling, crossing our diagonal from wing to piano as if we'd been doing it forever. Smile! Step! Swirl! Yes! A hesitation step, a spin, a dip, and Keith deposits me in safe harbor against the baby grand. Lights soften, music comes down, the piano plays my intro....

"Oh, God, I need this job."

My plaintive voice reaches out across the immense theater, pulls thirteen hundred people into the heart of my "Chorus Line" character as she prays before an audition. It's no reach to make these lyrics real. I've been there, done that, have the war wounds to prove it. As my song ends, there's barely time for applause before the tempo kicks into high gear and the dancers take off across the stage. Kathy has put together a show that breathes life into hope, heals broken hearts, sets a wrong world right, makes lovers of strangers.

The simple choreography Kathy arranged for me around the piano keeps me in motion but out of the way. A few times I cross the stage, to stand on a different spot. Elaine Burke, good to her word, dances close enough to stop me from heading off in the wrong direction. Somehow, she manages a radiant smile for the audience while calling "upstage left" and "Rockette kicks next" out the side of her mouth.

When it's time for my final number, the lights dim and the band plays the haunting opening notes. "Ahhhh," says the audience, falling silent, holding its collective breath. I open my mouth, and magic happens.

"Where is the little boy I carried?
Where is the little girl at play?

I don't remember growing older.
When did they?

It is my voice, and yet it's not. Not exactly. My real voice is a mix of sweet and gutsy, sort of Bernadette Peters meets Ethel Merman. But this voice is overlaid with a third sound—something bell clear, haunting. Something Angela. "A chance for ghosts," Ida called it. Perhaps the old woman had sensed Angela's spirit haunting the theater this morning.

The acoustics carry the magnificent "Fiddler on the Roof" lyrics out over the theater and I feel the audience wrap itself in the music. I take my time, caress every note. The song is perfect. Perfect. I hold the last note, fading it slowly as the spot dims, ending as the room goes to black.

At first, there's not a sound. Then I am hit by a thunderous wave of applause. Whew! Thank you, spirits of the theater, gods of the voice, lords of the dance. The lights come up. I take deep bows, right, left, center. Relief washes like floodwaters through my body. Nothing can hurt me now. Oh, how I'd love to wade in and wallow in this moment for a nice long time but the band strikes up and the ensemble dances onto the stage for a rousing George M. Cohan medley, finishing with "Give My Regards to Broadway."

When it's over, if the audience wants to stay and applaud, give us two standing ovations, so be it. And if several interested gentlemen hang around the dressing room door, it would seem rude to brush past without giving them a radiant smile and thanking them for their kind attention.

Even Jackie switches her bipolar self from vampire to vamp, stopping long enough to rest a hand on one gent's sleeve. An Armani sleeve by the cut of its jib, over a hand-tailored shirt with gold-and-diamond cuff links and perhaps just a glint of Rolex peeking out. As the daughter of Skokie Sam the Shoe Shop Man, I recognize the Italian leather shoes as the kind whose price gives my father heartburn. Lawsey me, honeysuckle, howsome ever did our l'il ole' Jackie target herself *the* most expensive pick of this partikilar litter? She's a right piece of work, she is. The gent takes her hand, presses it to his lips. She flashes a smile bright enough to land jets in dense fog.

Our second-show audience, considerably looser from two more hours of drinking time, is even more enthusiastic. Would that every show I did had these audiences. They make stars of us all. The performance flies past and once again we run offstage to the dressing room through a phalanx of male admirers. Mr. Rolex-Armani is here again, this time bearing long-stemmed roses, which he presents to the ever-so-surprised Jackie.

"I'll just be a tiny moment," I hear her tell him as I pass.

"Hurry," he says, pressing a key in her hand.

She throws the flowers and key on the dressing table, sitting next to me as she cold creams off her makeup. Everyone is in high gear after the show, laughing and joking as they change into their civvies. Everyone except Jackie, who seems enclosed in a world that doesn't include the rest of us.

I return my costume to Rosa, who runs a hand along the fabric.

"The costumes, everything was all right for you?" she asks.

"Yes. You and Rhea did a great job." I put my hand on hers. "And I watched a video of the show. You're right. Angela was very special."

I am packing up the last of my makeup when Kathy comes over. "Come on," she says. "We have a hot Scrabble game waiting." She takes me up on the Flamingo Deck where a couple of the musicians are already setting up the board. The first thing I notice is the balmy evening air. The second is that we're moving. The sea is calm. Still, I feel pressure balloon inside my head, press against my eyes, circle toward my stomach. I grab a table for balance.

"You all right?" asks Kathy.

"Been better."

"Maybe Scrabble's not a good idea your first night out. Come on, sailor, I'll walk you to your cabin."

I give up trying to remember the way as we serpentine to our quarters. The lower we go, the steadier the ride. It's a mystery to me why the most expensive cabins are the highest up. If I had to actually pay to sail, which I wouldn't, I'd book center steerage every time. Chain me to the anchor, stow me with the crew and the engines, bunk me where my ancestors' masses huddled in their frantic escape from the Cossacks.

The late-night halls are filled with crew kicking back after a long hard day. Kathy leaves me at my cabin. "You look beat," she says. "We'll shmooze tomorrow after rehearsal."

"Nine-thirty in the theater?"

"Yup. See you then."

SOMETIMES I SENSE THINGS I can't put a name to. As I unlock my door, step into my cabin, warning chills spider up my spine. The cabin feels deserted—no sign of Jackie—but there's something...

I leave the door to the busy hallway open, just in case, while I check things out. The cabin looks exactly the way I left it five hours before. Right down to the pair of ripped panty hose on the floor near the wastebasket where I missed an easy jump shot and was too rushed to pick them up.

Still, the room *feels* wrong.

One of the first things Roblings taught me when we began dating was not to ignore my intuition. "The best detectives use it all the time," he said. "It's the pure animal part of us that picks up hidden signals—a subtle shift of smells, a 'wrong' ambient sound, the change of the press of air on our skin. If a person, place, or situation feels wrong to you, it probably is. You have to learn to trust that."

I do. I check under the bed, in the bathroom, look through my clothing. Everything's the same...as far as I can tell. I'm not the neatest person in the world so it's tricky to determine if anyone went through my closet or drawers. I can only be sure no one is hiding in them. When I am positive no danger lurks, I close the door and lock it.

Maybe this disquiet I'm feeling is Angela's spirit. Perhaps people who die on cruise ships haunt the decks in search of one last nonfat yogurt vanilla-chocolate swirl. Not funny. More likely, I'm just beat. I lull myself to sleep watching the tapes Kathy gave me. Our next big show is the "French Follies" and it looks as if I'll have a whole lot more dancing to do. I watch it once through, then rewind and start again, falling asleep as a pair of Apache dancers—Keith and Jackie—burn up the stage.

A few times during the night, noises erupt in the hall. Laughter. Music. A scuffle outside my door. Singing. Although I am not seasick, I am also not a hundred percent. Jackie's plump mattress taunts my aching back. A custom number like that had to set her back a shekel or two. I could do serious sleep on a mattress like that. If she's going to sleep out every night, maybe we can cut a deal. The thought weaves in and out of my restless night.

The ship's subtle rolling puts pressure in my head, my throat. If this is as bad as it gets, I can manage three weeks. I say a small prayer to the sea-gods. They listen. I awaken after a good night's sleep to a world of calm seas, my roommate's unused bed—

—and an envelope slipped under my door.

DAY TWO

IT'S A JOKE, SON

STALKER.

The word strikes terror.

Stalker.

My heart tries to punch its way out of my body.

Stalker.

Roblings' word. His is a homicide detective's take on life. People slipping anonymous letters under private doors are *stalkers.*

The envelope taunts. I don't touch it. How many actors, athletes, politicians, rock stars fall victim to twisted fans? Mutilations happen. Deaths.

Stalker.

Has my Chicago "fan" found me? Followed me here? Can't be. I fold my legs up under me, stare down at the envelope. I don't care how innocent the letters seemed back in Chicago, how sweet the poems. There's nothing friendly or harmless about this.

Stalker.

Locked in this windowless, airless room without a phone, I feel the walls close in. What does he want? How did he follow me so far so fast? How can I perform, how can I function, knowing he's somewhere on board, watching?

Think.

The envelope moves, slithers closer. I take deep breaths. Easy. Slow.

Think.

It is impossible he's followed me on board. Impossible.

Think.

Who knows I'm here? My parents, Roblings, my agent, my friend Beth. None of them would tell some stranger I was here.

Think.

Even I didn't know I was coming until the last second. Was he watching my apartment, waiting? Did he follow from Chicago, fly to

Florida with me? My skin crawls at the thought of him on the same plane, maybe sitting in the next seat.

Think.

Even if that were possible, there's no way anyone could have booked last-minute passage. No way. Sean O'Brian said this cruise was so oversold they tucked college kids in the crew's quarters. Kathy said there were no empty cabins. *Get hold of yourself. Nice deep breaths.* I let my intellect beat my emotions into submission. *There now, that's better.* Reason and courage return.

I reach over and delicately lift the envelope by one corner. It's totally different from the cheap blue envelopes slipped under my Chicago door. I turn it over. "Morgan Taylor" is typed on the front, just below the *Island Star* logo. I pull out the "wire" inside:

Received 0700 hours: To: Ms. Morgan Taylor / From: Detective J. Roblings:

So this duck walks into a pharmacy and says, "Got duck food?" "No," says the clerk, "this is a pharmacy." The duck leaves. Next day, the duck comes back. "Got duck food?" he asks. "No," says the clerk. "I told you yesterday this is a pharmacy. We have no duck food." The duck leaves. The next day, the duck walks in. "Got duck food?" The clerk starts screaming. "I told you yesterday and the day before, this is a pharmacy. We don't sell duck food. If you come in again I'm going to nail your little webbed feet to the floor." The duck leaves. The next day the duck comes in. "Got nails?" "No!" yells the clerk. "Good," says the duck. "Got any duck food?"

Can you tell I've been spending time with your dad? He's been hanging around the station. Likes the coffee. No accounting for taste. Speaking of which, I miss you.

I did a quick check to see who's policing your ship. Security Chief is Gene Davis, he's good people. Used to keep Denver safe from the bad guys before he retired. We go back a way. You may want to look him up if you can take time from your busy sun-bathing schedule.

Send your itinerary when things settle down. I miss you. Let me know how you're doing. Oh, yes, did I mention I miss you? JR

I press Roblings' letter to my breast, feel its warmth flow through my body. He spent a fortune to wire me one of my dad's terrible jokes. A normal boyfriend, if inclined to send a gift, might opt for candy or flowers or jewelry. Not Roblings. He understands that what brings me joy has nothing to do with things money can buy. I'm a sucker for bad jokes and good puns ("an oxymoron," insists Grandma Ruth) and I'm snowed by a man who spends time schmoozing with my dad even when I'm not around. So, what is it about our relationship that frightens me? Why am I running away?

—*I'm not running away.*

—*Oh, yeah? Then why are you here while he's in Chicago?*

—*It's cold back home. I'm just taking a little working vacation.*

—*Cut the bull. This is me you're talking to.*

The cabin door bangs open. Jackie stumbles in, last night's mascara raccooning her eyes, hair matted from sleep or lack thereof, eyelids barely open. Looks like something the cat dragged—

"Morning," I say.

"Mmmnn." She kicks the door shut, sets a container of coffee and a jewelry box on the desk, and disappears into the bathroom.

"I really enjoy our little conversations," I say.

The shower goes on. I hear her step in. Then nothing but the sound of water sloshing around. How can a person not sing in the shower? Especially this metal shower with its stunning acoustics? Un-American, that's what it is. I'll have her brought up on charges. I go into the bathroom, splash water on my face, brush my teeth. Steam pours out from behind the curtain. My hair kinks. I'll need to comb it with a weed whacker. I'd like to dab on a little makeup but, no matter how hard I wipe, the mirror won't defog. The world will have to take me au naturel. Scary thought, that.

I dig shorts and a T-shirt out of my drawers, pull on a pair of sandals. My side of the cabin is a disaster compared to Jackie's. But then, it's easy to keep things neat if you're never around to mess them up. Looks like Jackie and I are in for a three-week run as the Odd Couple. Guess which character I play? I wonder if Angela was the tidy type.

The aroma of Jackie's coffee wafts over, triggers my hunger switch. Her cup must have a crack. A thin line of coffee trails around the jewelry box and across the top of the desk. I grab a couple of tissues and fold them underneath. And, just to be sure the coffee isn't damaging whatever's in the box (me, curious? nah), I gently lift the top.

A fabulous Christmas bracelet, braided ribbons of rubies and emeralds set in gold, glitters inside. The stones look almost real, especially to someone like me, who knows nothing about fine jewelry. I set the box back in place. Of the two items on the desk, I most covet the coffee.

I still have an hour until rehearsal, plenty of time to grab a bite of breakfast and maybe soak up some morning sun. I debate making my bed and hanging up my clothes but they can wait until later. Right now I need coffee.

YOU PUT YOUR RIGHT HAND IN,
YOU PUT YOUR RIGHT HAND OUT

IN THE BOWELS OF the ship, in the monotonous metallic shell the crew calls home, no portholes exist to signal day or night. Four in the morning and four in the afternoon, blinding rain and sunny days all look the same. It reminds me of the surrealistic timelessness inside Las Vegas casinos.

In time, I'll learn to read the sounds of the ship, but I've forgotten the language in the years since I last worked cruises. I become lost immediately. None of the crew-filled hallways are familiar from the day before. Where is Chief Supply Officer Sean O'Brian when I need him? Refilling the ship's sick-bag holders, no doubt. I scan the hordes for his Greek sailor's cap adrift in this sea of blue uniforms and caps. Neither hide nor hair. The frustration of being perpetually lost gains a toehold. I am doomed to wander this maze forever.

Maze. I put my right hand on the wall and start walking. When I was a little girl, my mother taught me that to find my way out of a hedge maze—

—"Why would I need to do that?"

—"Fair question. Okay, so say you're kidnapped by a crazed English gardener and he tosses you into the middle of just such a maze?"

—"Ah."

—"So, if this happens, simply put your right hand on the hedge to your right and keep touching it as you wander in out and all about. Eventually, you'll walk out of the maze."

—"Will it work with my left hand touching the left hedge?"

—"If I tell you every single thing you need to know in life, you'll never learn to learn."

Mom never said her trick would work on a seafaring metallic maze, but it's worth a shot. I walk, hand to wall, in search of stairs. A stampede of crew roar out of a doorway ahead wheeling rusty contraptions resembling bikes. It's like the running of the bulls in Pamplona. I flatten myself against a wall, staying out of their way. Doesn't do to get between horny gobs and shore leave.

As soon as there's a lull in traffic, I peek around into the bike hold. Bent relics lean every which way in long racks. Arctic air chills my bones. A steady stream of crew roll bikes out. The cavernous hold smells of rusty metal, grease, and oil. Didn't Kathy say Angela's body was found near here?

I step inside. What a cold place to die. Poor Angela. I circle the room. There is no welcoming place here, no softness. It is all cold concrete and colder metal. It's strange to feel such powerful sadness for someone I never met. Maybe it's the intimacy of slipping into her costumes, feeling the same fabrics that pressed against her body pressing against mine. Maybe it's because I know her spirit from watching her on the videotapes. Understand her heart from the way she opened herself to audiences. See how loved she was by the ensemble and by people like Rosa in Wardrobe. Even an old salt like Sean O'Brian teared up when he talked about her. We are connected, she and I, and her death has meaning in my life.

This bike hold is a metallic wasteland. Hers must have been a horrible end. I shudder, moving in deeper, half expecting to find some tribute…flowers perhaps…like the floral offerings that mark roadside deaths. Stop this. Why am I letting this crawl up inside of me? My brothers grew up complaining I was overly dramatic. Well, yes, that's what I do for a living.

I walk to the back of the hold and look out toward the door, feel the enormity of this space. A group of stage crew come in to grab their bikes, clowning around like kids let out of school. Their voices echo off the walls and fold in on themselves. When you consider how tight space is on a ship it's nice that the cruise line sets aside this area for bikes.

A solid block of body odor drifts back to me followed by the smell of food and just a hint of something else. Something vaguely familiar. It reminds me of the camping trip Dad took us on when I was ten. I can't think why. I'm obviously standing at the vortex of the hold's airflow, hit all at once by exhaust from one of the kitchens, a bathroom, and perhaps the laundry. The rich aroma of coffee comes to call. My stomach begs for a cup.

The "right hand on the wall" maze technique takes me to where humid breezes flow. Hundreds of crew—some wheeling bikes, some carrying duffels brimming with beach towels, thermoses, swim fins, and snorkels—move toward an opening in the ship's side. Sunlight pours in. It occurs to me I have no idea what our itinerary is.

"Where are we?" I ask one of the crew.

"¿Como?"

I scan my high school Spanish. "¿A donde estamos?" I say.

"Ah, Nassau."

"How long will we be here?" I think I say.

He responds either, "There is a man departing with trays," or, "We leave tomorrow at three." Serves me right for writing Gil Leavitt's name a thousand times in the margins of my high school Spanish book instead of paying attention to Señora Seid. After rehearsal, I'll find a secluded beach, lay out all afternoon, bake to a golden brown, sleep until I wake. Ah, paradise.

I catch sight of Paco adrift in a crowd of laughing young sailors. He looks a thousand times worse than he did yesterday in my cabin. It's obvious his buddies have told him about Angela's death. He's taking it hard, eyes puffy red, shoulders slumped, as he shuffles down the gangway.

Dominic, looking less Andalusian gypsy and more frantic giant, pushes through the crowd. He looks relieved to see me. "Ah, you...er—"

"Morgan," I say.

"Morgan, right. You're rooming with Jackie, right?"

"Yup."

"Where is she?"

"She was in the shower a little while ago."

"I knocked on the door," he says. "No one answered. Did she say anything about rehearsal?"

"Nope."

"She was due half an hour ago. I mean, how does she expect—" and he's off, ladies and gents, Gulliver through the Lilliputians.

I check my watch. My rehearsal doesn't start for another forty minutes. What harm in sneaking off-ship a few minutes, setting my feet on terra firma? I join the exodus down the gangway.

WHAT'S UP, DOCK?

NIRVANA! The morning sun burns off the chill of the bike hold. I inhale the fruity fragrances wafting on warm air, sway to the lilt of island voices. I think each of us is born either a desert person or a water person. Most of my Chicago friends escape to Arizona for winter vacations. I'm definitely water. Tropical climes may crimp my hair and jump-start my sweat glands, but the press of sultry air on skin is undeniably sensual. Roblings, Oh Roblings, wherefore art thou? My good detective once spoke lovingly of visiting Sweden, burning in the dry heat of a sauna, then rolling naked in the snow. If we become a serious item

—*I thought you were.*

—*Stay out of this.*

then Sweden is a trip he'll have to do alone. I'd rather languish on a sun-kissed beach and cool off in the sea.

Other cruise ships line the massive port. Passengers scurry on the dock, cranes load and unload containers. Colorfully dressed straw sellers sit in the shade of a large tree, chatting as they weave green leaves into baskets, hats, and purses.

"Easy, up, up." Sean O'Brian, Irish tour guide to the stars, races around with his odd gait, directing the loading of yet more huge containers onto the ship. I amble over, joining the gaggle of kibitzers oohing and aahing as the crane lifts a forty-foot container car and swings it up into the ship's hold. Painted a deep red, this one is marked with an Oriental character set into a circle. *Asia House Rice* is stamped underneath. Three Chinese kibitzers next to me talk excitedly when they see the logo. Asia House must be a popular brand, a bit of home away from home. I understand their excitement. I felt that way when I saw a McDonald's in Mexico. Another container is painted with sugarcanes and says *Sweet Sarah, Inc.* A ship this size must have one heck of a shopping list.

Sean pounds on the side of the crane, yelling something at the operator, motioning the other hand toward the container. What an amazing job he has. Back home, I constantly forget to buy the few supplies I need to keep my small apartment going. I've been down to my last few squares of toilet paper more times than I care to remember and once, okay, I'm admitting this, I was extremely grateful to have the latest issue of *Variety* in the bathroom. How the heck does Sean organize supplies for an entire floating city? We're talking three, maybe four thousand people when you add in everyone. That's a lot of toilet paper.

Sean sees me in the crowd, comes over breathing hard. "Mornin', darlin'," he says, pulling off thick work gloves. "Why aren't you out splashing in the surf?"

"This is much more fun."

"Each to her own." He smiles at the kibitzers, the audience for his particular kind of theater. One of the Chinese men bows slightly, asks a question in Chinese. Sean returns the bow, answers in Chinese. "He asked," Sean tells the crowd, "how much beer we stock each trip. That would be eight hundred cases." Before he leaves he answers questions in German, French, and Russian, each time translating them to the rest of us in English. "A thousand pounds of butter, five thousand pounds of bananas." I am mightily impressed. I can *sound* like I'm speaking other languages, but my words are all pretend. The crane revs and Sean hurries off to supervise the off-loading of a few small crates. Out with the old, in with the new.

I stroll along the dock, which seems strangely quiet considering the thousands of passengers all these ships brought in. Most tourists must be off on excursions that departed immediately after breakfast. I pass a row of taxis, the drivers calling out to disembarking stragglers.

"Best tour of the island...."

"Hey, lady. You like to shop? Jewelry? Luggage? I take you."

"Snorkel, dive? What you want?"

"No problem. Don't worry. I make you best deal."

The drivers ignore me. My *Island Star* name tag, a brass rectangle staff must wear at all times, gives me away as a ship employee who gets her excursions gratis. It also says I'm Angela Parker. Kathy promised my own name tag will be ready the next time we pull into Miami.

A sleek black limousine stands apart, its driver sitting quietly inside. Smoke trails out the rear window. A hand reaches out, fingers flick ashes off a cigar, tap impatiently against the window frame. Sun glints off a Rolex. Might this be Jackie's gent? My nosey self ambles over, nice and casual. The man inside leans forward, looks out the window toward the staff gangway. Yes indeedy, ladies and gents, it's the ever-elegant bracelet-buying Mr. Rolex-Armani. Now, boys and girls, can you guess who he's waiting for?

I jump as a voice sneaks up close behind me. "You've been to Nassau before?"

I turn to the owner, a stranger, tall and handsome in a *GQ* sort of way. His clothes are elegantly casual—baggy linen pants, braided leather belt, bloused raw silk shirt. His black hair is fashioned in the kind of razor cut preferred by models, gangsters, and cops. He is, in short, exactly the type a gal might hope to meet on a cruise, if a gal were in the market.

"No," I say, "this is my first time."

"There's a lot to do here. Nightlife, beaches, shopping." He extends a hand. "Mike Polsky." His is a nice handshake, firm, friendly.

"Morgan Taylor," I say.

He squints at my *Islander* name tag, seems unsettled by the name. "It says Angela."

"It's a long story. But I really am Morgan."

"I see we're on the same ship. I'm on Christmas break. English teacher."

"Ah," I say.

"Minneapolis."

"Uh-hah."

There are a million questions I could ask to keep the conversation alive:

—And what grades do you teach?

—Are you traveling with family? With friends?

—What is the meaning of life?

I don't ask any of them. Since Roblings entered my life, I've lost my taste for casual flirting. I know I said I'm trying to work through my feelings but reading Robling's letter this morning—bad joke and all—gave me a warm fuzzy that hasn't gone away. Until I sort things out, it's better not to muddy the romantic waters by leading Mr. Mike Polsky on.

An urgent car horn shatters the air. A van hurtles down the dock, its horn bleating like a wounded sheep. With one headlight missing, the other dangling from its socket, the van looks like a mutilated monster. A mangled front bumper, lashed to the grill with pieces of twine, bounces wildly. Slashes of assorted paints crisscross the chassis—Jackson Pollock on wheels.

The van swerves erratically. The driver stops honking and hangs out his window waving, shouting.

"Something's wrong," I say.

"Looks like his brakes gave out."

He swerves toward us. Before I can think, Polsky yanks me violently to the left as the van jerks right. We watch in horror as it hurtles past us toward a basket seller stretched out dozing among his display of straw baskets, hands folded on his chest, straw hat over his face.

"Look out!" I shout. "Look out!"

Other people see the danger, begin yelling. I hold my breath as the basket seller leaps to safety milliseconds before the van drives over where his legs had been. The van decimates the corner of his display. Smashed baskets fly up like startled birds. The shocked basket seller stares at his ruined merchandise.

"Ho! Yo, ho!" The driver's yells echo along the dock as he caroms toward the ship.

"Oh!" I brace for the crash.

"Christ," says Polsky.

A few feet from the gangway the van screeches to a stop. A waiting gaggle of passengers rushes toward it. It's Ichabod and his mismatched entourage. The van's driver, a short round man in a sweat-stained shirt, jumps from the van, effusively greeting the group.

"Wha—?" I stare in disbelief.

"Idiot," says Polsky.

The only thing wrong with the van is that the driver is late picking up his group. "He nearly killed that poor basket seller," I say.

"And us."

"That, too."

I roll my head trying to loosen the sudden knot of muscles in my neck and shoulders. Ichabod's group loads an assortment of boxes and bags into the van. They help a wheelchair member up into a seat, the rest of them folding inside like circus clowns. No shorts and T-shirts for this crowd. Long-sleeved shirts and long pants protect arms and legs, serious hiking boots are laced up where sandals should be. Cloth hats shade their faces.

"Uh-oh." Polsky nods toward the young basket seller who, recovered from his shock, runs screaming at the driver, waving remnants of destroyed baskets. The two men get into a shouting match, circling each other, arms waving, fingers jabbing. No one on the dock moves to interfere. "This could get ugly," whispers Polsky.

I'm thinking the same thing. My instinct, from early years spent refereeing my fighting brothers, is to wade in, stop things before they get serious. Grandma Belle, a live-and-let-live kind of gal, says I've inherited my mother's Good Samaritan gene. She doesn't mean it kindly. I stay back. This is none of my business.

The shouting grows louder, the jabbing harder. I'm wondering if I should run and alert ship security, when Ichabod climbs out of the van. By this time, the basket seller is tearing pieces off his ruined baskets and throwing them to the ground. The van driver stomps on them and waves wild hands. Ichabod moves in, steps between the two men, takes out his wallet, and, after some animated deliberation, hands the basket seller a bunch of bills. In seconds, the group disperses, the van rattles off, and the dock returns to normal.

"That was fun," I say.

"Nothing like a little drama to start your day in paradise." Polsky rumples his hair, which immediately goes back in place. "How 'bout I buy you a cup of coffee?" he says. "There's a cute little stand just—"

"Thanks. But I have to get back on-ship."

He looks disappointed. "Someone special waiting?"

"Actually, I'm here helping a friend, filling in for one of the performers for a few weeks."

"Ah." He nods at my name tag. "Might that be Angela?"

"Right."

"Now I'm sorry I missed last night's show. I'll come see you tonight."

"Don't think so. This is Theme Night. Country Western. You passengers do the work. I'm rehearsing for Tuesday's show."

"Well, at least I can walk you back." The smell of ripe pineapple swirls around the dock as we head to the ship. "I've heard," he says, "that entertainers are a pretty tight clique."

I consider this. "I suppose. We tend to sleep late and stay up until the wee hours. It's not a schedule most civilians find appealing."

"You can't have much of a social life on board a ship."

Uh-oh, ladies and gents, here comes the pitch. "Oh," I say, "the entertainment staff sort of hangs out together."

"A friend of mine once worked a ship. He said there were a lot of romances between entertainers and officers."

"I can't really say." I flash my staff boarding card at the gangway guard and head up. "It was nice meeting you."

"Same here. See you later."

"Great."

Not great. I'm desperate for some serious R&R. After the last eight months, working too many hours each week, trying to fit in enough time to create a relationship with Roblings, agonizing over what that relationship is, all I want is sun, sand, and fun with friends. Period. I am not in the market for a new complication. This may mean doing a little buck-and-wing to sidestep the obviously interested Mr. Polsky. It's for his own good.

The vampire, freshly showered and in full makeup, passes as I board. Her red mane sways as she walks, hips swish her little silk dress the color of ripe strawberries. Who said redheads shouldn't wear red? I catch a whiff of 24 Faubourg which, when I worked Nieman's, retailed for three hundred dollars a quarter ounce.

"Off on an island adventure?" she asks.

"Maybe after rehearsal."

Jackie's penciled eyebrows arch in surprise. "Didn't they tell you? Rehearsal's been canceled."

"Canceled? I don't understand. I need to rehearse."

She fakes an amused laugh, tucks a long strand of hair behind her ear. The better to show off a large diamond stud, my dear. "Don't worry about it. You don't do the Follies until tomorrow night. You'll have plenty of time to rehearse tomorrow. Someone with *your* caliber of talent..." She trails off waving a dismissive hand, clanking an arm laden with the sort of Michelin-sized tortoiseshell bracelets Nieman's sold for six hundred bucks each.

"Dominic was looking for you before," I say.

"He's such a slave driver." She does a pouty thing with her mouth that looks much practiced. Probably hides her fangs. "Someone needs to teach that man how to have fun."

She floats away on a sea of crewmen's lustful glances. I still think she's scary-looking but I learned long ago that men and women rarely agree on who's sexy. As Grandma Belle pointed out the day my sixth-grade boyfriend dumped me for a gal who gave bare breast, "Mimi, baby, the same man who can't smell garbage rotting in his own kitchen can smell a willing bitch five miles away." Some grandmas bake cookies.

Well, since there's no rehearsal, I might as well pack a bag and head for the beach. I'm passing the staff mess when Keith bounds out juggling an armload of water bottles.

"Hey, sailor," he says, "how're you doin'?"

"Great...now that we're docked."

"That'a girl. A couple more days and you'll have your sea legs screwed on real tight. C'mon, we got five minutes."

"Until?"

"Rehearsal."

"But...I thought it was called off."

"You are such a hoot." He looks around. "Have you seen Jackie? She asked me to pick up some water for her."

"Oh, yes," I say, teeth clenched, "I saw her all right. She's the one who told me rehearsal was canceled."

"What a great kidder." His eyes go all puppy soft. "I'm telling you, she is so terrific."

I check for blinders. His are diamond-studded. Keith is head over heels in love with Ms. Manipulator of the Year.

"Let's go," he says. "Don't want to be late."

"I've got to get my gear. I'll meet you there."

The problem with being raised by a sweet-natured father who has an innate trust of humanity is that it makes me an easy target for the Jackies of the world. But I am also my mother's child and that street-smart lady taught me early on to let no evil done against me go unanswered. It may take awhile, but I'll figure out some small way to repay Jackie the favor.

A BLOODY SLEIGHT OF HAND

Across the main lobby, a gang of teenage boys roughhouse outside the theater door trying to attract the attention of teen girls who pretend not to notice. I know people who think high school was the greatest time of their lives. Their photos dominate my Niles Township High School yearbook, the Kings and Queens, Captains and Presidents of everything. I, on the other hand, spent those hellish four years battling industrial-strength acne, chronic nail-biting, and a serious inability to do math. My school activity photo, frizzy long hair cleverly draped over erupting skin, is buried in the Theater Department's "Cast" collage.

I'm not complaining, exactly. Weekdays after school I immersed myself in dance, acting, singing lessons and auditioned for everything. Since my parents limited me to appearing in two legitimate productions a year, most weekends I worked my brother Paul's magic act. My skin finally improved, braces came off, and curly hair became fashionable about the time Paul went off to college, which gave me my senior year to discover boys, and vice versa. By that time I had serious years of performing under my belt and had built an impressive bio. It's all worked out all right.

I slip around the testosteroned teens and open the theater door. A horrific scream slams into me. The teens stop roughhousing, look over with interest. Another scream. The boys jab each other, amble over for a look. These are not the kinds of sounds you want to share with passengers.

"It's a closed rehearsal," I say, quickly stepping inside the theater, pulling the door shut behind me.

Onstage, Dominic stands statue still, his gleaming metal saw halfway through a box. The screamer's head juts out one end of the box, long blond hair cascading to the floor.

She screams again. "You cut me."

"The blade's nowhere near you."

"I felt it."

"Ginger, please, will you just hold still and let me finish."

"Getmeoutgetmeoutgetmeout!"

"Calm down."

"I mean it! I mean it! I mean it!"

He pulls out the saw and unlocks the box. The waif clambers out, trembling, searching her skin for blood. The skimpy costume reveals a jut of hipbones. I can count her ribs from back here. Stick arms hang from knobs of elbows. Hands dangle from bony wrists. She looks as if she's starving.

"See?" says Dominic. "Nothing. Now, will you settle down and let's get through this?"

The little drama is ignored by the legion of dancers warming up around the theater. Legs stretch on brass railings, lithe bodies bend over stairs, chairs, tables. Upstage, Kathy works at the piano with a couple of singers. I climb up, toss my rehearsal bag on a pile with the others.

"Morning," I say.

She smiles. "Sleep all right?"

"Perfect." I nod toward Dominic. "What's going on?"

"Jackie never showed."

"I saw her a little while ago, told her Dominic was looking for her."

"She wasn't dressed for rehearsal, was she?"

I think of the Michelin bracelets, the strawberry dress. "'Fraid not."

"Didn't think so. I don't know what I'm going to do about her. Dominic's a wreck. I finally begged my buddy, the Head Chef, to loan me one of his kitchen crew."

The waif is backing off the stage. "I have to pee," she says, running out.

Kathy sighs. "I don't think show business is in her blood."

"I don't think blood is in her blood."

"Go warm up," she says. "We start in ten."

I find a space next to Keith. He slides his right foot up along his left leg, then extends it slowly over his head into a vertical split with no apparent effort. "Scuttlebutt is," he says, "we'll run into some weather tomorrow night."

My heart lurches. "Define 'weather.'"

"Don't get your tights in a knot. You'll do just fine."

"We're talking the 'French Follies,' right? Cancan, that sort of thing?"

"Right. If the seas get too rough we only kick waist high."

"Why not just call off the show?"

"Girl, you are a *stitch!*" He lowers his leg and slowly bends forward, folding in half until his nose touches his knees and his wrists rest on the floor. He's the Straw Man from Oz—no bones about it.

My warm-up begins with slow stretches. Since getting in shape for "Rent" I am in touch with every fiber of every muscle in my body. I'd love to stay this finely toned but it's a luxury I can't afford. Once I get back to Chicago I'll have to work my temp job at Junque and Stuffe, cleaning off dusty antiques, waiting on customers. I feel a pang of guilt, leaving Harold during the holiday rush. But my boss always has a waiting list of "between jobs" actors more than willing to take up the slack.

I ease into my floor exercises, starting with my toes and working my way up. Actually, my job at Junque and Stuffe comes in third. My second priority is my classes: voice, dance, the occasional scene study. And *that* comes after my top priority, which is auditioning for plays, movies, industrials, voice-overs. This is hardly the kind of schedule to allow me the luxury of staying in primo shape. It's also not great for serious romance. Although this thing I have going on with Roblings keeps trying to elbow its way to the head of the line.

I unbend from a deep stretch and catch Dominic staring at me. He's still center stage, waiting for Ginger to return. I smile. He smiles. Kathy pounds a few chords on the piano. "All right, everybody." She turns to Dominic. "We need the stage."

"I'm not through rehearsing. My new 'assistant' had to pee."

"Don't beat me up over this," says Kathy. "It's not my fault Jackie's not here. I'm doing the best I can."

"What about her?" He's nodding at me.

"Not a chance," says Kathy. "Until I find out what's going on with Jackie, it's Ginger or no one. Now, we need to rehearse. You can finish up backstage."

He slams the saw on top of the table and wheels it offstage.

Kathy grabs a cigarette from the pack on the piano, draws it slowly under her nose inhaling its aroma, sets it back down. I can feel how much she needs it. I can't even imagine this kind of willpower. I quit smoking when there were still places you could smoke. It would drive me crazy not to be able to light up at a tense time like this.

The "French Follies" is a full-scale production with five costume changes. If you've never seen performers changing offstage, picture frantic chaos times ten. Some shows' costume changes demand the same speed and precision of movement as dance routines. Kathy has asked Rosa and Rhea to come help me through my first dress rehearsal.

"Beautiful," says Rhea, helping me into my chanteuse dress.

"Just like my Angela," says Rosa.

I think the costume looks perfect but they flutter around, taking a stitch here, letting out a tuck there.

"Like it was made for you," says Rhea, reinforcing the left strap.

"You should have used the Forest Green," Rosa tells her.

"Too dark." Rhea bites off the thread, mutters, "Like anyone is going to see."

Kathy plays my cue as Rosa adjusts the Velcro waistband and Rhea smooths the skirt. "Go, go," they say together.

I dance onstage, remembering most of the routines from Kathy's videotapes. We run through each of my dance numbers three times, fine-tuning as we go. Elaine dances next to me, calling moves like a quarterback. I hope Keith is wrong about the weather. It'll be rough performing while I'm listing to lee side.

While the dancers break, I rehearse the ensemble songs with three other singers. Luckily, I sing melody, which requires nothing more taxing than staying on-key. We put everything together in one final rehearsal going straight through beginning to end with only a couple of small adjustments.

"Tomorrow morning, same time," says Kathy as we wrap. Groans come from all directions. "All right," she says. "I think we can do it with just the singers and anyone in 'Gigi' and 'I Love Paris.'" A few cheers go up as the ensemble scatters. I help Kathy pack her music.

"How about I buy you a day at the beach?" she says.

"Twist my arm."

"I'll pick you up in your cabin. Twenty minutes?"

I change into my civvies and return my last costume to Wardrobe.

"Here," says Rosa, pressing a batik bag in my hands. Vibrant red lizards crawl across a crackled black-and-green background. "Angela lef' this in Wardrobe. The strap it broke," she holds out the place where she restitched the fabric, "and I fix it for her. It was that day, that terrible day. You take it."

"Me? It's beautiful. You should keep it."

"Every time I see it," Rosa presses a hand to her heart, "it is a pain here. Your singing, you remind me so much of her. Please, take."

"Thank you." I put my arms around her in a giant hug. "I will treasure it."

ANGELA'S BAG is perfect to hold my beach gear. One problem. I forgot to pack a bathing suit. I walk down the hall, find Elaine's door open, ask if she has an extra. "Take your pick," she says, opening a drawer full of suits. I rummage through trying to find one that doesn't require a bikini wax.

Half an hour later Kathy and I walk down the crew gangway off-ship. The gangway guard, flirting heavily with a pretty basket weaver, barely looks as he waves us past. I've packed Angela's bag with towels, food grabbed from the deli stand, and enough money to buy an afternoon of frothy fruit drinks decorated with pretty little umbrellas. The limousine I saw this morning is gone.

"You know," I say, "it's possible Jackie went off-ship after I saw her. She was with this guy last night...."

"That would be so Jackie. While she's knee-deep in rum and Cokes, Dominic's stuck trying to teach yet another ding-a-ling the sacred tricks of his trade. She's always been difficult but it's gotten worse, lately."

"Why'd you hire her?"

"She's a convincing actress, comes off sweet and loving when she's a mind to. I've tried talking to her but..." Her voice trails off. "After New Year's, when I can get replacements, I'm going to have to let her go."

I feel a twinge of guilt, knowing I, Wanda, assistant to Margenon the Magnificent, could help Dominic work his act. A magician's craft relies on precision timing. His art is in making the audience believe what it doesn't see, and disbelieve what it does. It's hard to perfect all that if your assistant doesn't show up to rehearse.

We walk toward the taxi line passing the stall where the young basket seller was nearly run over by the renegade van. The stall is unmanned, strewn with crushed baskets. Can't really blame the kid. If I were nearly killed while enjoying my morning siesta, I'd take the rest of the day off, too.

SHARK!

THE MOST SOUGHT AFTER place to be is where passengers aren't. Cruise ship personnel ferret out remote beaches, private coves, and rocky inlets where they don't have to please anyone they don't want to. This means driving a goodly distance from the ship. To cut expenses, Kathy and I split a taxi with Elaine and a couple of the musicians.

Our driver, "Voodoo Vince," is a jovial mountain of a man who long ago sprung the seat springs, leaving him low in the saddle. His Medusa hair, wild and wooly corkscrews jutting in all directions, bounces as he talks and laughs. Which he does. Often. If his floral print shirt were music, we'd go deaf. The real music, CDs drifting through four Bose speakers, alternates between reggae and Miles Davis.

We head south for half an hour, hot air swirling in from open windows. The cab smells of tropical oils and musk incense. Kathy, the lone smoker in the bunch, rides shotgun, holding her cigarette out the window between frequent drags. A macabre line of chicken wishbones frames the inside of the taxi's windshield. Each has been dipped in white paint, then glued in place. Seven chains swing from the rearview mirror. One looks suspiciously like the skeleton of a rattlesnake. Two bear large crosses, one shocking pink plastic, one onyx. The others are the sort of cheap pop-beads my sister and I played dress-up with at Grandma Ruth's house.

From the banter, it's clear Voodoo Vince is a regular, picking up crew at the ship each week.

"You watch out for shark," he's telling us.

"Right," says Kathy, "the two-legged kind."

"No, now," Vince says, "you listen what I say. They find parts out where I take you."

Kathy shudders. "Parts?"

"Parts," says Vince.

"As in human body?"

"Fishes been eating on it real good."

"Anyone want my lunch?" I say. "I think I've lost my appetite."

"You'll get it back," says Kathy, "after a run on the beach and a swim."

"You mark me," says Vince, "don't you be swimming out far. I don't want nothing bad to happen to my friends." He lets us out at a near-deserted stretch of sand, arranging a pickup time before he leaves.

The creamy ribbon of beach undulates for miles before curving out of sight. Occasional chaises and umbrellas dot the distant landscape like miniature objects in a Grandma Moses painting. No jag of hotels disrupts the palmed skyline. No fancy shops, bars, or restaurants attract fun-seeking tourists. This is a remote area of no interest to any but sincere and dedicated sun worshippers. We trek along the sand and stake out a flat spot near the water.

"I have number thirty-five," says Elaine, slathering sun block on her freckles.

"Let me get a base, first," I say.

"Better use it," says Kathy. "This sun will fry you in two seconds."

Elaine tosses me the tube. "You haven't felt pain until you try pulling a scratchy costume over sunburned skin. Trust me. This is the voice of experience talking."

I spread a thin layer over my body to appease them. I rarely burn. I've inherited my Sephardic maternal ancestor's oily skin, which turns olive green in Chicago winters. The upside is I don't waste money buying expensive moisturizers and I always tan immediately. I know, I know, I've heard all the skin cancer warnings but (with apologies to Kermit the Frog) I just can't bring myself to stay green all year.

"You'll be sorry when you're my age," says Grandma Ruth. "My skin is like silk, it never sees the sun." This is because she never leaves the house. If having beautiful skin means living like a mole, I'd rather have elephant-hide.

Excuse me while I eat my words. Thirty minutes later my skin crinkles like papyrus and, when our group pitches in to rent a couple of large beach umbrellas, yours truly is the first to dive for shelter. I am spreading my beach towel in the shade when a taxi pulls up.

"Civilians," mutters Kathy as a group clambers out.

They run toward our beach carrying mesh bags bulging with swim fins, masks, and snorkels. It's impossible not to stare. The two women and three men look like extras for "Baywatch" or "The Love Boat"—perfect bodies, beautiful faces, the women tending to frolic in a particular breast-bouncing way.

—Lights! Camera! Cue the cuties in the fluorescent bikinis. Bring in that swarthy guy and his blond buddies. All right, people, Action!

As they approach, I recognize Mr. Michael Polsky from our little meeting on the dock this morning. If I thought he looked good in clothes, he's even more delicious out. The group spreads blankets and towels, making camp a few hundred yards away.

Kathy purrs softly. "Mmmmmnnnn, the one in the blue's a hunk and a half."

"Would you like to meet him?"

She peers at me over her sunglasses. "I assume that's a rhetorical question."

"Hey, Mike," I call. Polsky looks up, seems pleasantly surprised. I wave him over, dialing down my thousand-watt smile, reminding myself I'm not in the market, that somewhere in the wilds of Chicago, my own true homicide detective is braving blizzard winds and numbing sleet to make the world safe from crime. However, that doesn't mean I can't share with a friend.

I make the introductions. Polsky seems duly impressed that someone as young and attractive as Kathy is also bright and capable enough to be in charge of all the entertainers. "Mike thinks entertainers are cliquish," I say.

"Is that a fact?" says Kathy.

Polsky looks sheepish. "That's what I've heard."

"Well," Kathy pats the blanket next to her, shifts from friend to seductress, "we'll just have to talk about this."

He settles in between Kathy and me, sharing our shade. Sure there is a strict no-fraternizing policy onboard ship but, heck, if we happen to bump into someone on a public beach, it would be unsociable to ignore him. Polsky, fascinated by Kathy's job, asks her all sorts of questions, which she delights in answering. The troubling weariness I saw in her fades away, replaced by something bubbly and happy. There are few things like the undivided attention of an interesting, intelligent man to set a wrong world right.

I decide to run along the beach, give Kathy and Polsky time alone to get to know each other. Sand-running is a tough workout and my calf muscles, not entirely happy, complain early and often during the run. I keep an eye on the debris tossed up from the sea. Don't want to be stepping on unattached body parts. Voodoo Vince might have been kidding, but I'm not taking any chances. Half an hour later, as I run back, I pass the couples who came with Polsky, walking hand in hand along the beach. I'm glad Kathy and I were here to keep him from feeling odd man out. Sometimes, it seems everyone in the world is walking two-by-two. It's a comfort to run into other singles. By the time I return, Kathy and Polsky are engrossed in intense conversation, and I lie back closing my eyes, listening to their voices weave in and out of the lapping waves.

SUNKEN TREASURE

KATHY SHAKES ME awake. "Come on, Sleeping Beauty." She tosses down snorkeling equipment. "We don't have much time." I follow her and Polsky to the water's edge, pull on fins and snorkel. My skin sizzles as I ease in. The water feels soft and silky and completely wonderful. We kick lazily, arms dangling loose at our sides. Schools of small fish dart around us. I reach out. In a flick, hundreds of fingerlings change direction, seeming to disappear before reappearing swimming the other way. Schools of bigger fish follow. Voodoo Vince's warning intrudes. *"They found parts."* I scan for shark.

The sand-bottomed terrain shifts. We enter a world of jagged rocks and undulating sea plants. Dustlike particles hang suspended in the sunbeams piercing the water.

Ghostly forms catch my eye. Five bat-winged creatures, each the size of my hand, dance in the water below. Their gelatinous bodies, nearly transparent, give them an ethereal quality. Wings flutter, graceful as silk chiffon. Their heads look like squid but I always thought squid had tentacles. What do I know? In Chicago, any squid I see are swimming in garlic butter. What maniac first thought of eating such beautiful creatures? A cow, yes, okay, I can see eating cow. But these angels?

I want to show Kathy and Polsky but they've swum further along the rocky cropping. If I go to get them, I risk losing these creatures. It is a terrible moment, wanting to share something so magical and having no one to share it with. I ache for Roblings. He would understand how powerfully their beauty moves me. My attention is so focused, I don't feel the current washing me into an outcropping of jagged rocks until my leg bashes against it. Skin scrapes. Salt water burns. I reach down to rub the wound.

A shaft of sun glints off something shiny hidden among long strands of sea grass. I paddle back against the current until I catch the glint again. Definitely something down there. An empty beer can? A lost watch? A doubloon? I take a deep breath and dive, pulling against the water with strong, even strokes. The swim fins propel me down at a dizzying rate. I used to be able to hold my breath underwater for a little over two minutes. Even in bone-chilling Lake Michigan water I could do a minute twenty. In this tropic sea, following sunbeams down to the depths, who knows how long I can stay under?

Graceful grasses weave and wave like veils around the glittering thing. I swim down into the long strands, their feathery fingers trickling along my skin. Metal glints. I move in for a closer look. Sea vines thick as bullwhips twine my arms and legs. The metal is a lock on a duffel bag, which has become wedged between a jagged rock and a barnacle-encrusted anchor. I reach out to touch it. The current pushes me away. I swim back. My lungs complain for air.

I tug the lock. It won't open. I push against the bag. It doesn't budge. I can't stay under much longer. I walk my fingers under the bag feeling for a handle. The bag is filled with hard lumps, like rocks. My fingers find a hole the anchor has ripped into the underbelly. I reach inside, touch something soft and silky. It feels like the fringe on Grandma Ruth's piano shawl. I grab hold and yank. A few strands pull away.

My lungs won't wait. I swim toward the surface, kicking hard, feeling the panic edge of an old fear.

—*"Only stupid people swim without buddies,"* says my brother Paul.

—*"Or dead people,"* says my brother Art.

They have pulled the five-year-old me out of the Nippersink Manor swimming pool where I jumped into the deep end without knowing how to swim.

—*"You're lucky you're only stupid,"* they say together, leaving me gasping and embarrassed but alive on the side of the pool.

Kick harder! Sunlight sparkles on the surface above. I burst up and out, suck frantic gulps of air.

"There!" Kathy's voice yells far in the distance. "There she is! Morgan! Morgan!"

They swim toward me. Polsky is a strong swimmer. He reaches me quickly, clasping his hands under my elbows, holding me up while I catch my breath. "You all right?" he asks.

"Yes...fine."

"You scared us."

"Scared myself." My breath calms. "There's a duffel down there."

Mike smiles. "Buried treasure?"

I hold out my hand, still tightly fisted around the strands ripped from the bag. I uncurl my fingers. "Oh my God!"

"What the hell?" He reaches out, touches them.

I want to let go, to not see what I'm seeing, but I am frozen in place. Kathy swims up, looks at the treasure in my hand.

"Oh, no," she moans. "Oh, no. Please, no."

We stare, knowing, not wanting to know. A gentle wave washes over my hand, carrying away the unmistakable long, red strands of Jackie's hair.

ALAS, POOR JACKIE, I KNEW HER

THE NASSAU POLICE are most understanding. Chief Detective Kolby questions us on the beach as his divers search the area I've pointed out. It's not that he doesn't believe we saw what we saw, exactly. But he prefers to see proof. Elaine and the musicians have gathered up our beach gear and sit off to the side with a small crowd.

Winds pick up. Heavy clouds blow in. The police boat tosses on choppy waves. Watching it makes me queasy. A diver emerges, pulls the air hose from his mouth, and whistles the boat over. Kolby snaps to attention. The boat spews black exhaust as it slowly chugs backward toward the diver. It stops, idles, and unrolls coil from its winch. The diver grabs hold of a huge hook dangling from the end and slips back underwater. The boatman whistles three shrill notes toward shore.

"It would appear," says Kolby, "my men have found something."

Kolby waits on point. Impeccably tailored, a compact man with economical movements, he is worlds away from Roblings, who frequently looks as if he slept in his clothes. Yet both Kolby and Roblings exude the same quick instincts of natural blood hounds. I'll bet Kolby hates loose ends—either on his Italian linen pants or in his murder investigations.

Dalí would appreciate the surrealism of this scene. Here we wait, surrounded by palm trees, buffeted by warm winds, watching a search for a dead body. My internal clock ticks at a violent rate. How can I stand still? Shouldn't I be running around, *doing* something? Time melts, bends, drapes over fallen palm fronds and shifting sands.

Kolby turns to Kathy. "You say this Jackie missed rehearsal this morning?"

"We didn't think it was anything. We just thought she decided to take off."

"Is that usual?"

"Jackie could be...impulsive."

"She would go off without telling anyone?"

Kathy stares out at the boat. "Lately, she pretty much did what she wanted."

"Lately?"

"Jackie wasn't a team player. She never was really one of us. I'm not sure why she took the job."

"Why did you hire her?"

Kathy manages a wry smile. "She gave good audition."

A metallic screech rakes the air as the boat's winch reels in cable. I shudder at the sound, hug myself against a terrible chill. Kathy turns pale. Polsky puts a supportive arm around her. All eyes are fixed on the boat as the duffel breaks the surface. Strange fish up from the deep. The bag dangles from the hook, swings in wild sweeps as it rises off the water. Divers and boatmen struggle against wind and chop. It seems forever before they push and pull the duffel on board. Water pours out the jagged hole where I reached in and grabbed and yanked. My palm burns where I clutched the strands of hair.

The boat comes as close as it can to shore. Four divers float the duffel in on a rubber life raft, then carry it to the sand in front of us. Police push back the crowd of onlookers. Kolby pulls on clear plastic gloves, kneels next to the bag, and lifts off pieces of sea weed. The duffel's fat zipper sticks at first and he has to work it down little by little. Strands of red hair, caught in the teeth, trail out onto the sand like man-o'-war stingers. I press my hand over my mouth. I don't want to be here. I don't want to see this. Let me go home, now, please, thank you very much.

He works the zipper all the way down and gently separates the two sides. Inside, Jackie is folded in half, nose to knees. Her arms stretch toward her feet like a diver in mid-jackknife. Her skin glows the waxy white of plants kept too long from the sun. The jumble of jagged rocks weighting the duffel have gouged and torn soft flesh. Seawater has turned her strawberry silk dress the brownish red of dead leaves. Tiny crabs skitter all around.

Kolby reaches in, moving the head to one side so we can see. Particles of sand stick in odd places. Her eyes, partially open, stare vacantly. Her mouth forms an "o" as if surprised.

"Is this Jackie?" he asks.

"Yes," we say.

He looks at us, one to the other. "You're positive?"

"Yes."

The world presses in. I telescope somewhere outside of myself, look down at the scene as if from afar. On some level, I am aware of the sound of Kathy heaving up her guts, of Polsky soothing her, of crowds murmuring. Nearby bird shrill mixes with the *slap slap slap* of water against police boat. A sudden wind gust whips sand at my body like stinging nettles, blinding, choking. It is not until I feel like I'm suffocating that I realize I am holding my breath.

Kolby sets Jackie's head down and waves over an ambulance that crawls toward us along the beach. Lights off, siren mute, it inches through the push of onlookers. There is something eerie about a quiet ambulance. It is an emergency vehicle. Its very nature promises urgent speed and sirened warning. Its silence prickles the hairs on my nape.

Police lift the bag and set it on the gurney. The sides of the duffel gap apart. Jackie looks like an exotic pea in a pod. I realize what is wrong with the stark whiteness of her arms. "Her bracelets," I say.

"What?" says Kolby.

"The last time I saw her she was wearing an armload of expensive tortoiseshell bracelets. And big diamond stud earrings."

He reaches over, lifts strands of hair away from her ears.

Whoever killed her picked her clean.

A DEATH OUT OF TIME

TECHNICALLY, JACKIE'S BODY was found in Nassau waters, which gives local police jurisdiction of the case. Practically, Jackie was employed by the Islander Cruise Line and was seen alive and well as recently as this morning. The clues police need to solve her murder might well be on board. It is testament to the economic power of the cruise industry—which pours millions of dollars a day into Nassau's tourist-driven economy—that Detective Kolby escorts us to our ship rather than police headquarters. The last thing Nassau police or the cruise line want is to alter our itinerary. Passengers, many of whom scrimp and save for years to take a cruise, tend to become cranky if something disrupts their dream.

Polsky sits stone-faced in the front seat. Boy, did he pick the wrong two women to take snorkeling. I can just see his English class back in Minneapolis enjoying the heck out of his essay on "what I did on my winter vacation." Even though he said he never met Jackie, he was with us when I found the body, and Kolby lets him ride back to the ship with us. Elaine and the musicians taxied back with Voodo Vince. Kolby made them promise not to talk to anyone about any of this. Yeah, right. And I've got this bridge to sell you in Brooklyn.

Kathy huddles in the corner, trembling. I'm happy Polsky was on hand to comfort her when she heaved her lunch. I'm not good around sickness. I'm a lot better around death, which I was raised to view as a natural part of a great cosmic continuum. Though it's harder to reconcile a death out of time. Like a child's, like anyone's murder. My usual wisecracking self has the good sense to keep quiet.

Kolby sits in back with Kathy and me, taking notes. He'll get Jackie's background from her employment file on board. What he wants from us is personal information. He decides to start with me, give Kathy a chance to compose herself. I tell him about Mr. Rolex-Armani. How the gentleman came around last night, latched on to Jackie after the first show, brought her roses and his stateroom key after the second. I tell him about Jackie sleeping out last night and Armani in a limo on the dock this morning. "He was waiting for someone," I say. "I assumed it was Jackie."

"Is there not," asks Kolby, "a rule against fraternization between staff and passengers on your ship?"

Oops. Polsky's shoulders tighten. Not to worry, I won't rat on him and Kathy spending a lovely few hours on the beach. "There's the theory," I say, "and then there's the reality."

"Can you remember anything special about the limousine or its driver?"

I try to retrieve a single characteristic. I was so busy trying to get a look at the passenger that I didn't pay any attention to the driver. Can't even swear to color. Roblings would be disappointed. He's been teaching me to memorize physical details as a way of amusing myself during long hours spent waiting to audition. Exercise: walk into a room, glance around, sit down, close my eyes, and see how many details I can remember. If I'd known I'd be quizzed about my morning stroll around the dock, I'd have paid more attention. Kolby brightens when I say, yes, I can positively identify Rolex-Armani...right down to the angle of his razor-cut sideburns.

"And the last time you saw Jackie was?" he asks.

"This morning, near the gangway as I came back on-ship." And, "No, I didn't actually see her go off-ship but I assumed that's where she was heading."

Kolby turns to Kathy, who says she never saw the man, either last night or this morning.

"But," she says, "he sounds like Jackie's type. She had radar for men with money."

"You have many wealthy single men taking these cruises?"

Kathy shifts uncomfortably. "Jackie didn't exactly discriminate."

"Meaning?"

"It didn't seem to matter to her, one way or another, whether a man was single or married." My friend's face is bright red. For all her travels, Kathy has Old World values. It's one thing to know about a member of her staff's dirty laundry, but a whole 'nother matter to air it in front of strangers.

"So," says Kolby, "a man who tells his wife he's going off to play a five-hour round of golf might be playing at something else altogether."

"It's been known to happen."

"And you said these were men with money?"

Kathy bites the skin around her thumb. "Jackie liked expensive jewelry. Men liked to buy it for her."

Kolby stares out the window, digesting the information. The lush landscape whizzes past. "Might your friend have been involved with drugs?"

"She was not my 'friend.' And it's highly unlikely she did dope. I never saw any signs of her being high. And staff and crew are given random drug checks all the time. If anything showed up she would have, at the very least, been fired on the spot and put off-ship at the next port. And if she was dealing, she could end up doing serious time in a foreign jail. Jackie loved her comforts. I don't think she'd risk something like that."

An onslaught of ominous clouds roils across the sky. Palm trees bend in the wind, pointing the way to the ship. Fine particles of sand and dirt haze the air, muting colors like a Monet painting. In the distance, the line of ships in port looms like a range of white mountains.

Our car swerves suddenly, narrowly missing a convoy of crew biking back to the ship. Paco wobbles along near the back of the pack, sweating with the nervous effort of a beginner. Maybe his friends are teaching him to ride to take his mind off Angela's death. It might be working. At the moment he looks more terrified than sad.

Kolby presses Kathy for information about Jackie's personal life.

"Jackie never let anyone get close," she says.

"Sometimes," he says, "in casual conversation, people let things slip."

Kathy bites off a piece of thumb skin. A drop of blood wells around the nail. She sucks it absently. "This is probably nothing," she says, "but, when she first came on board, we were talking about how boring most people's lives are compared to ours. Jackie said something about working nine to five, then going home to a husband who was—how did she put it?"—she closes her eyes, retrieving the lines—"'a jobless slug who spent his days in front of the tube and never left his recliner except to take a piss or get a beer.' She said she ran away from home to join the cruise ship. But I don't know if it was just talk or if she really was married. Jackie's one of those people who would just as soon lie as tell the truth."

The police have radioed ahead and Lt. Gene Davis, the *Island Star* Chief of Security, meets us at the ship flanked by four of his men.

Roblings mentioned Davis in his wire, called him "good people," which I find a real comfort just now. The former Denver cop is a big man, six-three or -four, about two hundred thirty pounds, some of which seem to be growing a little soft around the middle. Early-to-mid-forties, he has affable features, which, at the moment, look troubled. Kolby fills Davis in as we walk to my cabin. The four security giants fall in behind. I know I didn't do anything wrong but this police escort makes me *feel* guilty.

"Allow me," says Davis, taking my key, unlocking my door.

The cabin is exactly as I left it, stuff thrown around in my rush to pack for the beach, Jackie's side surgically neat. The three of us enter, leaving the others guarding the hall outside. Davis closes the door. The small space shrinks with three people and Jackie's ghost inside. Two ghosts if you count Angela. Which I do.

"You said Jackie slept out last night," says Kolby.

"She came in around eight this morning."

"How did she look?"

"Like she needed sleep."

"Did she seem frightened, edgy, nervous in some way?"

"No. Just tired."

"What did she say?"

"She didn't."

"You didn't talk?"

"I said 'hello.' She grunted."

Kolby digests this as he looks around. "You will please show us what was hers?"

I point out her drawers, bed, and closet space, then show them the tiny bathroom. The three of us won't fit. They stand outside and poke their heads in while I point out her shelves. I squeeze past them back into the main part of the cabin. A knock on the door. I open it to a man carrying what looks like a small fishing tackle box. Lt. Davis points out the areas he wants dusted for fingerprints.

"You think the murderer was in this room?" I ask.

"I have no idea."

"Do you want me to stay?"

He nods. "In case we have questions."

I climb on my bed watching the detectives pull on plastic gloves and begin a methodical search. The print duster works around them, lifting samples from around the room. I know better than to touch anything until they've finished but I'm dying to put away this morning's damp underwear and rehearsal clothes balled in heaps on my unmade bed. Who knew I'd have company? I feel sudden empathy for the robbery victim Roblings told me about. He was working Burglary and went on a call to an elderly woman's apartment. Turns out, she'd discovered the burglary four hours before she called the police. When Roblings asked why she'd waited so long, she said the burglar left such a terrible mess she was embarrassed to have anyone see the place until she cleaned up. She even scrubbed off a nice clear set of dirty fingerprints the thief left on the door when he picked her lock.

Davis pulls a long metal lockbox from under the lingerie in Jackie's dresser. He unfolds the punch on his Swiss Army knife and pops the lock. Sheaves of papers on top have the look of legal documents. He lifts these out. Ribbon-bound handwritten letters line the bottom. Kolby pulls a large plastic bag from his suit jacket and holds it open while Davis drops the packets in.

"Those look like love letters," I say, dying to have a look.

Lt. Davis closes the lockbox and tucks it under his arm. The two men take one last look around. "This cabin is as you last saw it?" asks Kolby.

I try to remember. "This morning there was a Styrofoam coffee cup and a jewelry box on that desk. I didn't notice if they were still there when I came back to change for the beach." I describe the gold braided bracelet set with emerald and rubies that "I just happened to see" while wiping up a spill of coffee.

Lt. Davis checks the garbage can, finds the coffee cup but no jewelry box. Kolby thumbs through his notes. "From what your entertainment director told me..."

"Kathy Bloch," says Davis.

"Yes. She said Jackie had expensive tastes and willing suitors. We should find a large quantity of jewelry."

"Some of the staff keep safe boxes in the ship's bank." Davis jots a note on a small pad. "I'll check, see if she's one of them."

"Good. And I will do the same in Nassau. If her killer stole the jewelry she was wearing, it is possible she was also persuaded to give up other jewelry. If she stored it in a local bank, there will be a record of her visits. We'll see if she visited today."

The print man leaves. Kolby follows.

Davis gets ready to go. "Thanks for your help," he says, dwarfing the doorway.

I stop him. "I have a hello for you from Chicago. Detective John Roblings?"

He looks pleasantly surprised. "You make a practice of associating with unsavory characters?"

"As often as possible."

Davis has a warm smile. "Haven't talked to that sorry excuse of a skier for a dog's age. He something special to you?"

"We've been going out for about a year."

Something shifts between us. I am the girlfriend of a cop, which means I am not a complete outsider.

"Well," says Davis, "tell the man I say howdy. Wouldn't hurt him to pick up a phone every now and again."

"I will. Can I ask you something?"

"Shoot."

"When Kolby said Jackie might have been 'persuaded' to give up her jewelry, he meant tortured, didn't he?"

"We'll know after the autopsy. But, yeah, we had a real bad case here a couple years back. Some goons from a Miami gym kidnapped a guy, tortured him for a month until he signed over everything he owned to them. That guy escaped. But the goons figured it worked once, they might as well do it again. The next time things went wrong. They wound up killing the guy and his girlfriend. Cut off their heads and hands before dumping them in a ditch. The girl was identified by the manufacturer's markings on her breast implants. So, yeah, Kolby meant tortured.

"Listen," he says, choosing his words carefully, "I want you to keep an eye out. If you go off-ship, be sure you buddy up with someone. Don't take any chances. I know Roblings, I've seen him in action, and I sure don't want to have to face him if anything happens to you."

"I appreciate the thought."

I lock my door behind him and survey the room. I am gripped by an overwhelming and uncharacteristic urge to clean. It is the methodical method taught to me by Grandma Ruth. As a child, I tended to become distracted when cleaning, my mind wandering off mid-task to strange and wondrous places. *"You start at one end of a room,"* Grandma said, *"and clean speck by speck, not stopping to dance or sing or feed the fish or read a comic book or call a friend or eat a grape or go to the toilet—well, perhaps just that, but quickly—until you finish cleaning all the way around to the other end."* It takes supreme concentration and focus, like a meditation. Each swipe of the cloth, each fold of the garment, becomes part of a mantra.

I don't clean often but, when I do, I am thorough. I have no time to think about dead bodies or Rolexed murderers or the reality of what it means for one person to actually take another person's life. Television and movies numb us to what used to be unthinkable. In a single day we can watch murder by gun, knife, drowning, poison, neglect. Murder by friends, lovers, co-workers, strangers. Murder erupting from anger, anguish, revenge, love. Murder funny and murder serious. Murder messy and murder off-scene. And in the end of it all, someone dies, and that doesn't even touch us anymore.

Let me tell you something. The reality of a murder is something very different. It rages against you in powerful waves. It is troubling and scary and brings a particular sick feeling to your heart and stomach. And right now, the only weapon I have against visions of pale white flesh folded into a dark green duffel is a cleaning rag and a bottle of Formula 409.

GONE BUT NOT FORGIVEN

IT'S ONLY FIVE O'CLOCK, but I feel I've been up for days. I join the others trickling into the dressing room—ensemble members, musicians, Wardrobe, stagehands, everyone who worked with Jackie. A few officers, department heads, and other heavy hitters stand in a group in back. I recognize the two officers who worked gangway duty the day I arrived. Sean O'Brian comes in and joins their group. Something in their demeanor tells me Lt. Davis has already talked to them. They're probably here for moral support. Two of Davis' security men stand in front, studying people coming in.

"I think the news of Jackie's death should come from me," Kathy had told Kolby and Davis and they've given her the okay. At the moment they're in Personnel going over Jackie's records and questioning cabin stewards, trying to track down the Rolex-Armani man I described.

I sit up front with Kathy, keeping her company while the crowd assembles. She turns a cigarette and lighter around and around in her hand like worry beads. I search the crowd for Keith. My lanky dance partner's going to take this hard.

"Where's Keith?" I ask.

"I thought it would be best if I told him privately."

"How'd he take it?"

"He's a wreck." She rubs her eyes, already a weary red. "At first, he thought I was joking. Then he saw I wasn't. I swear I heard his heart break." She clicks the lighter lid open, closed, open, closed. "He started crying, couldn't stop. I finally asked the doctor to give him a tranquilizer. He's resting now."

"The police found some letters in our cabin," I say. "They looked like love letters, all tied with ribbon."

"Has to be Keith. He was so crazy about her. God, I hope he didn't sign them. It would be horrible if the police think he had anything to do with this." She flicks the lighter on, stares at the flame. "Can someone please explain to me why the sweet romantics are attracted to the sluts?''

Dominic rushes in, gets right up in Kathy's face. "Is this going to take long?"

"I'm just waiting for a couple more people."

"Some of us have work," he says, flopping into a chair. "Jackie better get her ass back here, because Ginger is useless. She has the memory of a carrot. There's no way I can get her ready in time for tomorrow night's show."

Kathy nods, tight-lipped. Elaine walks in with the musicians who rode to the beach with us. Kathy makes a circle of her thumb and middle finger, presses them against her tongue, and blows a shrill whistle. "Okay, okay," she says, "settle down." The room gets quiet. "I have some bad news," she says. She takes a deep breath. "Jackie's...dead."

Gasps all around. Dominic's head snaps up. "What did you say?"

"Jackie...she, um, her body was found near shore. You know that beach we go to?"

"She drowned?" someone asks.

Ah, yes, she drowned and folded herself inside a duffel bag, filled it with rocks, and zipped herself in before impaling the bag on an old anchor. Clever girl, our Jackie. I keep my thoughts to myself.

"Ah, um," says Kathy, "actually, it, ah, wasn't an accident. Jackie was murdered." More gasps, cries of surprise. Murmuring. Kathy lights the cigarette, a no-no in this room. No one complains. She sucks in a long stream of smoke, then puts the cigarette out. "There are Nassau police on board," she says, "who are working with Lt. Davis to gather information. They will be interviewing each of us. Whatever you can tell them about Jackie will be helpful."

Rhea the Wardrobe elf speaks out. "And just how exactly did she die?"

"We don't know yet."

Rosa crosses herself. "Do they know who killed her?"

"They don't know anything—"

Voices pour in from all directions.

"What are they doing to protect us?"

"Will the cruise be canceled?"

"What do the cops want to know from us?"

"I *thought* something was bothering her yesterday."

"Something was always bothering Jackie."

"Don't speak ill of the dead."

"Hey, I'm no hypocrite. I ragged on her when she was alive."

Dominic slumps forward, elbows on knees, his head resting on his hands. It looks as if he's stuck with Ginger.

Kathy rolls her shoulders in broad circles, tips her head side to side. She's wiped. I put an arm around her. "Hey, cheer up," I say. "The worst is over."

"Will you put that in writing?"

"You betchum, Red Ryder."

Suddenly, everyone talks at once. When we've a mind to, we actors can dissect someone up, down, and sideways with the precision of fine surgeons. It's obvious Jackie was no one's favorite. That's the danger in her kind of arrogance. The "little people" you dump on (and to the Jackies of this world, we're all little people) are more than happy to return the favor when given half a chance. Not one woman here considered Jackie "friend." The men found her sexy but aloof. "Gold digger," "Snob," and "User" are a few of the nicer comments.

As the group talks, some of Jackie's patterns start rising from the muck. In the four months she'd been on-board ship, she hit a number of people up for cash, loans she didn't seem inclined to repay. One guy admitted paying installments on her dental work. Entertainers are notoriously easy marks. We're so used to being broke that when we do get some money we spend it immediately. But the code is, if you borrow, you pay back as soon as you can. Jackie just kept taking. It would have caught up with her eventually, but she ran out of time.

The girl who was her cabinmate before Angela said Jackie loved to brag about expensive gifts men bought her, about her multiple sex partners, about how she never used condoms. Jackie claimed that the excitement of unprotected sex made men more generous at the jewelry shops. I think of all those unsuspecting wives and girlfriends waiting back home. My much-married Grandma Belle warned me early on that sexually transmitted diseases are "dirty little gifts that keep on giving."

Others talk about the way Jackie fought to make her roles bigger, little tricks she'd pull to make them look bad onstage. After Angela died, Jackie tried to elbow her way into the opening. When Kathy sent for me instead, Jackie grabbed the chance to jump from the chorus to the more highly visible role as Dominic's assistant.

The more secrets they unearth about my recently departed room-mate, the more I get it that she was one extremely nasty member of our species. I wish I could be a fly on the wall when these same people are questioned by the police. Will they gild the lily or yank off the petals?

It's a small blessing that Keith isn't in the room to hear this. I don't think he's strong enough to take the truth of her.

WORTH A THOUSAND WORDS

LT. DAVIS STOPS ME in the hall. "You said you could positively identify the man you saw with Jackie?"

"Yes."

"I want you to go to the photographer's studio."

"Now?"

"They're setting up the photos taken of every passenger coming on
board the ship."

"All two thousand?"

"Actually, twenty-two hundred. I'm hoping our man's in there
somewhere."

I clear it with Kathy. Tonight is Country Western and my job is to
help out with line dances, keep the party hearty. "It's not a problem,"
she says. "Come whenever you can."

One of Davis' men escorts me down into the catacombs twenty
thousand leagues under this sea. This is way too far below the water-
line for comfort. Millions of tons of water per square centimeter press
against the sides of the ship trying to crush it. The phrase "watery
grave" riffs in my head. A loud pounding echoes in the background.
Something's banging against the hull. A demented giant squid trying
to get in.

The spacious foyer of the "studio" stretches three inches by three
inches. Walls awash in glossy publicity posters heighten the claustrophobic effect. Beautiful people of all races romp, dance, sun, and
drink. None, I notice, is over thirty except for one stunning silver-
haired couple used by every advertising company in the universe every
time a client wants "a mature couple."

Normally, daily cruise photos are displayed in a large area near the
dining room where passengers are most likely to spend a little time
before or after meals. The photo concession is one of the most lucra-
tive on board all cruise ships. Not that you can tell from looking at
this space.

The three photographers working this cruise have pulled the passenger arrival photos. They've cleared a work space for me on the desk, which, like the chairs, tables, and floor, is covered with teetering stacks of photos. "Gotta get to work," one tells me, handing me a notepad and pen. "If you take any of the photos, just jot down the numbers stamped on the back. You'll want to leave the door open. It can get stuffy in here with the fumes and all. Just be sure the door locks behind you when you leave."

I settle in, devise a search pattern working clockwise through the piles. The overwhelming emotion pouring off the photos is "happy." These are people looking forward to enjoying every second of their vacation. I wonder what effect, if any, Jackie's murder will have on the cruise.

I get into the rhythm of the work. A lot of single women are on board, most traveling in groups—teachers, co-workers, friends, off for the holiday vacation. I toss these with barely a second glance. I pay closer attention to the men, no matter if alone or with other people, no matter how differently they might be dressed from the man I saw. Any time I find a man whose face is blurred or turned away from the camera or otherwise unclear, I pull the photo and set it aside.

"Gotta talk to you." A man barges into the small space, knocking over a stack of photos. In his seventies, immaculately groomed, he is dressed in the more formal blue-blazer-and-pressed-linen-slacks mode of people cruising in the forties and fifties.

"Stop!" I say as the photos splay out on the floor.

"Your prices for these photos are ridiculous." He topples another stack. I know that voice. It's the one I heard my first day on board arguing with the purser about his cabin.

"Sir, you need to stop, back up."

"Look, I know business. Instead of charging outrageous prices, you should offer a package deal."

"Sir," I jump up and grab his arm, "you must get out of here. Passengers aren't allowed. Be careful where you walk."

I get a death grip on his blazer and haul him out of the room. He's oblivious, keeps talking. "At the end of the cruise, you should let people buy ten photos for forty bucks, something like that. You'd make a fortune. No one's going to pay these prices." He's the type that doesn't listen because their mouths never stop. "Is that me?" He pushes back into the room, lifts a photo off a pile. "Nah." Drops it on another pile. Picks up a dinner table photo. "See, this is my group. I'll give you five bucks for it." He's reaching into his pocket.

"No. You have to go. I don't work here. You need to talk to—" He peels a five off a roll of bills. "You can't use money on board, sir, you know that. Everything is charged to your Cruise Card."

"I'm a stockholder of this cruise line, y'know." He presses the five in my hand, winks. "Just between you and me," he says, taking the photo.

He shouldn't have winked. People who think they can buy their way past me set my blood boiling every time. I rip the photo out of his hand, leave him holding a corner. "Look what you did," he yells.

"Yep. And if you don't get out of here, now, I'll call security. Have you thrown in the brig."

"What's your name?" He squints at my name tag. "Angela Parker. Well, Miss Parker, I think you'll be hearing from your superiors about the proper way to treat passengers."

"I look forward to it." He storms off.

Okay, so I'll never make Employee of the Year. Or of the Week, for that matter. I guess I could shoot for Day, but I'd have to be seriously motivated.

I get back to work. Rolex-Armani isn't showing his face. A couple of men sort of have his head shape or nose or hair. I begin to doubt some of what I remember, feel the onus of identifying a killer—possible killer. What if, in my desire to help, I pull the wrong photo, finger the wrong man? An hour later, I know I needn't have worried. Rolex-Armani's not in these photos.

"YOU'RE SURE?" asks Lt. Davis.

I stand in his office feeling like the key player who let the coach down. I've brought a handful of blurred and otherwise unclear photos but I know these men are not the man I saw. "Maybe he didn't want his photo taken," I say. "Maybe—"

Davis pops a pistachio nut into his mouth, cracks it open, sucks out the innards, and tosses the shells in a basket. "The two photographers working the gangway say they got everyone. But you and I know someone intent on slipping by could figure a way. It's no big thing to time a boarding with one of the big rushes or to hide in the middle of a tour group, or even have an accomplice create a diversion. All kinds of ways if you've a mind.''

"Sorry."

"Yeah," he says, "me, too."

A LITTLE BIT COUNTRY

THE STAR STRUCK ROOM is a mammoth space that, in the course of a single day, has more personality changes than Sybil. It's home to Bingo games, mechanical horse races, group dance lessons, celebrity seminars, excursion lectures, art auctions—an endless, ever-changing smorgasbord of activities spawned by the cruise staff's fertile imagination. Tonight the room is pure country, all gussied up with bales of hay in a wood wagon, saddles draped over railings, a portable stage erected at one end for the musicians, and wood squares locked together in the room's center to create a dance floor. Small tables with red-and-white checked tablecloths ring the room.

Some serious cowboy hats dot the landscape, weather-curled brims, sweat-stained bands. People flash enough silver and turquoise jewelry to stock the Phoenix Flea Market. The clunk of steel-tipped boots beats a do-si-do tattoo on the dance floor. Even people who refuse to play dress-up (you know the type) manage to don black Levi's and plaid shirts. A few, caught up in the wild abandon of the moment, have tied red or blue kerchiefs around their necks.

As I walk in, hundreds of cowboys and girls line-dance to "Elvira." Kathy and a couple of the other dancers demonstrate steps up onstage. A hint of color has returned to her cheeks and—though it might be wishful thinking on my part—I think I glimpse signs of her old perkiness. This show must go on and Kathy Bloch, entertainment director extraordinaire, is the one responsible for making sure it does. Hard enough to do when a gal's tired or harried or premenstrual. Really hard, I reckon, after witnessing the aftermath of a grisly murder.

The dance ends, and a fiddler, mandolin player, and banjo player launch into a bluegrass tune. There is a buzz of excitement in this air. I'm not up on country stars but it's clear these three are a name group hired by the *Island Star* especially for tonight. Cruising's a fun gig for celebrities. Perform a few hours, maybe give one- or two-day seminars about your work—country music, professional football, romance writing—then cruise for free in the best available staterooms. I wave to Kathy and she signals to meet her outside the room.

"Hey, pardner," I say, "how y'all doin'?"

"A whole heck of a heap better, thank ye kindly. How'd the photo hunt go?"

"Looks like Jackie's friend is camera shy."

She worries the fringe on her suede vest. "I was thinking," she says. "I know it's crazy. I mean, I doubt he would..." Her voice trails off.

"Could you be just a little more specific?"

"Oh, Morgan, you don't think he'll come back on board?"

The thought never occurred. Why would a killer return? Unless he's not the killer. Or unless he would want us to *think* he wasn't the killer. Like a kid at bedtime, Kathy doesn't want discussion, she wants reassurance. No, dear, there's no monster hiding in the closet. "No," I say, "I don't think he's coming back."

She looks mightily relieved. The worry lifts off her shoulders and settles directly on mine.

The musicians swing into a new tune. "Come on," she says. "I need you to circulate, pump up enthusiasm, get the crowd toe-tappin' and Texas two-steppin'."

I work the room, coaxing the timid to come give line-dancing a try. It doesn't take much. Just a smile and a welcoming hand. What's the worst that can happen? The worst that can happen is you'll step in the wrong direction. Think anyone will notice, or care? Not in this crowd. It's an easy sell. I keep my eyes and ears tuned for signs that passengers have heard about Jackie's murder. Nary a whisper. So far so good.

Near the end of the set, I see Ida Mills, the elderly lady I'd met in the theater my first day. She's sitting ringside, tapping the table in time to the music. I dance over. "Hi," I say.

She squints at me, reaches in her purse for glasses. "Oh." She smiles. "Morgan. Hello."

"Come on," I say, wiggling my fingers, inviting her up to dance, thinking she'll say no. But she's up in a flash, dancing close to the safety of the table, her cane dangling unused on the back of her chair.

"Lady," I shout, "you got rhythm!"

"I adore dancing." And she does a careful twirl, a shoulder shrug followed by a shimmy, ending with a hip twist that took me an hour to learn at Gus Giordano's dance class.

"Want to come out on the floor?"

"Much too crowded. Besides, I am quite out of breath." She settles back in her chair. "Not bad for ninety-three," she says.

"Seventy-three?"

She shakes her head, holds up nine fingers. A line of tattooed numbers peeks out from her dress sleeve. At first I think it's a stain, that she's set her arm in some juice or food on the table. My mind doesn't want to register what I'm seeing. I blink my eyes clear. The numbers stay numbers. I grew up seeing these at family gatherings, was instructed early not to ask questions. She sees me staring, smiles gently. "You go on, dear. Thank you. This was wonderful."

I give her a hug and head back to work. This day is an emotional roller coaster run by a madman. He doesn't seem inclined to stop and let me off.

A few times I glance over at Kathy. What a trooper. To look at my friend, so lively and enthusiastic, you'd never guess how violently sick she'd been at the beach. How hard it was for her to break the news about Jackie to the staff. Her fear the murderer might still be around. Of course, this particular music helps drown the demons. It's impossible to be sad when a banjo's playing.

Kathy suddenly jumps off the stage and dances out onto the floor. She dances through the crowd, smiling as she goes, moving like a shadow next to cowboy Michael Polsky, resplendent in hip-hugging Levi's and "shit kicker" boots, who's line-dancing like he was born to it.

SO THAT'S HOW IT WORKS

TONIGHT I OUTDO MYSELF trying to get back to my cabin. My mind, drifting against my will to Jackie's murder, refuses to pay attention. This time I get so turned around that, after descending a couple of stairwells I've never seen before, I'm not even sure I'm still on the same ship. I clomp along in cowboy boots half a size too large, bought for five bucks from my summer stock production of "Oklahoma."

A vague uneasiness works my stomach. No one else is walking these halls. If someone came at me... I tread more softly, wish I carried a big stick. My razor-sharp instincts tell me my cabin is not on this level. At this depth, I'm more likely to run into Orpheus descending than someone from waitstaff. I turn into a corridor that dead-ends at a massive metal door secured by three huge locks. I try a smaller door on my right. Locked. My heart rate cranks up, pumping little warnings. *"Find people." "Don't paint yourself into a corner." "Don't get caught alone and trapped."* I try a door on my left. This one opens onto an oval catwalk.

A wall of noise hits me, half the decibels of a Latino dance club, one stop short of deafening. The catwalk, as far around as my high school running track, encircles massive pieces of machinery rising at least three stories from the floor below. A handful of crew man their stations, attend gauges, write notes on clipboards. I relax. The presence of people means safety. And standing in the bosom of machinery feels like home. Like a moth to light, a monk to prayer, my dad to chocolate, I step onto the catwalk, welcoming the mechanical hum vibrating through my bones. I have stumbled into the glorious heart of the ship.

I lean on the railing, feeling the rhythm. *Ca chung. Ca chung a thung. Ca chung a thung a thung a thung.* You need to understand. I was raised by Skokie Sam the Shoe Shop Man. From the time I was a toddler, the shop's fancy retail area held no interest. It was the workroom in back that drew me—the smell and elegant movement of oiled cutting machines, sounds of special sewing machines punching needles through thickest oxfords and daintiest T-straps, the symmetry of stacked leather patches and Neolite heels. I knew the function of every tool hanging on the Peg-Board, could use them all by the time I was seven. To this day, I can build a house better than I can clean one.

Ca chung. Ca chung a thung. Ca chung a thung a thung a thung.

My feet start moving, Fred Astaire in "Shall We Dance," set against a backdrop of stark white boilers and engines, tapping out the rhythmic music of machinery. The Gershwin boys laid the groundwork for "Stomp" way back in 1937. I'm really getting into this odd-tempo beat when a sudden movement catches my eye. Nearly a football field away, two men step out from a doorway onto the catwalk. Sean O'Brian's uneven gait is unmistakable even from this distance. He and a square-built man with no neck bend toward each other in shouted conversation. This is an odd place to communicate. I can't work in *loud.* I once waitressed at Viva! but gave it up when screaming the daily specials at diners created nodes on my vocal cords.

It isn't until they've walked halfway around that the man notices me, touches Sean's arm, nods in my direction. I wave. Sean says something to him and the man turns back. My friend ambles toward me, smiling.

"I'm thinkin'," he shouts, "we need to give you bread crumbs to scatter. Help you find your way home."

"What makes you think I'm lost?" I yell. "Maybe this is how I get handsome men all to myself."

He laughs. "There's that. Well, now that I've got you in the belly of the beast, would you be interested in a tour?"

"I would, that."

"You'll be my second tonight," he shouts, nodding toward the man going back through the door they came out of. "I'm sort of getting the hang of this guide thing."

We circle around as he points out the function and purpose of the equipment below, mammoth pieces so clean and shiny it's hard to believe they're not stage props. Here live the powerful monsters that propel, heat, cool, and otherwise run this floating city.

A few of the crew watch as we circle. I recognize Paco's face staring up at me, frightened. Does Angela's friend think I'm upset about his coming into my cabin, mistaking me for Angela? Does he think I'm bringing the authorities? I smile and wave. Look, see, we're friends. Sean has already moved ahead on the catwalk. The young sailor understands that my presence here has nothing to do with him, smiles before turning back to his work. Maybe I should pick up his lessons where Angela left off. It might be fun teaching someone to sing. Though I don't think I'll let him teach me Spanish. I've tried to learn other languages, can "pretend talk" authentic-sounding Spanish, French, Italian, Russian, German, and Swedish. But my Teflon mind won't hold real words and grammar.

We've circled all the way around to the far side. For all his misshapen limbs, Sean O'Brian moves smooth and easy, like a thoroughbred with a playful gait. I clomp behind in my oversized boots. His gracefulness makes me feel downright inelegant. Sean opens the door from which he and the man had emerged. "My office," he shouts.

I step through onto another catwalk, this one running above a cargo hold at least as immense as the space we just left. The floor below looks like the final scene in "Raiders of the Lost Ark." A bijillion crates and container cars, piled two and three high, are stacked in endless rows. Sean pulls the door closed behind, damping the machinery noise to a low rumble.

We circle the catwalk at a good clip. "Don't want to be runnin' out of toilet paper in the middle of the ocean, now, do we?"

"Not unless you want a mutiny."

"Naw, mutiny happens when the booze runs out." He points to a row of locked metal cases. "We've stocked five thousand quarts for this trip. Our refrigerated containers hold twelve thousand pounds of meat. We'll pick up eleven thousand bananas along the way, stow forty-three thousand eggs."

"It's amazing you can keep track of all this."

"Not as amazin' as you rememberin' speakin' lines and dance steps. I'd never have enough nerve to get up in front of all those people."

"Don't sell yourself short. You're a great guide."

"Not many would care for this particular tour."

"You said you just gave one."

"That fella you saw me with. I found him wanderin' about, poking his nose into everything. We get them now and again. It's the same kind of fellow who fancies a peek into the airplane cockpit or the ship's bridge. Course, I don't get 'em as often as the captain, thank the Lord. Don't have the temperament to be nice when I haven't the mind."

"I met a passenger like that down in the photo office."

"They have you workin' down in the mines, do they?"

"No. I was trying to find a photo of a passenger I saw with Jackie."

He shakes his head. "Ah. That's such a terrible thing. Young girl like that. Did ya have any luck, then?"

"No."

Two crewmen stride through a door in the hold below wheeling a dolly. Sean and I watch as they load items from various-colored containers. "Those would be lightbulbs," explains Sean, "and those boxes he's pulling from the yellow container are the seasick bags. Ran out, if you can believe it, during last week's storm."

The draft from the open door carries odors from below. It's that same blend of food and body odor and something that reminds me of camping. "What are those smells?" I ask.

He cocks his head, sniffing. "Just the ship," he says. "Everythin' venting together. Sometimes, when we're not movin', this air below can get ripe as a boys' gym locker. Come on, let's get you headed on the right path."

A door off this catwalk leads to a good-sized storage area. Dominic's Vanish Box, saw box, and other big pieces of equipment share space with Entertainment Department props. A freight elevator stands silent in the corner. We pass through another door that opens to the back of the bicycle hold. I follow Sean past the rows of bikes and out into the hall. Things are starting to look familiar.

"Give me another hundred years," I say, "and I might find my way around."

"Where you from, then?" Sean asks, walking me to my cabin.

"Chicago."

"No, darlin'. That's where you live. Where are you from? Your people?"

"Russia," I say. "My mom's family's from Russ-Pole by way of the Spanish Inquisition. Dad's family's from Belarus, though I suspect some Mongolian blood explains the exotic slant of his eyes. What about you? Where're you from?"

"Sweden." We laugh. "Belfast, darlin', born and bred. What you see before you is livin' proof of the humanity of rubber bullets."

So that's what bent his body. "How old were you?" I ask.

"I was but a bump in me ma's belly. On her way to buy bread she was, in the wrong place at the wrong time. Tho', as she told me often enough, if that bullet had not been rubber, I'd not have lived to tell the story."

I think of my own ancestors, the terrifying hardships that drove them to leave the only homes they'd known and set off for strange new lands. "You must be happy they're so close to peace in Ireland."

"Been readin' the papers, have you now?"

"I know peace is iffy. There'll be flare-ups. It's like Israel and the Arab states. So many years of terrible losses on both sides. But, still, it sounds like things are really better in Ireland. Have you gone back?"

And he fixes me with a gaze so powerful, a wistfulness so intense, it's almost painful to look at him. "Oh, darlin'," he says, "can't you see I've never left? What you're lookin' at here is my sorrowful ghost."

And somehow we've arrived at my cabin door and Sean's off down the hall waving over his shoulder as he rounds a corner and disappears.

There are people you meet and, in two minutes, you know everything you need or want to know about them. And there are others you know all your life and still can't get enough of. Old friends are like that. And Roblings. And, most certainly, one Mr. Sean O'Brian.

TONIGHT, THE SOUNDS of crew hanging out in the hall are a comfort. I want people around, lots and lots of people. I lock my door behind me, check it, check it again. It's a little tricky walking around the room avoiding touching anything of Jackie's. Once, I brush against her bed. The feel of the fabric sends shudders.

I pop a couple of seasick pills and climb into a hot shower. No matter how hard I scrub, I can't wash away the feel of Jackie's hair twining my fingers, burning my flesh like a brand.

With my desk chair pushed against the door, I settle into bed to study the videotape of tomorrow night's "French Follies." This tape was made before Jackie left the ensemble to become Dominic's assistant. She is an accomplished dancer and, if you didn't know about the rot inside, you'd think her a remarkable beauty. It's easy to see why so many men were drawn to her. Won't you come into my parlor...

I run the tape again. The pills begin working their magic. My eyelids grow weights. By the time the tape ends, I've nailed the moves. I *own* this show. By next week, I'll have learned all of Angela's routines. By the end of week three I'll be able to perform all the shows in my sleep. And then I leave.

And I float away on a sea of wooze. Did I remember to lock up? I should check again. But first let me staple this string of white voodoo chicken bones around the cabin door like holiday lights. And oh, see the line of pregnant dancers do the cancan through the bike hold. Seaman Sean O'Brian, in tight Apache dancer pants, his Greek sailor's cap askew, kicks front and center, perfect long legs flying high over his head.

DAY THREE

THE MORNING AFTER

THE SCENT OF Roblings' skin reaches deep into my sleep, drags me awake. Spring earth and sea air mix with something musk. His is the perfect masculine smell, one never captured in any designer fragrance. Still inside thoughts of him, I open my eyes. Jackie's bed stares back, pillowed and pristine. I close my eyes, try to fall back into my dream, but it vaporizes.

The face looking back at me in the morning mirror is not a pretty sight. My sunburnt nose glows Rudolph red. Pillows of skin plump under each eye. The humidity has crimped my hair into comb-defying ringlets. I grab my toothpaste and brush out of the medicine cabinet, trying not to look at Jackie's shelves. How soon will they take her stuff away? *Who* will take it away? Will her family come? What kind of people raise a vampire? Other vampires? Or were hers recessive genes? Do vampires mourn their dead or eat them? No, those would be werewolves. Can the two species intermarry?

My morning mind's a scary place,
and none I think do there embrace.

Who invented morning, anyway? It's a brutal concept, cruel and unusual. Coffee. I need coffee. I pull on rehearsal shorts, a tank top, and dark glasses. On my way out, I grab the bathing suit Elaine loaned me. If I'm going to be on-ship for three weeks, I should buy my own.

Her door is decorated with a festive Christmas wreath, bright green-and-red plaid ribbons trailing down. Bing Crosby sings Christmas carols from the other side. I knock softly. "Elaine?" I say. "It's me, Morgan."

"Hold on." She unlocks the door. She's been crying. "Hi."

"You all right?"

"Yeah. Come on in."

She looks more fifteen than nineteen. Sodden tissues overflow the wastebasket next to her bed. Poor kid's having trouble dealing with Jackie's murder. It's a lousy break she was on the beach when I found the body. Murder on-scene is the stuff of nightmares. It's easier to take when it happens offstage. One of the perks of dating a homicide detective like Roblings is it helps develop certain emotional calluses. Not that I'm immune to the power of murder, I've just developed a bit of armor.

Elaine goes into the bathroom, blows her nose, splashes water on her face. The cabin, smaller than mine, has only one bed. Elaine has cozied the space with a crazy quilt hand-stitched from scraps of fabric and old clothing. All vertical spaces overflow with Beanie Babies.

A plastic shoe box filled with skeins of embroidery threads sits open on her bed. She's been cross-stitching a baby quilt from a store-bought kit. The top half is stamped with big block letters of the alphabet, the bottom half a menagerie of ducks and rabbits. She's working on the little blue x's that form the "D." I pull up the desk chair as she climbs back on her bed.

I hold out the swimsuit. "Thanks for the loan," I say.

She waves it away. "Use it until you leave. I've got plenty." She picks up her needlework.

"That's cute."

She tries to smile, doesn't quite make it, rests the stitching on her lap. "They're digging up Angela," she says.

"Angela?"

"An autopsy, you know?"

It takes me a moment to shift bodies. To understand she's upset about Angela, not Jackie.

"I talked to her mom last night. I've called every few days since...since she died. Angela and I were best mates, you know?" She stares down at the needle and thread as if wondering how they got in her hand. "This is so hard on her mom. She begged them not to disturb Angela's body. I mean, Angela's death was an accident, had nothing to do with this business. But the authorities contacted her yesterday, said they had to exhume the body, do the autopsy. Police down here want to be sure Angela wasn't murdered."

"This is because of what happened to Jackie."

"Yes." She jabs the needle into the cloth. "This is so like Jackie. Even from the grave, she found one last little way to hurt Angela. Won't let her rest in peace."

"I don't understand," I say.

Her voice turns hard. "Jackie was so mean to Angela, always thought she should star. Angela tried to ignore her but Jackie really knew how to get to people." She's stitching faster, now, pulling the thread too tight, making the fabric pucker.

"So why did they room together?"

"Mostly because no one else could stand Jackie and Angela wasn't a complainer. She never complained to anyone but me. I told her to ask for a move but she figured she was going to be leaving soon, could put up with it until her contract ran out. That way, she said, she spared the rest of us the horror of living with Jackie. I mean, she made it a joke. Angela was always real considerate, you know?" She pulls the short thread through to the back of the quilt, ties a quick knot. "I guess it wasn't so bad, not most of the time. Neither of them used the cabin much. Jackie played musical men and Angela pretty well stayed with Reggie."

"Her boyfriend?"

"Yeah, Captain Sensitivity."

"How's he taking her death?"

"Like he takes everything," she says. "Water off his back. I'm not passing judgment, you know? Angela was a big girl. Their arrangement worked for them."

She threads the needle and jabs the new strand up from the back. It will take many hours to finish this blanket. I started one like it for my niece when she was in utero. I'll be lucky to finish by the time she has a baby. I wonder, as close as Elaine and Angela were—

"Who's the blanket for?" I ask.

She stops, runs the tips of her fingers along the cross-stitched bunnies. "I thought I might as well keep working on it. It makes me feel she's still close by."

"Angela?"

She wipes a renegade tear. "She missed a couple of periods. Finally bought one of those pregnancy test kits. Made *me* buy it, in case someone saw. She was shy about the funniest things, like not being able to buy tampons if a guy was working checkout."

"My little sister's like that."

"Anyways, she took the test just before she...before her accident." She picks up a tissue, blows her nose. "As soon as she told me, I bought this kit in Miami, started it as a surprise."

So, Rosa the Wardrobe maven was right about Angela being pregnant. "She was going to keep the baby?"

"I don't know that she'd decided. But I'm always stitching something anyway, I thought I might as well get started. In case she did keep it, you know? If she didn't," she shrugs, "half my friends back home are popping out rug rats."

"Does Reggie know?"

"I think, when she died, she was still trying to decide whether or not to tell him."

"She didn't want to marry him?"

"Marry?" Elaine looks surprised. "Oh, I forget, you're new to this. Well, let me be the first to warn you. Shipboard romances have nothing to do with shoreside lives. No one working on a ship reads anything more into them than that."

My stomach starts keeping time to the motion of the ship.

"You don't look so good," says Elaine.

"Seasick."

"Boy, you and Angela. You should eat. Apples and crackers. It helps."

"I'm on my way. Can I bring you something?"

"Naw, I'm fine."

I'm opening the door when she says, "One of the worst things about this autopsy, you know?" Her voice is barely a whisper. "Angela's family's going to find out about the baby. What am I supposed to say to them then?" She looks up at me, tears running down her cheeks onto the little blue bunny with the yellow hat. "You know?"

SIGN LANGUAGE

WITH A MINIMUM OF wrong turns, I hunt down the staff mess and settle into a quiet corner table with coffee and a banana.

Sean O'Brian slips into the chair across. "Top of the mornin' to ya," says he, in his best Hollywood-movie Irish.

"And the rest of the day to yourself."

He crosses his sinewy arms on the table, leans forward. "One of the security lads just told me the sad news."

About Angela's autopsy? How could he have heard?

"About you, darlin', findin' that poor girl's body in the sea." Ah, he means Jackie. Can't tell your dead entertainers without a scorecard. "It must have been a powerful shock. When you think of that great wide ocean. I mean, what are the odds of something like that happening?"

"I've the luck of the Irish," I say.

"Of some of us, anyway."

The image of Jackie's white body begins to surface. I fight to push it back down. Sean squints at me, sees the struggle, covers my hand with his. It's a comfort.

"I've also seen death," he says. "I was four when my best friend Michael O'Malley was caught by a bullet shot through a bedroom window. Patrick, Jimmy," he runs a list of names as his gaze drifts off over my shoulder, "so many killed so many ways. It never gets easier." His eyes look back at mine, and I see the pain and sorrow there. "You'll be all right, will ya?" he asks.

"Yes, thanks."

"Well, then, you need anythin', anythin' at all, you come lookin' for me."

He leaves and I feel the walls of the mess closing in. There're still twenty minutes to rehearsal. I grab my coffee and climb up out of the depths in search of daylight. The passengers I pass in the near-deserted halls seem relaxed, normal. It won't be long now. Jackie's murder is too big. It can't be contained, even on a ship this size. What will happen when word leaks out?

I settle into a railside chaise. The Nassau sun warms without burning. More ships arrived during the night. Now we are nine. The dock below is pure chaos. Tour leaders call out shore excursions through a clash of bullhorns.

"Casino tour, here. Paradise Island casino tour over here."

"Close Dolphin Encounter people, here please."

"Cable Beach golfers. Leave your clubs on the blue cart. We'll load them for you."

"Catamaran sail here. Catamaran, green bus please. Sorry, only room for those already signed up."

"Spruce Cay people. Here, please."

It's amazing how effortlessly so many people can be herded onto buses and whisked off for a day of fun in the sun.

Ichabod and his group, looking like big game hunters in their safari shirts and multi-pocketed pants, gather on the far side of the pier loading equipment into the same beat-up van that nearly ran me down. Was that only yesterday? Seems like years. Across the pier, the young basket seller is back in his booth looking none the worse for his near-death experience.

"Morning." Mike Polsky stretches his perfectly toned body onto the chaise next to me. "Sleep all right?"

"I guess, all things considered. You?"

"Not really." He stares at the mob scene on the pier. "I keep thinking about the murdered girl. I mean, you read about murders in the paper, see stories on TV, but it's different in real life."

My palm burns. I check for red-haired stigmata. Nothing. I close my eyes, push death thoughts away, let the island sounds and moist air work their healing magic.

"Wasn't there another one?" Polsky says.

"Another?"

"Kathy mentioned another entertainer died?"

"Mmmm." I'm in no mood to discuss death.

"Her name was Angela," he says. "You were wearing her name tag yesterday."

"Right. Never met her. I was hired to replace her."

He is silent awhile. I hear his chair scrape back. "Well, I guess I'll go grab some grub. See you later."

"Later," I say.

A sudden smell of Opium body powder comes so strong I open my eyes to see who is standing over me. No one. I am alone. The phantom Opium lingers. Angela's Opium. They say smell is the strongest of all our senses, retrieves memories from our earliest years. For me, Opium will be forever Angela. That tiny spill of her powder left in my medicine cabinet makes her real to me. She was a living, breathing human being. How long does it take to exhume a body, to determine if a death is accident or murder?

I JOIN KATHY and the skeleton crew in the freezing theater. Another dancer takes Keith's place. "He was up all night," says Kathy. "I'm not sure when he'll be able to perform. I've never seen anyone this upset."

We run through a few songs and dance numbers. After yesterday's rehearsal, which laid down the groundwork, this one's a snap. It doesn't take long to smooth the wrinkles. When we finish, Kathy gives me a Walkman and audiotape of the music to back up the video I already have. "You okay with this?" she asks. "Do you need me to stay and work with you?"

"This should do it," I say.

"Great!" She grabs her gear. "I'm going to show Mike the Botanical Gardens. Maybe picnic on the beach."

One without dead bodies, I think, but don't say. "You like him."

"What's not to like? Gorgeous, bright, interested," she winks, "available. See you tonight."

I linger on the empty stage, plink a few piano keys. I hope for her sake Polsky isn't a theater groupie. At the beach, when I introduced him to Kathy, there was something almost urgent in the way he latched on to her. I may be an entertainer, but Kathy is the Grand Poobah of all the entertainers. Although, to be fair, when Detective Kolby unzipped the bag with Jackie's body, I noticed a shift in Polsky. He seemed sharper somehow. Less puppy, more guard dog. And I can't deny he's been great to Kathy since she met him.

I run my voice through tonight's songs. It's so great being onstage. I've loved it since Aunt Bertha first brought the three-year-old me to Sulie and Pearl Harand's School for the Performing Arts and lifted me up onto the stage. I'm energized by the nervous tremors running electric through my body, love the feeling that, up here, I'm someone special.

The air-conditioning kicks in again. My skin ices. The scent of Opium wafts in on the chill air. It is powerful, unmistakable. Angela calling out to me? A plea for justice from beyond the grave? It's not that I believe in omens...exactly. But as a direct descendant of Bubbe Dubbe Rissman, originally of Minsk, who brought a Maxwell Street peddler's dead horse back to life by a laying on of the hands, I also do not believe in thumbing my nose at a Sign from Beyond.

"All right, all right," I say, "I hear you."

I just wish I knew what the smell of Opium means. "Sometimes we don't understand signs until after," says Grandma Ruth, she of the Tarot cards and Ouija board. Unfortunately, if we're talking double murders here, understanding omens "after" may be a tad too late.

ON THE ROAD AGAIN

I STUDY THE "French Follies" video for half an hour before my cabin starts feeling more prison than sanctuary. Angela's ghost was bad enough, now I feel Jackie rattling around this space. I have to get out.

What I need is a nice long run, get back on track. My mind is muddled because I'm not getting the level of exercise I'm used to. It doesn't help that memories of Jackie's body wash over me at odd times. Like now. I shudder, push away a sick feeling. I lace up my running shoes, buckle on my fanny pack, pull on my Chicago Cubs baseball cap, and five minutes later I'm following the mob of bikes and beach-bound staff down the gangway.

The late-morning dock is a zoo crowded with nine cruise ships' worth of leftover passengers, those opting not to take morning excursions. I wend through ambling tourists who ooze like sludge on their way to and from the Straw Market and Rawson Square shops. Smells of sizzling barbecue and ripe fruits mingle with sounds of metal bands and straw sellers. I pass the bow of the ship where Sean O'Brian vigorously oversees the loading of two large container cars into the hold. I feel a little guilty. Some staff, entertainers like me for example, get more time off than most cruise employees. While some crew are confined to windowless cabins and work areas, putting in twelve- to fourteen-hour days, seven days a week, for less than two bucks an hour, entertainers sometimes have entire chunks of time off and can mix with passengers in certain areas on the upper decks. It doesn't seem fair. But, hey, I don't make the rules.

My need to run alone, so I can set my own pace, go my own distance, balances with my desire to stay around the safety of other people. The line separating caution and paranoia stretches thin at times and there's no harm straddling them for a while. I decide to warm up with a slow run down Bay Street to Mackey, then begin picking up the pace as I cut across the bridge to Paradise Island.

My body's not thrilled about exercising in this heat. I run alongside the road, moving against traffic, wary of jitneys, taxis, and horse-drawn carriages. The crowds thin as I go, but I am still surrounded by a comfortable cushion of tourists and locals. Hordes of mopeds buzz like angry insects.

Most of the traffic heads for the Paradise Island Casino. I take a left down Paradise Beach Drive picking up the pace a little more, hitting my stride, and letting my mind float. What is Roblings doing at this exact moment? Is some willing woman making herself available? Is she mesmerized by his eyes, their brilliant flecks of orange and gold and green? Is she seduced by the intelligence behind them?

A car horn blares. Startled, I dive out of the way as a taxi comes up behind me, swerves into my lane as it whips past a man on a moped. My foot catches in a rill in the dirt shoulder and I go down. Hard. My head bangs against the sun-baked soil. My ankle explodes with pain. Metal blood-taste fills my mouth.

I try to move. Thorny plants stab my skin. My aching brain warns my body to lie still. Sweat mixes with dust, burns my eyes. I wipe them, smearing the dirt, making the stinging worse. I can't see. My ankle's on fire.

"Oh, no, please," I whisper. "Please don't be sprained. Please. Please." No one stops. I try to stay calm. This needs time. In a few minutes, when my system moves out of shock, I'll sit up and assess my injuries. Right now, I'll lie still, cheek to soil, breathe slow and easy.

The putter of a moped slows. Tires crunch gravel inches from my head. I choke on exhaust spewing in my face. My stomach heaves at the stink of fuel, burning eyes refuse to open. A woman's voice calls over the noise of the motor.

"Are you hurt?"

"Yes, I think I may be."

"Good."

"Wha—?"

"I hope you broke something, you slut."

The engine revs, the moped races off kicking up more dirt, this time into my nose and mouth. I choke, coughing, gasping, fighting to sit up. My head throbs. I hold it with both hands to keep it from falling off. What was *that* about?

Again, a moped buzzes toward me. Is she coming back? Fear digs jagged talons into my stomach. Busy road or not, I'm an easy target should someone feel so inclined. I try to open my eyes. The sting is horrible. The moped comes closer. Who's to say Jackie's killer wasn't a woman? I'm the one who thought it was Rolex-Armani. What do I know? I scoot back from the road, into a nettle bush. This time the moped stops.

"Oh, my God. Oh, my God." A man's voice. I tilt my head back, flutter my dirt-caked eyelids. A blurry face with amazing bushy eyebrows comes close to mine. The brows hoist in surprise.

"Miriam? Miriam?" The West Side accent bends around my birth name. "Is this you?"

I squint. "Uncle Leo?" Can't be. Not on a moped. I squint harder. The blurry face is too thin. Besides, this guy's wearing a weird hat. No, not a hat. Long strands of hair flap like an open lid to one side of his head. It is. "Uncle Leo! Oh, thank goodness."

"Wha...what happened? You're hurt. Oh, my God. Let me get help."

"No. No. Just stay here with me." Protect me from weird moped-riding women. "Give me a minute."

He kneels beside me. "What can I do? Is anything broken? You were, maybe, hit by a car?"

"No, I just fell." I try to calm him. "I'll be fine. I'll be fine."

He unzips his fanny pack, pulls out a bottle of water and a large handkerchief. "How is it you're here?" he asks, wetting the kerchief, dabbing dirt from around my eyes.

"I was just about to ask you the same thing."

"I'm taking a cruise," he says.

"Me, too. Well, sort of. I'm working a few weeks on the *Island Star*."

He stops dabbing. "But that's my ship!"

"You're kidding."

"My hand to God. Careful. Keep your eyes closed. Let me get this shmutz out."

"Then, you and Aunt Bertha must have seen me last night in 'The Best of Broadway.' I was that gorgeous singer propped against the piano."

"Oh, I, ah—" He, quickly pours more water onto his kerchief, becomes very busy wiping dirt off my face. "I was...a little tired. All that traveling the day before. Getting to the airport in that blizzard, flight delay, waiting for luggage in Miami, fighting for a taxi. The whole thing wore me out. You know I don't travel much. At least I didn't. I'm thinking maybe I'll do more now. Tilt your head back. That's a good girl.''

My eyes still sting but the fresh water clears my vision. Uncle Leo looks awful. The clump of hair he combs so carefully from above his left ear over the bald spot on top to the right ear has come totally unstuck. It flaps in the tropical breeze like a matted dead thing. His usually rosy skin is ashen. Once-round cheeks sink inward like deflated balloons. Small patches of white stubble mark the places his razor missed. Uncle Leo has always been a cherubic little man. Quick to smile. Impossible to anger. Which is just as well since he's married to my mom's big sister Bertha the Bombast. But it looks as if he's been through a terrible illness. Can't be. Mom would have said something. I'll have to call home, find out what's going on.

"Is Aunt Bertha out shop—"

A gang of teens, riding three abreast, buzz past on mopeds. One nearly clips Uncle Leo. "C'mon, Mimi," he says, helping me up. "We'd best move."

I test my ankle. It's sore but bears a little weight. "Hop on," he says, holding the moped still for me. "I'll take you back."

THE RIDE TO THE SHIP on the back of Uncle Leo's moped is surreal. Here's a man I've known my entire life. He's as cautious as Aunt Bertha is wild, a man who believes two-door cars are too small to be safe. He'd be last on my list of "guess who I saw bombing around Nassau on a moped?" In fact, he'd be way down on my Nassau list as well. In grammar school when I had to make a family tree and write what each member did, my dad told me to put down that "Uncle Leo test-drives La-z-boy recliners for a living."

Always a lousy driver, Uncle Leo's even worse on a moped. We move in fits and starts, his foot frequently reaching for a brake that isn't there. I hold on to him for dear life, shutting my eyes against the sting of his windblown hair whipping my face. A disturbing thought hits me broadside. Maybe Uncle Leo's been given a month to live and has decided to throw caution to the wind. That would explain his gaunt appearance and the moped. He asks me something but I can't hear over the motor's noise. We make the ride back to the ship in silence.

Uncle Leo slows as we ride onto the dock, the moped lurching inches from a steel drum player before sputtering to a stop. He fires it back up. "Where to?" he asks. I'm about to point out the crew gangway amidship when I realize there are too many people around. Uncle Leo's bound to take out one or two.

"This is fine," I say, wincing as I dismount.

"You'll be all right?"

"I'm sure I—"

But he's not listening, he checks his watch. "I have to return this thing or they'll charge me another hour."

"Thanks for—"

"You'll have dinner at my table one night, yes? How do I reach you?"

"You can leave a message at the Entertainment Office and they'll—"

The moped bolts like a horse returning to the stable. Uncle Leo goes with it.

I wonder what Aunt Bertha is up to today. She of the diamonds and furs, manicures and makeup, is hardly the moped type. But, until today, I didn't think Uncle Leo was, either.

PIER GROUP

I LIMP TOWARD my ship. Straw sellers, their clothing ablaze in fiery clashes of reds, oranges, and yellows, prowl the dock, enticing returning tourists with towering stacks of woven hats, purses, and baskets.

I keep weight off my ankle as much as possible. Thank goodness for Uncle Leo coming along when he did. But what was with that woman on the moped? I've been called a lot of things, "ham" mostly, "kook," "showoff," "zany." But this was my first "slut" and I didn't much like it. I could laugh her off more easily if I hadn't discovered a dead body yesterday. A thing like that tends to make me edgy.

A few passengers in wheelchairs board in a special line, their ramp less pitched than the others. Crew working gangway duty help board them quickly. Dominic moves in behind them wheeling his hand-painted Vanish Box. It's an upscale version of the box my brother Paul, aka Margenon the Magnificent, used when we performed at parties. The thing weighed a ton and was miserable to lug up and down apartment stairs. I swear only people in third-floor walk-ups booked our act. Dominic's box is even bigger and fancier and he doesn't have a little sister to help him shlep. I doubt his assistant Ginger-the-waif would be much help. He follows the wheelchairs on board, maneuvering the box up the ramp as if it were weightless.

I join the flow of crew walking their bikes toward the crew gangway amidship. Every step hurts my ankle. I hate being injured, have no use for it, become depressed when I'm in anything less than top physical shape. Unfortunately, injury is first cousin to dance.

"BAAAA-ssss-kets. BAAAAA-ssss-kets."

An amazing voice sings out over the dock. Bob Marley meets Harry Belafonte. I search for the source.

"BAAAA-ssss-kets. Beautiful BAAAAA-ssss-kets."

The voice belongs to an energetic straw seller singing enticements to passengers and crew waiting to use a bank of pay phones. I should try to call Mom, make sure Dad didn't garble my message about working on the cruise ship. I'll also ask if Uncle Leo has been ill. And I can try to reach Roblings, casually mention the body I found. Murder is the sort of thing he finds interesting. That and Shakespeare's comedies, and smelt fishing, and astronomy, and an endless slew of unrelated subjects. Damn, I miss him. I check my watch. Still plenty of time before I need to board.

The afternoon sun beats in earnest, burning my arms and legs. I hobble into the phone line behind part of Ichabod's group, two safari-shirted men pushing a third friend in a wheelchair. The long sleeves that looked so untropical before make perfect sense now. These men won't be needing jars of "aloe gel for the relief of sunburn." One of them lights up a pipe of pleasant cherry tobacco. I smoked pipes and cigars when I was trying to quit cigarettes. It was a bad move. I inhaled everything.

"BAAAA-ssss-kets. Beautiful BAAAAA-ssss-kets." The straw seller gloms onto the men, who are a whole bunch more polite than I would be. It makes me positively claustrophobic when salespeople push into my face. The seller opens his baskets, one after the other. The men look in with interest.

"Some of these men are so handsome." A thirtyish woman behind me is appraising a couple of officers at the head of our line. I check the guys out. They're Nordic giants from one of the other ships, blond hair, robust complexions, square-built bodies nicely filling their dress whites. Not my types. But, then, I've got a thing for the Jacks Palance and Nicholson.

"It's the uniforms," I say.

"You think?"

"They're probably nothing special without clothes."

"Is that how you like your officers?"

"Without clothes?" I laugh. "That's cute." She doesn't smile. Good deadpan. It's one of the harder stand-up comedy techniques.

Her hair is the monotone black of shampoo-in hair color. The roots growing in are light, probably premature gray. She should try going blond, the roots would be less obvious. Like I'm one to talk. I've been tweezing out occasional white hairs for three years now. First one or two, then it just growed like Topsy. If I'm not careful, there will come a time when I'll either have to color my hair or go bald. It's like Uncle Leo and his comb-over. He started years back with a little bit of hair combed over a tiny bald spot. The bald spot grew and his side-part sank lower. These things just take on lives of their own.

The line moves. I step up, trying not to put weight on my bad foot.

"Which ship are you on?" she asks, trying to make out my/Angela's name tag.

"The *Island Star*. And you?"

I fall off-balance, gasp at the sharp pain.

"You're hurt," she says.

"It's nothing serious."

She looks dubious. "Are you traveling with someone?"

"Two thousand of my nearest and dearest. I'm one of the entertainers."

"That must be nice. No house to clean, no food to cook, no kids to run after."

"That's the upside. The downside is I have no house to clean, no food to cook, no kids to run after." A part of me—the nesting, biological-clock-ticking part—actually means it.

Either my shoe is shrinking or my foot is swelling. The mid-day sun sucks every soupçon of moisture from my skin. Energy seeps out my pores. My skin shrivels to dust. *I'm melting, I'm mellllllllting....*

The safari suits become so entranced by the singing basket seller that they follow him to a blanket where he lays out his baskets for closer inspection. I try balancing on my good foot but that shifts my body so off-killer, a new pain erupts in my hip. I'd better rest before tonight's performances. As much as I want to phone home, it will have to wait.

I hobble out of the line, start limping toward the ship. "I will and bequeath my space to you," I call back to the gal behind me.

"Wow. And you hardly know me."

Again, that wonderful deadpan. She'd be fun to get to know. Is she cruising on the *Island Star?* Did she say? I can't remember.

GINGER SNAPS

WALKING DOWN STAIRS is excruciating. An elevator would be wonderful but I have no idea where to find one. I should tape my ankle, but guess who forgot to pack tape? Seven lipsticks, three mascaras, a nail repair kit, peel-off facial mask yes, but tape? After I rest I'll try to track down the ship's doctor. I know I've passed the office, I just don't remember where.

By the time I reach my deck, I'm fantasizing a soothing shower followed by a huge ice pack on my elevated ankle, and perhaps, dare I dream, a lovely nap.

Ah, the best laid plans...

A note marked *URGENT* is taped to my door. "Come to my cabin as soon as you get this! Kathy."

I stop in my cabin long enough to splash water on my face, wipe a damp washcloth over the Nassau dirt and gravel embedded in my legs, and change from running shoes to sandals. Back out in the hall, I shoulder my way through crew rushing to ready the ship for our afternoon departure.

Kathy's door stands open. She sits cross-legged on her bed balancing a pad of yellow legal paper on her knees with names written and crossed out and lines going every which way. Dominic slouches against a wall, flipping a quarter back and forth across his knuckles.

"What's up?" I say.

Kathy shakes her head over the list of names. "We've lost Ginger."

"What happened?"

"Jackie's murder spooked her. She went back to kitchen crew."

"It's spooked all of us," I say, sitting on her bed.

"Yeah, well," says Dominic, "being the Einstein she is, Ginger figures if she works for me she'll be murdered next."

Kathy rotates her head in slow circles. Tight neck muscles crunch. Dominic flips the coin from right hand to left, begins the knuckle roll again. My ankle throbs. I tuck a pillow under it to help take down the swelling. Kathy gives it a hard look.

"What'd you do?"

"Twisted it a little. Nothing major."

She lights a cigarette, studying the list as if she expects to see something new. She looks at me, my ankle, the list. A little warning bell sounds.

"And you wanted to see me because—?" I ask.

"Because," says Dominic, "until our production company comes up with a new assistant, which might take weeks, I'm out of work. Meanwhile, I have financial responsibilities. I can't afford to be laid off."

I shift the pillow under my foot, wince at the pain.

"That looks bad." Dominic kneels at the bed, rests cool hands on my burning ankle. "You can't dance the cancan on this."

"I'll be fine. I'm going to ice it and—"

"A glacier couldn't make this ankle ready for tonight's show." He sounds nicer now, concerned. It puts me on guard. "You know," he says, "I have a repertoire of illusions you can do lying down or sitting."

"Some of the contortions would kill my ankle," I say. "I know. I've worked magic."

"Yes, Kathy mentioned you assisted your brother."

I give my friend the evil eye but she's busy picking lint off her bedspread. "You're welcome to jump in any time," I tell her.

"I hate to admit it," says Kathy, "but he's right. Dancing will make that worse. It needs to rest."

"What about the show?"

"I'll figure something out. Keith's a wreck, anyway, so we're basically one couple short as it is." She flops back on her bed. "Why didn't I listen to my father? He begged me to become a teacher. Regular work. Decent hours. Summers off. Pension."

"For one thing," I say, "you're a pushover. The kids would run all over you. You also can't spell and you hate math. Besides, you get nervous when you stay in one place too long."

She moans. "This has been the worst couple of weeks. Bad luck on top of terrible luck."

"Does that include me?" Mike Polsky leans in the doorway.

"Especially you," says Kathy.

He smells of sun lotion and aftershave. A new Kathy takes over the old Kathy's body. The replacement glows. Sexual energy pours off her in waves. Polsky radiates interesting waves of his own. Bubbe Dubbe could see people's auras. These two must be glowing like the northern lights. The air in the small cabin charges electric. Polsky settles on the bed next to Kathy. Heat crackles where their bodies touch. I should make a break for it before they spontaneously combust.

"So," says Dominic, "can we get started? We need to work on tonight's act."

"If I help Dominic," I say to Kathy, "who will you have to replace me? Unless you want me working both."

"I thought about it, even before you hurt your ankle. But doubling up won't work with the costume changes spaced the way they are. Dominic's performance comes in the middle of the show, when you'd be changing from the 'Paris Taxi' number to 'Lovely Lido Ladies.' There's no way you could make it. I might be able to rig something in the other shows. If you're willing."

"I can do anything for three weeks," I say. "Especially when it pays time and a half."

"You wish."

Sean O'Brian pokes his head in. "Looks like a right party," he says. "Who's buyin'?"

"I've got half a can of warm diet Cherry Coke," says Kathy.

"Well, now, that's mighty temptin', but I'd best not drink while I'm on duty." He cocks his head toward Dominic. "You're lookin' like somethin' my cat wouldn't bother draggin' in. You all right, then?"

He's right. Dominic's face has gone sickly white. "I'm fine," says Dominic, fumbling the quarter. "Fine," he says again.

"You lot have gone through a nasty business, you have. Amazing, you are. The show must go on and all that. I want you to know, from the rest of my crew, all our hats are off to ya." He starts to leave, then stops. "I completely forgot why I came. Kathy, love, I've just come from security and they've asked me to send you up to converse with the constabulary."

"I don't understand," says Kathy. "I already talked to them."

"That's the trouble with being such a charming lass." He tips the brim of his cap and leaves.

"C'mon," says Polsky. "I'll keep you company."

We create a small traffic jam, all trying to leave the cramped space at once. Worry lines mar Kathy's face as she locks up after us. I want

my old Kathy back, the one with the quick smile and boisterous laugh.
It's not fair that so many events have conspired to suck the joy from
her life. I wish, for her sake, I could fast-forward a couple of months
to when life will return to normal...however normal hers ever is.

My mom used to say it's easier to experience pain yourself than to
see someone you love in pain. There's truth to that. It's hard for me
to watch Kathy, still struggling to deal with the death of her mother,
trying to handle Angela and Jackie's deaths. A massive force, death.
All the stronger when it's laid out on the sand in front of you.

The idea of going home flares like flash paper and disappears.
Granted, my ankle's hurting too much for me to dance. And I have a
Vanish Box looming large in my future. And I am definitely missing
Roblings more than I ever thought I would. But I can't leave Kathy
like this. I am stronger than her, can deal with this better. The least I
can do is stick around and offer support until things straighten out.
There aren't that many people I care deeply about in this world and
Kathy's right up near the top of the list. I'll see this through to the
end. It helps that Polsky happened along when he did to provide a
strong shoulder if Kathy feels the need to lean.

I limp back toward my cabin, Dominic trailing close behind.

"So," he says, "which illusions have you worked?"

"I still haven't said yes. Doesn't anyone care what I think?"

"Honestly? No." He stops. "Please. I'm desperate. You're my only
hope. If it's a question of money..."

"That's not—"

"I'm sure I can arrange to get you a little extra—"

"It's not about money—"

"You have to help. For Kathy. For me. For the good of the ship."

"For God and country."

"That, too."

"Why not do your act solo?" I say.

"You saw the size of the theater. I have to work big out there.
Besides, audiences love to watch beautiful assistants. You distract
them when I need them distracted. And you know there are illusions
I can't do alone."

"You were alone this afternoon."

His mouth tightens. "Where?"

"Coming back on board with your traveling trunk."

"Oh, that. That's a charity thing I do at hospitals. Kids' ward, old people. Mostly a lot of close magic: cards, coins, scarves, the odd rabbit.''

"Then why shlep that big box?''

"I, um, do a few other things. Kids love when I make their nurses disappear.'' His face turns red. I guess he's embarrassed I discovered he does something nice, like volunteer at the local hospital. "So, tell me,'' he says, shifting the spotlight to me, "what kind of magic did you and your brother do?''

I give him a quick rundown. He looks relieved. "Perfect. It's all the same basics. You'll pick it up right away. Tonight I can stick to sawing you in half and the Vanish Box. Tomorrow we can rehearse—''

My ankle gives. I grip the handrail to keep from falling. "I should tape this,'' I say. "You wouldn't happen to have an elastic bandage you don't need?''

"In my cabin. Be right back.''

He moves gracefully through the crowds. If I'm a giant among the mostly Filipino crew, Dominic is a Goliath. At six feet plus he towers over everyone. He stops at a cabin far down the hall.

Kathy's *URGENT* note is still taped to my door. As I pull it off, the door swings open. I must have forgotten to lock it in my hurry to get to Kathy's cab—

A message in thick black felt-tip is scrawled across the far wall: *"YOU SALACIOUS WHORE. YOU'D BETTER GET YOUR HOUSE IN ORDER. YOUR DAYS ARE NUMBERED.''*

CALL ME, ISHMAEL

IT IS THE TIMING we can't figure. "It's obviously meant for Jackie," I say, staring at the wall while Lt. Davis takes Polaroids.

"Why threaten a dead woman?"

"Because whoever did this doesn't know she's dead."

He chews on this. "That would mean at least two people—her murderer and this clown—had it in for her. Not likely."

"I disagree. From the things I've heard about her, I'd say the odds are pretty good."

He checks the Polaroids, waves them in the air to help the images come up. "You know, this could also be meant for you."

"Me? I just got here."

"Have you rubbed anyone the wrong way?"

"No one with such nice penmanship."

"Funny lady." He slips the photos in his pocket. "I don't like this. You watch your back. Meanwhile, I'll send someone to clean this up. Is there anything I can do for you?"

I feel an urgent need to call the people I love most in the world. "A phone would be nice."

"You got it." Ten minutes later he sets me up in the telephone room off the Purser's Office. "Make all the calls you want," he says. "It's on us. And remember, keep your cabin door locked. If something happens to you, I'll have to answer to Roblings. Personally, I'd rather jump into a vat of angry rattlesnakes."

I sit at a desk stocked with large pads of doodle paper and a mug crammed with Islander Cruise Lines pens. A long laminated sheet of dialing instructions, including international access codes, is chained to the phone.

Grandma Belle says, "If you want to learn about a person, don't listen to what they say, watch what they do." What I do is dial Roblings first. I figure this cuts to the chase about his importance in my life. His partner answers.

"Feldman."

"Hey, good-lookin'," I say.

"Hey, gorgeous. You back home?"

"Not for a little while."

"The man's gonna be pissed he missed you. He called two minutes ago, on his way in. Give me a number."

"It's easier if I call you. About twenty minutes?"

"I'll nail him to the chair."

Sounds of the station seep in, phones, voices, radios. "How's he doing?" I ask.

"Too many broads, too little time."

"Ho-ho."

"Between you, me, and my bookie, this serial killer thing's getting to him. He'd do better if you were here."

"That works both ways."

I hang up. I've covered the doodle pad with hearts. JR and MT in block letters fill the centers, bright on one side, long shadows on the other, as if a spotlight were hitting them. I tear it off, slip it in my pocket, and call my folks.

Mom picks up. "Hey, sweetie, how's life on the Love Boat?"

"A little strange." I give her the edited version, detailing Jackie's death, leaving out the message scrawled on my cabin wall. Mom's good with murder once removed, can investigate and write it as well as any reporter working Chicago's crime beat. But she doesn't like the mean streets coming up to her door.

She asks about Kathy, who was like one of our family when we were at Northwestern. "She sends regards," I say. "I think this job's starting to get a little old."

"Ain't we all?"

She wants to hear more about the murder but I'm afraid she'll be on my back to take the first plane home. I do an end run around the subject. "You'll never guess who's on the ship," I say.

"The King of Prussia."

"Close. Uncle Leo." The silence runs long and deep. "Mom? You there?"

"Where is he?"

"Here. On board. He's a passenger."

"Thank God."

"You didn't know? What's going on?"

Her voice turns hard. "My sister..." She lets it hang.

"What?"

"Bertha's really done it this time. I'll let her know he's there."

"She's not here?"

Pause. "What has he told you?"

"We haven't had time to talk—"

I hear their front door slam in the background, my father's voice call out. "Dad's home," she whispers. "We'll discuss this another time." To my father, "Sam, pick up, it's Mimi."

"Great!" he shouts. "I'll get it in the living room."

Her voice to me is quiet, urgent. "Don't say anything. Dad doesn't know."

"Doesn't know *what?*"

"R.Y.!" It's our childhood command to shut up, *now!*, the sort of secret code necessary in families with five verbal children who frequently say embarrassing things. Literally, it means "red in Yiddish," "speak Yiddish," which none of us can. Practically, it means stop *immediately,* no questions asked. I stop.

Dad picks up. "Hey, Sport." And he's off and running about the paintings he doing for a Miami show, a new technique he's developed, which requires a dozen egg yolks per canvas. It's unclear if the yolks are mixed with his paints, basted on after, or cooked for breakfast. He's a talker, my dad. His friends call him "Soaps" because you can walk out during one of his conversations and come back a week later picking up right where you left off.

I press the phone to my ear, doodling Aunt Bertha's name in block letters. Normally Mom ends her calls by catching me up on my siblings and cousins, especially the married ones, the happily married ones, the happily married ones with children. But this time I don't hear her voice again until fifteen minutes later when we all say good-bye.

The clock hands crawl. I'll give Roblings another five minutes to get to the station. I dial Beth. Her machine picks up on the first ring. "Lyle and Beth are out—" I leave a message thanking her for getting my mail, watering my plants. Two minutes down, three to go. I consider calling Paul, letting my brother know that working as his assistant all those years ago is finally paying off. But Paul cannot manage a phone conversation in less than half an hour. I'm not up to it.

There's really no one else I want to talk to. I stare at the phone, push the buttons in different patterns, down, up, across. Hands on the clock tick away one minute, two. I dial. He picks up on the first ring.

"Roblings."

"Hey," I say.

"You sound far away."

"Too far."

He laughs. "You got that right."

I hear something in his voice. "What's going on?"

"We're rewriting the book on serial killers. Looks like we've had three, maybe four working the South Side right under our noses for years."

"How can that be?"

"Because we're so damned smart we know what serial killers look like: white, twenty to forty, single, loners who are also outgoing, likeable. We had them pegged. Made it real easy for these guys."

His voice is gravel on silk. I could listen to it all day. I want to tell him all the things I couldn't tell Mom but his plate is so full right now I'm afraid to dump more stuff on top. "You met Davis?" he asks.

"Yes, I—"

"Good cop. Lousy skier. If he hadn't retired when he did, that whole Jon Benet investigation would have a different ending. And don't you believe anything he says about me."

"How you killed a crazed grizzly with your bear hands?"

"Ho-ho," he says.

"No one here gets my puns."

"Then come home."

"Soon."

Someone barks his name. "Hold on," he tells me, covering the receiver, then, "I have to go."

"Miss me?" I ask.

"Truth?"

"I can take it."

"Yes."

"Me, too, you."

A tender silence stretches out between us. His voice, when it comes, is soft and husky. "Gotta go catch bad guys," he says. "Call me again."

"I will."

He hangs up.

"I love you," I say to the empty air, trying it out. It's easier than I thought.

THE BUZZ AMONG the staff is, "Will we or won't we sail?" Murder is serious business, after all. But the engines fire up and we sail off into the sunset exactly on time. The one good thing the murderer did was kill Jackie off-ship, which leaves the mess in Kolby's capable lap. He could possibly detain us if he wanted but there's no point. He's got Lt. Davis working this end and, if he needs us, he knows where to find us.

I'm dressing for rehearsal with Dominic when my cabin steward brings a note.

Come for dinner. First seating. I'll put a shrimp on the bar-b (or, better, a matzo ball in the soup). I cleared it with the entertainment director, who said you could come as long as I promise to let you go in time to get ready for your first show. See you tonight.

Love, Uncle Leo

Absolutely not. Not now, not today. I'm in no condition, can't handle one more thing. But, at the same instant I'm thinking "no" I know I'll go. First, because—while it's possible to refuse an invitation from the Captain of the ship, the Queen of England, the president of the U S of A—in my family, you never ever refuse an invitation from one of your own. And second, I'm dying of curiosity. Just what is going on between Uncle Leo and Aunt Bertha?

OH, I AIN'T GOT NO BODY

I CAN'T BREATHE. Scrunched into the secret compartment, the press of velvet hot against my skin, I ration air slowly in through my mouth, let it trickle out my nose. Dominic's Vanish Box works beautifully, top quality hinges oiled to perfection, nary squeak nor creak. But the stench in this airless place—body odor, vomit, roadkill—combines with the ship's rocking. Rehearsal better be over pretty soon. I can't stay in here much longer.

A couple of Lt. Davis' security henchmen stand guard on the stage apron. The two muscled mountains, more used to dealing with raucous drunks and rambunctious teens, fidgeted self-consciously onstage, shifting from foot to foot until we were ready to rehearse. They weren't thrilled when Dominic pulled the curtain, shutting them out, refusing to allow them to see his secrets.

Dominic's already sawn me in half a couple of times. He has this shtick where he holds up a rusty jagged-toothed saw and is about to cut me in half when he has an idea, and, abracadabra, the old saw changes into a brand spanking new chain saw. It made me seriously nervous at first, that roaring machine cutting down through my tender body, but Dominic's extremely good and I am, after all, a professional.

We're nearly done, just need to nail this vanish. I strain to hear his patter, to pick out the key phrase that's my cue to reappear. Except for my churning stomach, rehearsing with Dominic for tonight's show has been great therapy. Illusion is all about precision of movement and timing. Performance of magic takes absolute concentration. Learning the show keeps my mind too occupied to dwell on death and the disturbing threat on my cabin wall. *"YOUR DAYS ARE NUMBERED."*

Dominic's voice comes muffled through the thick cloth and layers of lacquered wood. I think we're near the end. My brother's Vanish Box was a cheap piece of secondhand junk bought for bupkes at a Magic Convention. But at least I could hear my cues loud and clear.

Dominic's voice stops. I think. Maybe it's just a dramatic pause. I press my ear against the side. Nothing.

My skin heats to burning. The plush velvet lining turns to sandpaper. Sweat trickles. Tickles. Mixes with Ginger's old sweat. And Jackie's.

The creepy crawly heebie-jeebies spider up my skin, remind me I'm rubbing up against remnants of the former occupants, one now majorly dead. "Nothing passes through this world without leaving a trail," says Grandma Belle. She means that physically, spiritually, and philosophically. How many times did Jackie compress herself in here? She was limber. Oh, yes. Limber enough to fold her nasty self into a duffel and sink to the bottom of the sea.

Out! Get me out! My vertebrae weld. I need to unbend, stretch, uncoil the full length of my body.

"Dominic! Dominic!" The velvet sucks up sound. I yell louder, banging on the side of the box.

"Dominic!" Where is he? What if there's a fire? What if there's a maniac bent on doing me bodily harm? "Dominic!" The air in the compartment is running out. I run my fingers around the panels, along the corners, frantically feeling for the release. Can't find it. I press the floor panel. Something sharp jabs my finger. "Dominic! Anyone! Help!" I try to breathe slowly, ration the air that's left. I pound on the side as hard as I can.

The hidden panel releases and I fall out, sucking in deep breaths of air. The two security men barge through the curtain as Dominic comes in from the wings.

"You all right?" he asks.

"Do I look all right?" Hysteria jacks my voice up a few octaves. I sound like Olive Oyl on pure oxygen.

"I...it's..." He holds up a cotter pin. "This must have fallen out when we were bringing the stuff onstage. I couldn't get your panel to release without it. I had to go back and—"

"I'm out of here," I say, limping through the curtain, onto the apron, down the stairs. The security guys look at each other, unsure whether or not to follow.

"Morgan! Wait. Hey, I was just—" Dominic chases me into the darkened theater where a thousand plush seats stand in mute witness. "I'm sorry. Really. And stupid. Please, don't walk out. I have no act without you."

I limp up the aisle toward the door. In the half-light, I see Ida dwarfed in the same aisle seat, her cane hooked over the chair in front of her.

Dominic reaches me, falls to one knee. "You've got to make the show," he says. "Please."

I weigh this. I've never in my life quit a show. "Don't you ever, *ever* leave me like that again, you understand?"

"Right."

The ship pitches. I grab a seat for stability. "I've got to get something from the doc for this nausea," I say. "You might consider cleaning the Vanish Box every millennium or so. It smells like something died in there. In fact, if you don't scrub it out by performance time, I'm not getting back in."

"Yes, okay, whatever you say."

Ida's smiling. Maybe she thinks Dominic's proposing. "One more thing," I whisper.

"What?"

"That pack of cards you carry around?"

"Yes?"

"See that nice lady back there? I want you to go over and do some close magic for her."

He squints at me, looks about to refuse.

"It's a deal breaker," I say. "Just a couple of tricks. You'll gladden a wonderful woman's heart. It might even make you feel good."

He mutters something I don't quite catch. Probably just as well. But he goes back to my friend and, settling into the seat beside her, takes out his deck of cards and fans them with a flourish.

I love negotiating from a position of power. It happens so rarely in an actor's life.

FOOD, GLORIOUS FOOD

THE SHIP'S MAIN dining room is the size of Rhode Island, with roughly the same population. I stand in the doorway, scanning the acres of diners for Uncle Leo. I'd enjoy this a lot more if I had no show to do and my ankle wasn't hurting and I had nothing more pressing to think about than which dressing to put on my salad. An elaborate ice sculpture of Neptune ringed by succulent-looking giant shrimp dominates the center of the room. Waitstaff carrying massive trays piled high with dinners race back and forth like sprinters through the room.

Halfway across the cavernous room, a man jumps up wildly waving both arms in my direction. My real Uncle Leo would never make such a display of himself. Why wasn't Mom more explicit about what's going on with him and Aunt Bertha? I wave back and limp through the room, which rings with laughter and lively conversations. I wonder what will happen when word leaks out about Jackie's murder. Which it's bound to.

It's tricky ducking waiters when the floor keeps moving under my feet. I'm still a little groggy from the shot the doctor gave. It could make my hair turn green, for all I care, as long as it keeps the seasick feeling away.

"Oh, this is wonderful, wonderful!" Uncle Leo hugs me. "I'm so happy you could make it." He waggles his eyebrows, which, earlier today, grew like thickets. They've been trimmed, I notice, as has his thick crop of ear and nose hairs. His hair mat, however, is still combed over ear to ear.

"I can only stay a little while," I say.

"However long we can have you. Everyone," he says, to his table, "this is my niece Mimi Tiersky."

"Hello." I smile at the six strangers. No one in my family calls me Morgan Taylor. I've given up trying.

He pulls out a ninth chair, which has been squeezed into the table for eight. "Actually, her birth name is Miriam. But we've called her

Mimi since she was a baby. Mimi is an entertainer. The best. You name it, she does it. Sing, dance, act—everything.''

These are more words than I have ever heard at one time out of that particular man. Aunt Bertha never let him get a word in edgewise, sideways, or any other way. This new Uncle Leo's a real Chatty Cathy.

He reaches over and squeezes my hand. "Mimi," he says, "I'd like you to meet—" He goes around the table, making introductions: Annette and David, a young London couple on holiday; a sixtyish woman and thirtyish man with the easy intimacy of old friends; a mother/daughter taking their first vacation since the husband/father's death the year before. One chair remains empty. Someone too seasick to come to dinner, no doubt.

My stomach heaves, but this time it's not from the ship's motion. I've never seen my uncle this way. Aunt Bertha is the talker, the one who stirs things up. Uncle Leo is the thinker, the listener, the easygoing partner.

"You look wonderful," he says, passing me oven-warm rolls, molded butter, and a trough of coleslaw. "How are you feeling after your terrible accident?"

"I'm fine."

He glances down, sees my taped ankle. "You can dance all right?"

"I'm not dancing tonight. Maybe for a little while."

He brightens. "You can, maybe, come explore the islands with me?"

"I'm still working. They're just accommodating my injury. I'm the new Magician's Assistant."

"An act like you and Paulie used to do?"

I laugh. "This one's a little more upscale."

The waiter takes our orders. I order a baked potato, salad, steamed vegetables, food I know I won't eat. It's easier to order than to fight Uncle Leo.

"Get more," says Uncle Leo. "You can order the whole menu, up and down both sides, if you want."

"Not if I hope to perform tonight," I say.

He turns to Mario. "Add a steak, medium rare, and a big piece of apple pie to the young lady's order." He bends and whispers in my ear, "I'll get you a doggie bag for your cabin so you don't go hungry in the middle of the night."

I honestly mean to tell him I talked to Mom, who has probably already called Aunt Bertha and spilled the beans about Uncle Leo's whereabouts. But this is neither the time nor place. Besides, people at the table are pumping me for information about how it is to live and work on a ship.

Coward.

Yup.

I TRY TO SATISFY my tablemates' hunger for the "untold" stories, juicy love affairs, exciting travel destinations, dangerous moments. I do some heavy editing, sharing what little I know and throwing in anecdotes remembered from my Hawaiian cruising days. I avoid mentioning dead bodies and threatening graffiti. I am halfway into the story of how a ship's entertainers saved passengers' lives on a flaming Greek cruise ship (after the captain and crew escaped on lifeboats) when Uncle Leo suddenly jumps up to pull out one of the empty chairs.

The cool blond who'd talked to me on the dock before we boarded glides over, graces Uncle Leo with a smile that would melt Antarctica, and settles on the chair. She is stunning, her perfect figure poured into a simple silk floral dress. "Mimi," says Uncle Leo, as if I weren't in mid-story, "I would like you to meet Miss Susan Gayle."

"We've met," she says, warm smile, charming voice, extending a perfectly manicured hand, which embraces mine in a nice firm grip. "You probably don't remember but we chatted a bit on the dock."

"Of course I remember," I say, unable to keep the frost out of my voice. What gives her the right to sit in Aunt Bertha's chair? Is she the reason Aunt Bertha isn't here? Home-wrecking vamp. How can Uncle Leo be so cavalier about introducing me to her? How long has this been going on? Why didn't anyone in my family say anything to me?

—Aren't we, perhaps, jumping to all kinds of erroneous conclusions?

—I don't think so. My uncle just deforested sixty-five years' worth of facial hair, for God's sake. What more proof does one need?

"If you'll excuse me," I say, "I must get to work. It was nice meeting all of you." I bend over, kiss Uncle Leo's forehead. "We'll talk."

"Certainly."

"After tonight's show?"

"Perfect."

"You're sure I'm not interrupting plans?"

"What could be more important?"

We set a time and place. One way or another I'll find out what's going on in my family. Maybe, when I was still back in Chicago, if I had called Mom as often as she'd like, she would have kept me informed.

ANOTHER OPENING—

I WATCH NERVOUSLY from the wings as the ensemble swings into a high-energy rendition of "The Night They Invented Champagne." The ship rocks-'n'-rolls in rough seas and I cling to a wall of ropes to keep upright. I fear for the dancers. Any second they could tumble like a row of dominoes.

Dominic and I are scheduled to fill the space midway through the "French Follies." This will give the ensemble breathing room while they change costumes and the crew changes sets. Every dancing fiber in my body—except for my whiny ankle—hungers to be on that stage rompin' and stompin' to this grand old music. The ship pitches. The troupe moves into a single row, long legs kicking the cancan waist high.

Keith anchors the center. It's an old Rockette's trick. Putting the tallest dancers in the middle makes the troupe's heights appear more uniform. Keith, more shadow than substance, makes halfhearted kicks and lame arm gestures. With a phony smile pasted under sad eyes, he looks more scarecrow than ever. It's a miracle that Kathy, the great persuader, managed to coax him out of his cabin. With any luck, just trying to keep his balance during the show will take his mind off Jackie's murder. But, there's performance and there's performance. Keith is phoning this one in.

Kathy "the show must go on" Bloch has dusted off her dancing shoes and stepped into my place—Angela's place. Luckily she's kept her dancer's body in shape, doing daily workouts with the troupe. But years of cigarettes have sandpapered her vocal chords. Her singing voice comes out a little Edith Piaf, a lot Carol Channing—not a bad sound for this particular show. The audience loves it, stomping and clapping as the troupe kicks its way offstage.

My usual performance jitters move in as Dominic bounds onto the stage performing an inventive series of scarf tricks. I remove the tape from my ankle and roll my foot in slow circles. Dominic finishes and with a flourish in my direction—"Ladies and gentlemen, my beautiful assistant, Morgan Taylor"—I trot onto the stage as gingerly as possible, nodding toward the applauding audience, gracefully extending my hand to allow Dominic to escort me into the Vanish Box.

He forgot to clean it. The stench of vomit and body odor is sickmaking, especially now when it's amplified a thousand times by the pitch and roll of the ship. If not for the doctor's magic shot, I couldn't do this. I smile at Dominic as he shuts me inside the box. "Lysol," I say.

He winces an "I forgot" look as he spouts his spiel. I'm doing fine until he starts spinning the box, preparing for my disappearance. The whirling mixes with the effects of the seasick shot and throws off my timing. I miss my cue. Dominic looks surprised when he opens the box and finds me where he left me. The audience laughs, thinks it's part of our act.

Dominic makes a joke of it, plays his disappointment broad enough to be seen in the last row. "Reminds me of my ex-wife," he says, "can't get rid of her, either." The crowd groans. He closes me back inside and this time diverts audience attention to give me the millisecond I need to disappear. After a little more stage business, I "magically" reappear from the wings stage left. Applause, applause. I wheel the box offstage into the wings.

No, I won't tell you how it's done. Yes, I know all about the superhyped television show that exposes magicians' most sacred secrets. My brother Paul, his Margenon magic act retired years before, became so livid when the show first aired he wouldn't talk to anyone for a week. He finally fashioned a wax doll in the shape of the turncoat magician, and stuck rusty nails into the heart and certain sexual places south. Despite that televised aberration, the rest of us are still bound by magicians' sacred code of secrecy.

While Dominic amazes the masses with rabbits and snakes, I open the back of the Vanish Box to let it air. I'm not getting back into this thing until it's fumigated. Maybe, if the fabric is stapled instead of glued, we can rip it out, scrub the wood, and put in fresh fabric. The light is too dim for me to see. I feel around the floor of the box, find a fold of fabric in one corner, and tug. The fabric gives easily. It'll be a cinch to rip out. Something sharp jabs my finger, probably a staple come loose. I dig into the tight corner fold, tease the thing out with my nail.

It's some kind of metal charm with part of a leather string still attached. I hold it up to light from the stage. It's an Oriental character by the look of it, probably worn as a necklace. Hardly the sort of jewelry Jackie would wear, though it might belong to Ginger.

I sense someone pressing into my comfort zone. A square-built house of a man with no neck and garlic breath peers over my shoulder into the Vanish Box. His nose has been mashed into his face, and I've seen his slanted brow on a couple of apes at Lincoln Park Zoo. He breathes through his mouth in erratic spurts. The sound crawls up my neck.

Security is supposed to keep passengers out of this area. I quickly close the false door and push the Vanish Box back out of the way. Dominic would kill me for leaving his secrets hanging out where any old civilian could see them. I wheel the saw-the-lady-in-half box up in place. I have to work around Garlic Breath, who now stands facing the stage, hypnotized by Dominic's act. I've seen him before. He was the guy up on the catwalk, the one Sean found poking around the engine room. Some people are just plain nosey.

"Excuse me," I whisper but he doesn't respond. His pucker-sleeved suit and steel-reinforced shoes are the type worn by recent Eastern European immigrants moving into my neighborhood. It's possible he doesn't understand English.

The drummer plays a tension-building roll as Dominic throws a scarf into the air. It flutters down, becoming two doves. Mr. Garlic Breath still hovers, hands clasped behind his back, riveted by the bright lights of the stage. I slip the Oriental charm into my bra and await my cue. Dominic bows to the applause, then turns toward the wings and sweeps an arm in my direction.

"Coming through," I say, bumping the man as I wheel the box onstage.

Dominic's eyes grow wide, his face freezing in a grotesque smile. Is my bra strap showing? Something hanging from my nose? I do a quick body and costume check. Everything's in place.

And then I feel what he must have intuited.

A sudden pitch of the ship rips the two hundred pounds of lacquered wood and brass fittings out of my hands and sends it hurtling downstage toward the audience. I chase after, pain knifing my ankle, catching it just as it hits the edge of the apron, one wheel miraculously snagging on a floor light. The musicians in the pit below look up, terrified. The coffin-shaped box teeters over their heads. They keep playing in the face of disaster. The *Titanic* comes to mind.

I lean back, pulling my weight against the box, my ankle screaming. My legs dig in, upper back and arm muscles strain, abs and glutes work to the ends of their strength. For a suspended moment, I balance the weight of the box giving it every ounce of everything I've got. The exact instant my mind knows I can't hold on one second more, the ship rocks back and the box retreats from the pit.

Applause, applause.

Now the box chases me, gathering speed as it rattles past Dominic on its trip upstage. The audience roars. My Second City improv training kicks in and I'm "in the moment," morphing from dainty Magician's Assistant to burly longshoreman. As soon as the box slows, I roll up imaginary sleeves, spit on my palms, and rub my hands together. With a waggle of determined ass, I hunker down and push the box center stage. I work it for laughs, Laurel and Hardy pushing a piano up a steep California hillside. The theater rocks with laughter.

I hit my mark and quickly stomp down on all four wheel locks. This thing's not moving until I say so. Dominic's sweating. Can't blame him. Forget about the musicians we almost crushed. He just watched a few thousand dollars' worth of primo magician's equipment nearly smashed into matchsticks.

Kathy gestures wildly from the wings jabbing a finger to her wrist. Time. We have to get on with this. The second-seating diners are munching through entrees on their march toward dessert and we still have half the "Follies" to go. I double-check the wheel locks. It could get messy if I start drifting away while Dominic's sawing me in half. He helps me into the box, my ankle complaining as I pretzel inside. Dominic is still sweating, pasty, trembling.

"You all right?" I ask.

He locks me in, lifting up the old rusty saw, starting his patter. I relax my neck muscles against the padded opening in the end of the box, let my head fall back, swish my hair. Legs wiggle out the opposite end of the box. Dominic begins his shtick, holding up the old saw, switching it for the new. I open my mouth and eyes in mock horror. He pulls the saw alive, lowers the buzzing blade toward the box. The ship rolls. Dominic falters, clanking the chain saw against the box. I have visions of limbs lopped off. My horror turns real.

"Use the manual," I say out the side of my mouth.

"I'll be fine."

"I'm not asking. I'm telling. Just pretend the chain saw won't fire up."

He pulls the cord once, twice. Nothing. He's about to try again. "If you fire that up, you're out one assistant," I say. That registers. At this moment I'm all that stands between him and unemployment. He shrugs at the audience and puts down the chain saw.

"Coward," shouts a man from the audience.

"Want to change places?" I shout. This gets a laugh. Dominic's still shaking but is able to cut me in half the old-fashioned way and paste me back together. We finish, pushing our equipment off one side of the stage while the dancers cancan in from the other.

Mr. Garlic Breath has not moved, stands hypnotized by the sexy flash of gorgeous legs kicking in fishnet stockings. "Coming through," I say, which he can't hear over the music. I reach an arm across, gently but firmly pushing against him to indicate he's blocking our way. His size twelves must be bolted to the floor because he doesn't even sway. But at least he understands that we need to move past him and, with a flash of bad teeth and blast of garlic, "Sorry," he steps back. He does speak English, in a guttural Boris Badanov sort of way.

Dominic brings up the rear. As he passes, Garlic Breath tilts off-balance, knocking Dominic into the ropes. "Sorry," the man says. This seems to be his one big word. Maybe that's because he has to use it a lot. Dominic struggles to regain his footing. The man watches but doesn't offer a hand. I guess he reckons an apology is enough.

A couple of stagehands come to help Dominic pack and stow his gear. I help load the freight elevator that leads directly down to storage. "We'll work on levitation tomorrow," Dominic says, blotting stage sweat, loosening his tux tie.

"How about, 'Thank you, Morgan, for helping me out tonight'?"

"What? Oh, yes. Well, yes. Certainly, thank you. Tomorrow," he says, his handkerchief sodden, "I'll have to let you know when. I have some, ah, things to take care of."

"I can hardly wait."

He pulls the grate closed and hits the "down" button, sinking slowly into the sunset. I sit on a stool and retape my ankle. Garlic Breath turns and watches with interest.

"Do you mind?" I say.

"Excuse me?"

Some things aren't worth the breath they'd take to explain. I remember how unnerving it was in Italy when men in cramped elevators would turn their backs to the doors and stare at me the whole ride up.

For some reason their culture doesn't consider staring rude. Mr. Garlic Breath is another case in point. I limp off, looking for security as I go. Someone should escort that man out of there.

I don't see one security person all the way back to my cabin. How comforting is that?

LOUNGE LIZARDS

I HOPE I HAVEN'T kept Uncle Leo waiting too long but I couldn't meet him without cleaning up. The stench inside the Vanish Box permeated my clothes like smoke from a cheap cigar. While I was performing, my cabin steward scrubbed the threat from my wall as best she could, leaving a note that engineering would slap a coat of paint over it tomorrow. "SALACIOUS WHORE," particularly resistant to cleansing, remains a shadowy reminder. I take a fast shower, toss on slacks and T-shirt, and lock the door as I leave. Halfway down the hall I turn around, go back, double-check the lock. What, me nervous?

This time I really concentrate, following the markers I memorized to get me from point A to point B. Still, I somehow miss a marker, overshooting the Tropical Cove Deck and coming out on the jogging path above. It's eerie up here at night without runners and walkers. This is the witching hour on-board ship, the changing of the guard, night people replacing day people. Somewhere below, passengers at the end of their day (mostly older) join cruisers just starting out (mostly younger) around the late-night buffet. So many passengers traveling on the same cruise never experience the same cruise.

I've run this track a couple of times, remember an outside staircase at the bow. I follow the curved track past curtained stateroom windows. The cushioned running floor sucks up sound. My own footsteps disappear into the black. All that's left is the wind whistling down the passageway and the distant slap of water against ship. Where is everyone? The soft pad of a runner's feet comes up behind me. I back against the wall to make room for them to pass. The footsteps stop. I look back. The track stretches long and empty toward the stern. I was sure...

I walk as fast as my ankle will let me. This ship's too new for ghosts. Although it's off to a good start. Angela, Jackie. "Bad things always come in threes," says Grandma Ruth. "That's fact, not superstition.'' The footsteps begin again. My ankle complains as I speed up. I risk glancing back as I reach the stairs. No one.

> "'As I was coming down the stair
> I met a man who wasn't there
> He wasn't there again today
> Oh how I wish he'd go away.'''

Saying the poem gets me safely down to C Deck. A couple sit in the dark, bare feet up on the railing, holding hands.

"Ho, ho, ho," says the woman.

I look closer. "Kathy?"

"Yup." She and Polsky wear Santa hats plundered from Wardrobe. A bottle of nonalcoholic champagne ices in a bucket. "You shouldn't be wandering around alone," she says.

"There're a million people around," I lie.

Polsky pops the cork, launching it over the railing. "Incoming," he shouts.

"Join us?" asks Kathy.

"Can't. I have a hot date."

I cross the pool deck, a clutter of sunbathers during the day, now nearly deserted. Ichabod and his cronies have commandeered a dim corner, pushing together several tables. Something prehistoric crawls around under their chairs. An iguana. Like the one the director of Daniel Pinkwater's "Lizard Music" kept backstage. It's not a bad pet if you're partial to scaly things whose claws are long enough to scratch your back from across the room.

Uncle Leo sits alone at a small table overlooking the sea. Two empty highball glasses, one with ice cubes, sweat on the table. He waves me over and signals the drink girl.

The first order of business is for me to fess up. "I wanted to tell you at dinner, I talked to Mom. Mentioned you're on the ship. She's going to tell Aunt Bertha." He nods, as if he expected this. "I'm sorry," I say. "I didn't mean to cause trouble."

"You haven't."

"I didn't realize your being here was a secret."

"It's not. I just didn't bother telling Aunt Bertha. The way she didn't bother telling me some things. A good many things, it would appear." He pushes the dirty glasses to the far side of the table. One,

I notice, is marked with lipstick. The cool blonde's, perchance? He pulls out a handkerchief, blows his nose, puts it away. "It's new to me, this not telling. I'm seeing if I like it. So far, I have to be honest, it's not so bad."

The drink girl comes over, flashes Uncle Leo a thousand-watter. "Another double scotch, neat?" she asks.

"Better make this one on the rocks," he says, handing her his aqua *Island Star* charge card. "And for my favorite actress?"

"Sparkling water with lime," I say.

She clears the glasses, sets out napkins. There is a break in the clouds and a full moon hangs close enough to touch. The iguana, attached to Ichabod's wrist by a long leash, crawls up and down and around. Another man sports an iridescent lizard boutonniere that begins crawling up his collar.

My uncle and I are quiet together, watching the moon dance on the waves until the clouds return. I'm trying to think how to start. I'm not used to prying into the private lives of close relatives. Movie stars, yes, athletes, tell me all. But how much do I really want to ask the person who read books to me for hours? Who came to every performance from the time I was in pre-school? Who treated me like the child he and Aunt Bertha never had? There's no good way to go about it. The truth is, it's none of my business. The bigger truth is, I want to know. I screw on my courage and ask.

"Unc—"

"I hear you had trouble," he's saying. "A young girl died? One of the entertainers?"

Which young girl? Angela or Jackie? "Yes," I say. "How did you hear?"

"Miss Susan Gayle, the woman at my dinner table. An intriguing woman. Beautiful, don't you think?"

"If you like that type."

"Type?"

"A little too perfect, if you ask me."

"Funny thing about physically beautiful people," he says. "So many blessed with good looks are insensitive to the needs of others. It's as if they expect the sea to part for them, because it always has. Your Aunt Bertha was that kind of beauty."

"She's still beautiful."

He skips over this as if I haven't spoken. "What intrigues me is that, when you find someone who is as beautiful inside as they are out—like Miss Gayle—you'll almost always also find something powerful in their past that shaped them. Severe poverty, for example, debilitating illness, death of a parent. I hope to learn what it is that makes her so sensitive to all the people at our table, and to me, I would say, in particular."

My uncle is smitten. I don't like it. "Have you known each other long?" I ask.

The question puzzles him at first. "Ah, you mean did I know her before this cruise? Was ours, perhaps, a pre-arranged assignation? No, Miss Nosey, we've just met. But I do feel as if I've known her a long while."

The wheelchair member of Ichabod's group rolls past our table, a small woven basket perched on his lap.

"I am not exactly a movie star type," says Uncle Leo. "And my clothes, although new and bought with the assistance of a fashionable young man at the Men's Warehouse, are not, after all, Neiman's. My intellect, of course, I will put up against the best. But how many women of Miss Gayle's beauty ever find the intellect of particular interest? Still, when she realized I'd be waiting up here for you all alone, she offered, no, *insisted* on keeping me company."

Ichabod's group shifts around to make room for their friend. He lifts something out of his basket and sets it on the table. The men lean forward.

"We sat out here nearly an hour this evening talking about Eastern Philosophy and literature, biotechnology, and recent developments in Indonesian politics. And, in conversation, she shared a little of the ship's gossip. Actually, she mentioned two deaths related to this ship. One which may have been a murder?"

"She seems to know an awful lot."

"I take that as a yes. And don't look so surprised. Miss Gayle's is an interesting intellect. So many people today form worldviews from reading *Time* and *People,* watching television and movies. She, like myself, prefers the elegant simplicity of information gleaned from primary sources. She knows five languages, you know. But one of her most attractive attributes is, she is a marvelous listener. After a few minutes in her company, people can't wait to tell her things."

"Like about someone being murdered?"

He nods. "Her cabin steward might have mentioned it."

"And have you told this wonderful listener what's going on between you and Aunt Bertha?"

Our drinks arrive. Uncle Leo signs the chit. A burst of laughter erupts at Ichabod's table. The man in the wheelchair jumps up, grabs something from the ground, puts it back on the table. I blink, not sure I saw what I did. He stands again. Maybe he's like Uncle Jake, who can walk but whose "bad ticker" makes it necessary for him to use a wheelchair.

The drink girl cruises toward Ichabod's table, oohing and ahhing over the iguana. I squeeze lime into my sparkling water, wishing it were vodka. Uncle Leo takes a huge gulp of scotch.

"Did you," I ask again, "confide personal things to this total stranger, who means nothing to you, a person you met two days ago?"

"It is sometimes easier to share with strangers."

"That's because," I say, "you can lie to strangers."

"What, you can't lie to family?" He bangs his glass on the table. "A wife can't lie to her husband, to the one person who's loved her and only her with all my heart for forty-four years?" His hand trembles violently as he raises his glass. Scotch splashes out over his hand. He shoves the glass away, stands.

"Sorry, Mimi, I've had too much drink and too little sleep. I think, tonight, the disco will have to do without me." An exit cue if ever I heard one.

"I'll walk with you," I say, slipping my arm through his. We stroll across the deck. "I'm sorry I upset you," I say. "I just don't understand what's going on."

"It will be all right." He gives my arm a reassuring squeeze. "One way or another. This is not for you to worry."

The turbulent front that churned the waves so violently passes, dark clouds moving off like a blanket pulled from the sky. The immense moon shows off its craters.

"Don't be upset that Miss Gayle told me about the murdered girl," he says. "There's no such thing as a perfect vacuum. Secrets seep out."

I have no idea, anymore, what we're talking about, murder or marriage. I think both.

We kiss goodbye and he strides to the elevators. He's looking better, my uncle, less haggard than when he picked me up on the moped. A lizard shedding dull old skin. And, despite the turmoil that brought him here, he seems to be having a fine old time. Which is not, I think, the kind of news Aunt Bertha will want to hear.

DAY FOUR

SEAS THE DAY

LITTLE-KNOWN FACT: The Marquis de Sade invented "A Day at Sea." Cruising, if done at all, should be like musical chairs where you don't leave one port until the next is safely in sight. Ideally, you'd sail under cover of night, awaken each morning already tethered to the next dock.

Granted, this seems a minority opinion, especially among people on cruises. Round about eight in the ayem, when I stumble out to find coffee and check the weather (a room with a view not being a luxury afforded us working stiffs) all the passengers I pass seem to be enjoying the heck out of sailing. The weather, by the by, is fabulous (as opposed to very fabulous, very *very* fabulous, or "Grab the camera, Maude; the folks back home aren't gonna believe this!").

I fill a huge Styrofoam container with coffee, cut with enough skim milk to keep my bones from curving into a question mark, and head back down to prepare for the day.

I feel no connection to this cabin. Usually, when I have a gig on the road, I drape scarves over tables and lamp shades, set out photos of family and friends, put Chicago snow globes and trolls and funny little trinkets around to cozy up a space. But I packed for this trip in such a rush I came away without anything.

It doesn't help that the heavy hand of the law has left its print everywhere in the room. Lt. Davis and Inspector Kolby methodically sifted through Jackie's possessions, destroying her immaculate organization. Our cabin steward, a timid Filipino girl, cried so hard the first time she stepped into the cabin that I told her to forget cleaning for now. She came back to scrub the graffiti off my wall, but that's been it. Once Jackie's things are taken out, it will be easier. Until then, I'll keep the cabin tidy enough.

I step into the small shower cubicle, turn slowly to let the powerful spray massage my back and shoulders. I lean forward, bracing my hands and forehead against the wall. A single red hair clings to the wall between my eyes. I jump back. Jackie was in this shower the day she was murdered, scrubbing off the remnants of her night with Rolex-Armani. A water droplet rolls down the wall, hits the hair, makes it squiggle.

And which role were you performing for him, Miss "I've played Broadway"? Were you enchantress, vixen, slut, wide-eyed girl, conniver? What bauble did you think This Week's Flavor would buy for you? And now, for the one-billion-dollar question, What did you do, or not do, that made him angry enough to kill?

Another drop trickles down, carries the hair along. The gossamer strand undulates snakelike, sidewinding down toward my bare feet. I jump out of the stall, staring as the hair inches toward the drain, then disappears. I grab a towel and start wiping. Damp. I've grabbed Jackie's towel, left neatly triple-folded on the bar, still damp inside from her last shower. I shudder, stuffing it into the laundry bag. I've got to move out of this cabin. Where? There's no space. Maybe I can bunk in one of the lifeboats. Someplace. Any place.

An *Island Star* notice has been slipped under the cabin door: "To: Staff From: Lt. Gene Davis, Chief of Security. Please report to my office at the following times." What follows is a list of cabin numbers followed by interview times. I'm slotted for nine-thirty.

KEITH, ELAINE, and a couple of other dancers wait in chairs outside the Security Office. "He's running late," says Elaine.

I take the chair next to Keith. "How you doin', pardner?"

"Shitty."

He looks it. I rest a hand on his. "If there's anything I can do…"

"You're a sweetheart. I keep thinking Jackie's murder is so unreal. I mean, murder is something on the news. It happens to other people. We're entertainers, for Pete's sake. We're harmless. Who kills entertainers?"

"Critics," I say.

That gets a smile. It's not fair. There are a million nice girls out there. Jackie didn't deserve this kind of devotion.

One of Lt. Davis' honchos hands me a clipboard with a questionnaire attached. I print my name and shoreside contact information, then scan the questions. *How long have I worked on this ship? How long did I know Jackie? What was my relation to her? Did we ever spend time off-ship together? Do I know her friends, family, profes-*

*sional acquaintances? When was the last time I saw her? Under what
circumstances?*

I stare at the sheet trying to figure if "spending time off-ship" with
Jackie includes my finding her body.

When and where was the last time I saw her? Do they mean dead
or alive? I write: "On-board ship near staff gangway."

Lt. Davis steps into the hall. "Ms. Morgan," he says, "if you don't
mind." I shrug, a little embarrassed, as I pass the others who have
been waiting longer, all of whom would rather be anyplace else.

"How're you doing today?" he asks, leading me to a small room.

"Pretty good. I talked to Roblings yesterday, he sends regards."

"I'll bet." He motions to a desk buried under piles of papers. More
piles are stacked on the floor. "Copies of passports, birth certificates,"
he says.

"You don't want—"

"'Fraid so. A person can possibly come on board without having
their photo taken, but they can't get on without giving us some form
of I.D. like a passport, visa, birth certificate, driver's license, credit
card. These are the photocopies. Your man's in here someplace. I need
you to look. Like some coffee?"

"A cauldron would be great, with milk."

"I'll send it right in."

This is harder work than looking through the photos. Passport photos, awful to begin with, become downright scary when photocopied.
What if I make a mistake, finger an innocent man? I could destroy a
life, get a man fired from his job at the widget factory. Mr. Garlic
Breath stares up from the page. His real name, typed into a real American passport, is Wilbur Tompkins. Wilbur? Sure doesn't sound Russian. Maybe it was changed when he was processed through whatever
passes for Ellis Island these days.

Three-quarters of the way through, Uncle Leo's face smiles up at
me. His passport photo, taken a few years back, shows the round and
jolly man I grew up with. If this were a new photo, and I hadn't run
into him in Nassau, I never would have recognized him, would have
flipped past without a second glance. I'm afraid it's going to be the
same for Rolex-Armani. Not one passport photo resembles the man I
saw.

Once again I bring Davis the bad news. He doesn't look surprised.
"What about his cabin?" I say. "He had to sleep someplace. And, if

Jackie spent the night with him, you can bet he had one of the fancy staterooms. One of the stewards must have—''

"Very good, Watson." Davis swings his hand-tooled cowboy boots up onto his desk. "In point of fact, your mystery man booked the best suite on the ship. It's empty now, of course. The stateroom was booked and paid for under a fictitious name by someone using a bogus passport. I had the cabin steward go through the same photos you just did. The guy didn't make either of your lists. Here." He picks a photocopy of a passport from his desk. "You passed right over him."

I study the square-shaped face, wide-set eyes, broad nose, old-fashioned aviator glasses. The thick black wig is styled all wrong and the eyebrows run in a straight line like a fuzzy caterpillar crawling above the eyes. "That's not him," I say.

"It is and it isn't." He jabs the photo. "This here's the face he came aboard with. Easy enough to doctor hair, thicken eyebrows, create a caricature of a face to match phony papers. This joker's passport's as bogus as everything else about him. Which says to me he came on board my ship with intent to kill. I take that real personal."

One of his security men comes in. "A couple more people waitin' out here, Chief."

"Be right there."

"So, he's not on board," I say.

"No."

"I'll tell Kathy. She was worried he might still be around."

"And you weren't?"

I let that pass. "Who do you think scrawled that message on my wall?"

"Don't know. But, like you said, Jackie had enemies out there. Maybe one of them didn't hear she'd died."

"What should I do with her stuff in the room?"

"We're tracking next of kin. Maybe you can have your cabin steward pack it up, stow it someplace until Jackie's family gives us instructions. No reason you have to look at it every day."

My thought exactly.

THE GAMES PEOPLE PLAY

TODAY I'M A FLOATER, which is what cops call a dead body in water. On a cruise ship it means going around and helping run the nonstop games designed to keep passengers amused during our day at sea.

I look over the railing down to the pool deck to see where I might be needed. A crowd surrounds the smallest of the ship's three swimming pools. Little inner tubes bob on the surface, each painted with a number: 100, 200, 300, 400, 500. At the shallow end, a bubbly Elaine brandishes a golf club and two plastic balls. She's working the crowd, pumping up enthusiasm, cheering the contestants, and keeping the kibitzers involved. She says something that gets everyone laughing. This is not the same person I saw crying over a baby blanket, distraught by the exhumation and autopsy of a beloved friend. There are all kinds of courage in this world, and Elaine's is classic variety "the show must go on."

It looks as if she has this activity under control but I'll check. I head for the stairs, taking a wide berth around the two-story-high climbing wall. A group clustered at the base cheer encouragement as four climbers crawl their slow way to the top, their clothes dripping sweat, their fingers white with the strain of gripping and holding onto the sheer rock face. I'd give rock climbing a try except I can't get past the fear of working heights without a safety net. It's less sexy but a lot safer to hit golf balls into a swimming pool.

"All right," Elaine's saying to her crowd, "we have Tiffany ahead with four hundred points." She swirls a hand over her head and the crowd cheers. A twelve-year-old girl with braces and acne blushes, tries to smile with her lips pressed together. It doesn't work. Braces glint in the sun. "Tiffany's beaten out every adult so far, including Frank," she gestures to a large man, "who swears he's an eight handicap." Elaine winks broadly as the crowd hoots.

"This isn't real golf," mutters Frank, trying to look like a good sport. "Give me my own club and a real ball and I'll show you how it's done."

"Are we still talking golf?" asks Elaine. The adults laugh. "So far, Tiffany is beating you and our other twenty-three contestants fair and square. How many left?" One man raises his hand. "Great. Our last contestant is...?" She places the club into the hands of a thin bald man who looks very familiar.

"Leo," he says.

Leo? Uncle Leo?

"Let's hear it for Leo!" says Elaine. The crowd cheers. "All right, Leo. Let's see what you've got! Everybody move back. Leo looks like a hitter."

I shield my eyes from the sun and take my first gander ever at Uncle Leo au naturel. The skin on his head, white from years in hiding, gleams as he sets down a ball. His is a beautifully shaped head. A gray band of freshly cut hair rings the back. The mutton sideburns he's worn for years to distract the eye from traveling up have been shorn into submission. Uncle Leo is, in point of very surprising fact, a handsome man. Who woulda thunk it?

He does a funny fanny waggle, which delights the crowd, then hits the ball with the grace of a Tiger Woods, give or take forty years.

The whiffle ball sails toward the 500-point tube, veering off at the last second, hitting the center "0" of the "500" painted on the side and bouncing out into the pool. "Awwwww," says the crowd.

"Bad break," says Elaine. "Give it another go."

He does another funny waggle and, with a glance at Tiffany, who has her fingers crossed and is biting her lip, he hits the ball. *Whack.* Again it sails toward the 500, veers, hits exactly the same place.

"Awwwww," says the crowd.

"Too bad, Leo," says Elaine, "but you're in good company. Better luck next time. Let's hear it for Leo." Applause, applause.

Uncle Leo shrugs, shakes Tiffany's hand. "Congratulations, Champ," I hear him say. Her braces shine as she goes up to accept her first-place trophy and a many-zippered Islander Cruise Line sports bag.

"Water balloon toss next," calls Elaine. "Everybody's welcome. We'll meet back here in twenty minutes."

I sidle up to Uncle Leo. "I like your new do," I say.

"Yeah?" He runs a hand over the bare skin. "I have to tell you, I'm feeling naked. But Susan, Miss Gayle, suggested the other look was maybe old-fashioned. It's nothing I even thought about. And I figure it's only hair. If I don't like bald, I'll grow it back."

We watch the lifeguard dive into the pool to rescue the golf balls. "I know you threw that game," I say. "You can out-trick-shot Chi Chi Rodriguez."

He smiles, doesn't say yea or nay. Uncle Leo used to have us kids set out shopping bags all around the backyard, then hit balls into them. He'd have us launch Hula Hoops and hit balls through them on the fly. He could even knock out a flying Frisbee. "That man can hit the eye out of a fly at ninety yards," my dad would say.

Yes, he can. Which is why I know he cheated. "You could have nailed that inner tube twice for a thousand points," I say.

He nods at Tiffany, who is showing off her trophy to her parents. "There are different ways of winning," he says. "Sometimes you can do it without raining all over someone's parade." He checks his watch. "Blackjack tournament. I'm signed up. Wish me luck."

And he's off to the casino with a hearty "Heigh ho, Silver, awayyyyy." Who is this masked man?

Elaine's packing up the golf equipment. "What can I do to help?" I ask.

"The Captain's usually here by now for the 'Day at Sea' drawing. People really wait for this, a free cruise for two, champagne, really good stuff. I'll go ahead with the balloon toss. It will buy me some time. But then I'm going to need the Captain, or *someone* official-looking, to pull the winning tickets."

I TRY THE BRIDGE FIRST. A group of passengers crowd around the high-polished brass gauges, listening to a lecture on the workings of our ship. I don't see the Captain. I approach a uniformed officer I recognize from the port of Miami, where he and his buddy greeted passengers on the gangway. He's even more gorgeous up close and personal. I explain what we need.

"The Captain's with Lt. Davis," he tells me. "Will I do?"

"You'll be perfect."

"Just hold on a sec, let me get something out of my cabin."

I follow his broad shoulders into a big stateroom. "This won't take long." He sits at his desk, making notations in a log. Family photos line a shelf along one wall. Most are of a much younger him alongside a stunning blond woman and four little children.

"You have a beautiful family," I say.

"Thanks. Those photos are a little old. My big guy just started high school." He runs a hand through his graying hair. "Hard to believe I'm the dad of a teenager."

Don't you just love when guys fish for compliments with a harpoon? Now I'm supposed to say, "Oh, you look much too young to have a child that old," and we'll be off and running. He seems disappointed I don't pick up the cue. This is a man used to being stroked. He probably keeps old photos because new ones would remind him he's aging.

His wife knows her way around makeup, can romance the camera. Several professional head shots show her sweet, sexy, exotic, cute. She's as chameleonesque as Madonna. If I didn't see the photos grouped together, I wouldn't recognize her as the same person. "Is your wife in theater?"

"Was. Met the little woman when she was in 'Cats' on Broadway. She gave it up, of course, when we married."

Yeah, sure "the little woman" gave it up. Like she'd give up breathing. "That's quite an act of love," I say.

He tosses this off. "A woman can hardly have an acting career and children."

This is not something I care to hear. Acting is more than my work, it's who I am. Annette Bening can do both, and Susan Sarandon, and...I run my list of heroines like a mantra.

He finishes his work and comes over, pressing inside my comfort zone. I am eye level with his name tag. Reginald Flagg. Reggie. Angela's boyfriend. He's reading my name tag, too. Angela Parker. His face goes slack. "Why are you wearing that?"

"Mine isn't ready."

"Take it off."

"I have to wear one."

"Then tape your name over it." And he strides strong and angry out of the cabin, not turning to see if I'm keeping up.

I stop to close his door. The outside has been keyed, an angry line gouged into the paint one side to the other. Was it this way when we came in? I wasn't paying attention.

—*Who keys a door?*

—*Someone, I reckon, with no car handy.*

I shake it off. I'm seeing things that aren't there. A million different things can cause a scratch on a door. I hobble after Reggie, follow him all the way to the pool where laughing passengers toss water-filled balloons until everyone is thoroughly soaked.

AFTER LUNCH in the mess, Kathy posts assignment sheets for the afternoon activities. Some of the troupe are still being interviewed by Lt. Davis so she's had to juggle us around. Keith and I are in charge of Trapshooting from two to four.

"It's easy," he says, leading me up top. "Just keep the targets flying and the rifles pointing away from the ship."

A large group of passengers wait their turn to demolish clay disks. We keep the rifles loaded and padded vests strapped on. Some of the people shoot wild. Others don't hug the rifle tight enough, letting the recoil bang into their shoulder. A surprising number do all right, missing just a few disks here and there. That's pretty amazing considering we're on a moving ship.

The last customer of the day is Mr. Garlic Breath, who has spent the last two hours sunning himself, watching others shoot. He steps up to the line, takes the rifle, loads both barrels. "Pull!" he shouts. It's not so much a word as it is the sound a person makes when they're punched in the gut. I hit the button. A clay target sails out from the ship. The shotgun blasts and the disk disintegrates. "Pull!" he says again. And again. And again.

Garlic Breath, aka Mr. Wilbur Tompkins, whose American passport says he is a longtime citizen even though the recent make and model of his Soviet shoes disagree, does not miss. He stays calm, not moving a single centimeter more than necessary. His facial expression stays stone cold as he hits every clay disk dead solid perfect. Don't ask me why, but this man scares the bejeepers out of me.

Keith and I pack up the equipment and lock it away. Happy hour is under way and we thread through throngs of travelers swigging fruit drinks garnished with umbrellas and fruit chunks. Posters announcing tonight's "Debbie Reynolds' Star Studded Review" are displayed everywhere.

"Want to catch the late show?" he asks, as we head to our cabins.

"Doesn't Kathy need us?"

"Nah. Reynolds brings her own entourage. She's something special. I caught her act in Vegas. Picked up a few moves from her dancers. Some of our guest stars are so-so, you know? But she's really fine. Why don't I swing by your cabin, pick you up around nine-thirty?"

I think about him coming to Jackie's old room, all the painful memories that might stir. "Let me pick you up," I say, dropping him at his door.

"Done."

I start limping toward my cabin. "Hey, Keith, it's good to have you back."

"I'm not all back. But I'm workin' on it."

MURDER MOST FOWL

THE STENCH HITS like a fist. I grab the doorjamb to keep from falling over.

Ransacked! My cabin's destroyed. Feces, smeared like brown finger paint, leave trails across beds, pillows, blankets. A dead chicken lies in the center of the floor, its broken neck flopping to one side. Bloody guts spill from its belly as if it were ripped open by some wild thing. The stiletto heels of Jackie's "fuck me pumps" are jabbed like chopsticks through its heart. Stumps of pinfeathers jut at awkward angles.

"SLUT!!" "WHORE!!" Giant red letters scrawl the walls, the spray paint dripping like blood onto desk and floor.

I stand frozen in the doorway, my hand pressed to my mouth, my mind refusing to understand what I'm looking at.

Piles of feathers pour out of slashed pillows. Clothing, mine and Jackie's, is strewn everywhere. Drawers have been ripped from the dresser and hurled across the room, shattering into pieces against the far wall. Cabinet doors dangle from broken hinges, the shelves emptied. A dusting of body powder coats the room like light snow. Bottles of shampoo and conditioner have been poured on top, mixing the powder into paste. Multi-colored bottles of nail polish drain their contents over piles of clothes. High heels have been snapped off shoes. Sport shoes are gashed. Bras have been slashed to shreds, delicate panties ripped apart, their elastic hanging useless from waist and legs.

My stomach heaves at the sight of the desecrated chicken. Waves of adrenaline scream "run" but my legs won't move.

I am dimly aware of commotion in the hall behind me: voice fragments, bodies pressing in trying to see. There's no way I'm going into the cabin but I also cannot leave. Something holds me. This is my room. A sick feeling twists inside. Time warps. My mind won't focus. I lose track of my place in the continuum. The *chug-a-thug* of blood pumps through my veins, echoes in my ears. I feel the valves of my heart open and close, open and close, open and—

A minute, an hour, a day later, Lt. Davis' voice booms down the passageway. I sense people clearing away. He moves in close behind me, looks into the room, catches a whiff of eau de hate.

"Shit," says Davis. I'm not sure if it's explicative or observation. He grips my arms. "You all right?"

As soon as he touches me, I realize how violently I am trembling. "I've been better."

"Wait here."

He enters the cabin. I've been staring at it without really seeing. I force myself to focus. Every inch is covered with something ugly. "SLUT!!" "WHORE!!"

My body is rigid with fear and anger. Which is a good thing. It keeps me from collapsing.

A solid block of gapers crams the hall. Dominic comes out of his cabin, pushes his way to the front. "What's going on?" He looks inside my cabin, recoils. All around us, crew and staff press in to view the wreckage. Sure, everyone shows up after the accident. Where were they before?

A couple of Davis' men arrive, pulling on plastic gloves as they go in. Davis comes out, pulls the door closed, puts a comforting arm around me. I try to deep-breathe fear and nausea away.

"Is this some kind of Tropical Welcome Wagon?" I ask.

"If it is," he says, "they've outdone themselves. Is there someplace quiet we can talk?"

"Use my cabin," says Dominic.

We do.

NOW YOU SEE IT...

I SIT ON Dominic's bed hugging my knees to my chest, trying to stop shaking. Davis leans against the dresser where a caged white rabbit sleeps. The good lieutenant studies me, absently stroking a knotted chain of chiffon scarves tied to a drawer pull. I breathe through my mouth, unable to shake the stench of my cabin.

"So," he says, "do you want to tell me what this is about?"

"Me? I have no idea."

"None?"

"None."

"I'd say you've made someone angry."

"That's crazy. I haven't done anything to anyone."

"This looks like a retaliation of some kind. A vendetta."

"You can't think it's meant for me?"

"You think it's for your roommate?"

"She's dead."

He nods. "My point."

My mind scans possibilities a million miles a second. "Maybe whoever did this doesn't know she's dead." He doesn't look hopeful. "All right then, maybe whoever killed her did this as an exclamation point. A warning to others. Like the mob tossing a dead fish on the body of a hit. You know."

"You watch way too many Hollywood movies."

A few rabbit hairs attach to his navy shirt. He picks them off one by one. Dominic's boa constrictor rouses from its perch on the bedside shelf. We've disturbed its nap. It flicks its tongue, testing our smell.

"Look," I say, "this is my fourth day on board. It usually takes me at least a week to make someone angry enough to disembowel a chicken on my floor." He's not amused. "That was a joke, Lieutenant."

"Nice to see you've still got your humor. But I hope it doesn't mean you're taking this lightly. This is no random act of destruction, Morgan. Someone wants to scare you."

"Well, they're doing a bang-up job."

The snake sways back and forth toward Davis, toward me. Deciding something, it leans over the edge of the shelf and slowly slides down onto the foot of the bed. Davis, busy brushing rabbit hairs, doesn't notice. He tries another tack. "Do you have any idea when this happened?"

"I haven't been in my cabin since after lunch."

"Everything in order then?"

"As much as my things ever are. Then I worked Trapshooting from two to four. When I came back...when I came..." Bitter fluid burns my throat. My lunch salad clambers to revisit. I swallow hard, trying to keep it down.

Two white doves coo in a cage hanging from the ceiling. Their soft song is totally wrong. This scene begs for Lon Chaney, the mad "Phantom of the Opera," wildly attacking the organ. The snake drops the rest of its body onto the bed. Davis sees it, jumps back, banging into the dresser, sending up a new cloud of rabbit hairs. They attach to his shirt like metal shavings to a magnet. The snake winds its slow way toward me. This boa is bigger than the one I worked with in Paul's act and a lot cuter. It glistens with the iridescent colors of a recent shed.

Davis stares at me, at the snake, back at me. I would have thought a cowboy from Colorado would be more comfortable around reptiles. "The words spray-painted on your wall are explicitly sexual," he says, eyeing the snake's progress toward me. "This kind of rage is very powerful and very specific." He shifts uncomfortably. "Morgan, I have to ask you something personal. It's a little awkward, my being a friend of Roblings and all, but is there someone else? Another man in your life?"

"No."

"An ex-boyfriend, maybe. Someone jealous of Roblings."

"My ex-boyfriend is now happily married to my little sister. One of the reasons I broke up with him was I like a little edge to my men, and Adam was much too nice. He could never do something this hateful."

The snake pauses, bobs its head at Davis, continues on. Davis swallows hard, clears his throat. "All right, then, Roblings and I haven't kept real close contact these past couple of years. Could he have an old girlfriend who's upset you took him away?''

"No."

I say this without being a hundred percent sure. Roblings and I have been working hard to build a relationship. Why dwell on our respective pasts? No need to detail for Roblings all the mistakes I've made. It's enough that I've come away from every relationship with another piece of the puzzle in place: what I do and don't like, what I can and cannot stand, how much or how little I am willing to put up with before calling it quits.

Davis paces the small cabin, examining Dominic's wands, top hats, metal cups, balls, and cards. A canister of antibacterial wipes is stored next to the bed. I take one out, press the clean antiseptic smell under my nostrils, inhale deep and long. I pull out another wipe, begin scrubbing the skin on my hands, cleaning off the acrid stench of my room. There's a way to get rid of skunk smell. What is it? What is it? Orange juice? Tomato juice? Something. I'll have to look it up.

"Okay," says Davis, "let's come at this another way. What about since you came on board? Might you have offended someone?''

"Like I said, this is only my fourth day."

"Whoever redecorated your cabin is not balanced. It wouldn't take much, either real or imagined, to set them off. Sometimes, harmless flirtations can be misconstrued. Perhaps you were nice to some man and his wife or girlfriend read more into it."

I scrub the web of skin between my fingers. "I did thank the soft-serve yogurt server a bit profusely."

"You're making light again, Morgan."

"Sorry. I get a little wiseass when I'm nervous."

"You're nervous?"

"You betcha."

"Good. I hope it makes you watchful."

"I still say this has to do with Jackie. Kathy said that men bought her jewelry. Did you ever find any of it?"

"We're working on it."

"See. Maybe someone—maybe the person who killed her—came looking for it, then trashed the room as a cover-up."

He's not buying. "Until we know for sure otherwise, you and I need to assume this is personal. I have a murdered woman whose body you found, another young woman who died on board—whose death we are investigating more closely—and now this. I'd like to find a common thread.''

The rabbit rouses in its cage, shakes off sleep, sending up a flurry of white hairs. They, too, float to Davis' shirt. With a blink of pink eyes, the rabbit turns its back and hunkers down to nibble a wilted piece of lettuce. Davis moves away and resumes picking off the hairs. ''Could this incident have to do with something back home? Chicago? Do you have enemies there?''

''I once cheered for Green Bay during a Bears game. But, hey, I was young, had a couple of beers, and—'' He gives me a hard look. ''Sorry.'' I scan my larcenous past, come up empty.

''Think,'' he says.

I do. ''Before I left, someone was slipping notes under my apartment door. Poems, mostly. All very sweet. Nothing sick like this.''

You have a stalker. Roblings' word, not mine. Still...

Davis runs his knuckles under his chin, thinking. ''That might be something. We found a few packets of poems in Jackie's belongings. Adolescent wet dream stuff with a liberal dose of S&M. Nothing any woman I know would want to keep around. Could be a connection there.''

The poems have to be from Keith-the-romantic. He's the love-letter writing type. But he loved Jackie. He'd never hurt her. ''Any idea who sent them?'' I ask, casually.

''No signature. They're postmarked New Jersey. Date back eight years.''

Not slipped under Jackie's door at all, but mailed to her. ''See,'' I say, relieved. ''I told you this was all meant for her.''

My ankle throbs. I unroll my elastic bandage and begin rewrapping. ''How'd that happen?'' he asks.

''Twisted it jogging. Nassau's roads aren't exactly—'' I gasp.

''What?''

The woman on the moped. *''I hope you broke something, you slut.''* The memory of her voice chills. ''I'd forgotten.''

''What?'' he asks again.

I tell Davis what little I can. ''No,'' I say, ''I don't know her. I'm sure...at least I was sure when it happened that she mistook me for someone else. I have no idea who she is. I wouldn't recognize her if I saw her. I was lying on the ground in pain. My eyes and mouth were full of dirt.''

The snake tests the air around the pillow behind me and, finding it to its liking, slithers into its dark shadows and curls up for a sleep.

The bandage won't cooperate. I've wrapped injured body parts all my life but suddenly my hands aren't working right.

"You're wrapping that too tight," says Davis. With a nervous glance at the slumbering snake, he perches on the end of the bed and unwraps what I've done. "Go home, Morgan. Back to Chicago."

"I have a job to finish here."

He smooths the bandage over and around. "You can't dance on this ankle."

"I'm working with Dominic until this is better. Kathy needs me. I'm staying."

"How's that feel?"

I waggle my foot. He's done this a time or two. "It's good," I say. He keeps wrapping. "This would be a good time for you to leave."

"The thought never occurred."

"It should have been your first."

"Well, I'm not running."

Davis folds the end of the elastic bandage, fixing it in place with a couple of metal clips. For a moment, he holds my foot and applies firm pressure.

"I can't protect you. Not full-time. The best I can do is keep an eye on things, but this is a big ship, and I have many responsibilities."

"I understand."

IT ISN'T UNTIL I walk out that I realize I have no place to go. My cabin's not an option, not in the condition it's in. Not ever. The hall is mobbed, everyone wanting to know what happened. Kathy rushes at me. "Oh, God, Morgan," she says and throws her arms around, squeezes hard. "Dominic told me. I don't know what to say. This is awful, just awful. I'm so sorry."

And I'm shaking like I'm freezing, my fine-tuned body jerking totally out of control. Kathy holds me tighter, keeps my limbs from falling off. I'm crying. I never cry.

"We've never had anything like this," she says. "Never. Oh, God, Morgan." She helps me down the hall as if I were a fragile doll instead of a tough-talking wiseass. I cringe every time I brush up against one of the onlookers. What if he's still here, watching, loving how upset he's made me? I scan each face for the attacker, see guilt in every eye.

—*A little paranoia with your disemboweled chicken, my dear?*

—*Thank you, no, I'm feeling quite full.*

Kathy's voice is soft, soothing. She leads me to the door with the wreath. "You're moving in with Elaine. She has the biggest single. We've rigged a mattress in her cabin. It's a little tight but—"

I nod, shivering, unable to talk.

"Elaine's going around to all the girls collecting clothes you can wear until you replace the stuff that was...that was...that you lost. A bunch of security guys are still in your cabin but, as soon as they finish, I'll send in a cleaning crew and have them rescue anything useable. We'll clean it up, bring it to your new cabin. No need for you to go back and see that...that... Oh," she says, pausing for breath, "I mean, oh."

As she opens Elaine's door, I hear Lt. Davis in the hall behind, asking questions of people, the same people who live all around my cabin. No one seems to have seen anything. How does that happen? How does someone come into your life and destroy it and not one single person comes forward to bear witness?

DAY FIVE

IS THERE WATER ON THE OTHER SIDE OF THIS ISLAND?

ELAINE SLEEPS like a little girl, snuggled up with a soft blanket in a circus of stuffed animals. I've had all night to study her sleep habits. I tried closing my own eyes a couple of times but there are some seriously scary monsters lurking in the dark, just waiting for a chance to pounce.

Red numbers glow from her bedside clock. I've watched them crawl from night to morning. This last hour I've tried to exactly count the seconds to the next minute. *One hippopotamus, two hippopotamus, three hippopotamus.* The hippopotamus has the largest mouth of any animal. *Four hippopotamus, five hippopotamus.* The African hippopotamus kills more people each year than the lion or elephant. *Six hippopotamus, seven hippopotamus.* Timing homicidal hippos helps detour my thoughts around pulverized poultry.

Le Question de jour: What kind of maniac kills a chicken without making soup?

Ten hippopotamus, eleven hippopotamus, twelve hippopotamus.

Question part deux: If the chicken killer knows Jackie is dead, the destruction of our cabin must be some kind of warning. About what? To whom? And if they don't know Jackie's dead, then someone beside her killer intended savage violence against her. Roblings says some people are trouble magnets, the way some people are accident-prone. If you break it down, dig into it, you often find underlying reasons. Primary causes. I know Jackie mostly through other people's eyes and what they saw was bone-chilling ugly.

Question part trois: If the carnage was intended against me—

This thought runs smack into a dead end. I'd know if I'd upset anyone that much. I'm an innocent bystander. Lt. Davis isn't sure about that, but I am. Absolutely positive. Ninety-nine, one hundred percent purely positive.

Thirty hippopotamus, thirty-one hippopotamus, thirty-two hippopotamus.

There is killing time, and there is strangling it to death. I limp to the bathroom, tape my ankle, and pull on the same slacks and T-shirt I wore last night. Luckily, the fashion police rarely roll out before the crack of noon. I leave Elaine snuggled with her menagerie and slip into halls busy with crew preparing for a new day.

A few couples on deck cuddle on chaises under blankets dragged up from their cabins. No need to book an expensive outside cabin when you can have the whole outdoors to yourself. The star-filled sky is still dark, the horizon on the verge of first light. I breathe deep. Sea air, faint floral smell. How is it possible for the world be so stunningly beautiful after the horror in my room? Breathe again, feel the morning air clear out remnants of the carnage. I have an uncle, still recovering from the effects of fighting in Vietnam, who recently went back with a group of other vets to visit, try to heal. "What struck me most," he said, "was how beautiful that country is. I never thought so, back then. You have to wonder why humans take God's beauty and defile it."

In the night sky off the starboard bow, the faintest outline of an island emerges, two low hills separated by a valley. It looks like a shadow drawing of a camel's back. A groggy couple join me at the railing, the blanket pulled tight around them. Her mascara didn't make the trip from disco to dawn, forms dark smudges around her eyes. His hair spikes at odd angles.

They stand inhaling the dawn. An aching for Roblings rams me like an eighteen-wheeler. He should be here. This big tough cop who spends his days wading through the muck and slime of man's inhumanity also cries at the beauty of a sunrise. We celebrated our first summer solstice together at a spot he found at the southern tip of Lake Michigan where you can watch the sun rise and set. We filled the hours between with walks and books and talk and silence. He knows how to be still, my detective. He belongs here with me, now, being still, sharing this.

The sky takes on color, deep purples, dark blues. Palm trees pop from the shadows like dots on the camel's humps. A band of sand glows white along the water, snaking the shoreline. We're sailing fast toward the island. Beyond the horizon, rays of sun reach long fingers into the sky. Hallelujah, it's a new day dawning.

A sprinkling of people come out on the deck, stand at the railing, more walk out onto the deck below. Uncle Leo passes under me, joins a small group gathered at the bow. I nearly call out to him, stop myself in time. He's known me since I was born. He'd smell the stench of chicken and shit clinging to my clothes, my hair, my psyche. He'd notice how jumpy I am, how I keep looking around for whatever or whomever. How can I act as if nothing's wrong?

—*Because acting is your work. It's what you do. It's who you are.*

—*I'm not that good.*

—*Sure you are.*

—*No. Not right now.*

I angle myself behind a post that shields me from his sight line, just in case he should turn and look this way. I'm too edgy to manage polite social conversation just yet. Lack of sleep doesn't help.

"Ooooooooohhhhhhhh." A soft hosanna arises from the blanketed couple next to me as the edge of the fireball rises from the ocean.

"Wow," says the girl.

"Yeah," says the boy.

And we're quiet with the beauty of it.

"Yo! Stan!"

Well, almost quiet. They shout their friends awake and now we are a gathering. The sun doesn't rise as much as pop up from the sea. The island snaps to life in the light. Brilliant flowers glow neon against lush foliage.

"It's beautiful," whispers the girl.

"Yeah?" says Stan. "Wait 'til you got two thousand tourists crawling all over it."

"Can't scare me," she says. "Six days ago I was shoveling my car out of fourteen feet of snow."

They laugh. Beauty is in the watery eye and frostbitten toe of the beholder. And for these huddled masses, you can't get much prettier than one private tropical island, owned and operated exclusively for its passengers by Islander Cruise Line.

Our ship steams full speed toward Eden. The crowd around us grows. There is strange symmetry to the stands of palm trees, neat rows never designed by nature. The odd shapes on the sand that I couldn't make out come clear in the new light. Evidently, when Adam and Eve moved out, Sportmart moved in and planted rows of Jet Skis, parasails, windsurf boards, beach chairs, and umbrellas.

Straw sellers arrange woven wares inside thatched huts. The ship slows, stops. The deck under my feet hums with the vibration of chains reeling out anchors.

"There you are!" Kathy brings me coffee. "Thought you could use this. Get any sleep? Of course not, how could you? I didn't." She holds her cup under her nose, inhales the aroma. "Everything's falling apart. At least, it feels that way."

"Bad stuff comes in threes," I say. "Angela died, Jackie died, my cabin was trashed. It should be all right now."

"I want that in writing." We sip the coffee. Caffeine. Just the thing for jangled nerves. "I wish I could go on the island with you," she says. "I don't know why I thought I could get away for a couple of hours. I have to rehearse the passengers who are performing in the talent show."

"I'll help."

"You can help later. But I want you to at least get off the ship for a little while. This island is so beautiful. It will do you good to walk around. And there's tons of people everywhere so you'll feel nice and safe. This island is one of the reasons I invited you to come. I wanted to share the beauty." She lights up a cigarette, and we inhale. "This wasn't the cruise experience I had in mind for you."

"A little like Peter Pan," I say, running a finger along my scar.

"Yeah, a little like that." She stubs out the new, perfectly good cigarette. Smiles at my expression. "I'm trying to quit. At least, cut down."

"This wouldn't have anything to do with a certain nonsmoking passenger of the male persuasion, would it?"

"You know, Sherlock, you've gotta stop dating that detective. He's teaching you all sorts of bad habits."

"One can hope."

TENDER MERCIES

I'M IN ELAINE'S CABIN sorting through the pile of clothing Elaine scrounged from coworkers when Lt. Davis stops by. He leans against the jamb, his bear-sized body filling the doorway. "How're you doing?" he asks.

"I'm starting to feel more angry than scared. First, because someone violated my space. And, second, because he ruined the few clothes I have. I know beggers can't be choosers, and I don't mean to sound ungrateful, but..." I hold up a purple ruffled blouse with matching Capri pants. "I mean, a lot of this is stuff I wouldn't be caught dead in...you should excuse the expression."

"I see what you mean. Why don't you pull a few things from the shop upstairs, tell them to send the bills to security? We'll pick up the tab."

"Thanks."

He works a toothpick around his mouth. "A passenger was seen down in this area yesterday," he says, "chunky guy. A couple of musicians saw him, say he looks like Gorbachev."

The Russian association clicks. "Could be Garlic Breath," I say. "He was backstage when we did the 'French Follies,' kind of hanging around, getting in the way."

"Garlic Breath?"

"Like you wouldn't believe. He must chew whole cloves. When I was looking through the passport photos, I saw him listed as Wilber something. He's Wilber like I'm Natasha."

"Anyone else see him?"

"Dominic. He tripped over the guy's feet. And I'm pretty sure I saw the same guy the night I got lost in the boiler room."

This gets his attention. "What was he doing there?"

"The same kind of thing, I think. Just poking around, seeing how things work."

"Anyone see him there?"

"Sean O'Brian wound up giving him a tour, said passengers wander down there from time to time."

"I'll check it."

"You're not thinking he trashed my cabin?"

"Nah. The guys who saw him don't remember him carrying chickens. It's the kind of thing I'd think you'd notice."

"Evidently not."

I finish going through the clothes, set aside a few wearable pieces. "What are you up to today?" he asks.

"Kathy is forcing me to tour the island. If that's all right with you."

"Good. Pretty place. It'll take your mind off the other stuff. Who you going with?"

"Kathy says a bunch of staff are already there. I'll hook up with them."

"Watch your back." I shudder. As if I need reminding. "Do you want to call anyone?"

"Tell Roblings how much fun I'm having? Not yet. He's got some heavy-duty stuff on his plate just now. This isn't the kind of distraction he needs."

"Let me know when."

He's nearly out the door when I remember. "One thing," I say. "Elaine told me they're exhuming Angela's body."

"That'd be right."

"Do you think she was murdered, too?"

"We mean to find that out."

"I told Inspector Kolby she may have been pregnant," I say.

"He passed that on."

"Well, I found out for sure she was. You know about her and Reggie."

"There're not many secrets on this ship," he says.

"Right."

"Keep me posted if you hear anything else."

"I'll be knee-deep in piña coladas if you need me."

THE WATERS AROUND the island are too shallow for the ship, so we anchor offshore. I board one of the double-decker tenders ferrying passengers to and from the island. It reminds me of the fishing charter Dad took us on when I was ten. That also stank of old catch and new bait, kerosene and rank exhaust. We'd barely left the pier before I tossed my French toast all over the deck. The Captain swung back and handed me to Mom, who'd had the good sense to stay on land.

I stand at the bow. This morning, while I was playing dress-up, the early settlers landed, racing to commandeer chairs, umbrellas, water toys, patches of sand on "secluded" beaches. Fantasy Island lives.

I lean into the wind, trying to inhale unfueled air. Gum would help. I rummage through Angela's batik lizard bag, which was the one item security pulled unscathed from my cabin. I've stocked it with provisions for my island visit: gum, hard candies, bottled water, towel, suntan lotion, cassette player with five tapes of musicals. I fold a stick of gum into my mouth. It takes the edge off the nausea.

A woman joins me holding her large straw hat to keep it from blowing off. Strands of pitch-black hair peek out from the back.

"Hi." She smiles, peering over the tops of her sunglasses. "Remember me? Nassau? We waited together in line for the phones?"

"Right."

"How's your ankle?"

"Better, thanks."

"You were the Magician's Assistant, right?"

"Right."

"But you're really a dancer, when you're not injured."

"Right."

She laughs. "I knew it! I was a dancer. Course, that was BC, Before Children. But I could tell by the way you move." She extends a hand. "I'm Pimm," she says.

"Morgan."

She frowns. "I thought..."

"What?"

"Oh, it's just I thought I heard someone call you by another name."

"Another—? Oh, that must be my Uncle Leo. To him, I'm forever Mimi. Morgan's my stage name."

She smiles. "Unfortunately, Pimm's my real name. My dad named me for the drink he courted Mom with, Pimm's Cup. Could have been worse. He's now drinking Kettle One."

I laugh. "Are you enjoying the cruise?"

"So far, it's everything I'd dreamed it would be. What about you?"

Murder, mayhem? "I'd have to say it's more than I expected."

A couple in their eighties, the woman bearing a striking resemblance to Margaret Mead, stroll toward us arm in arm.

Pimm waves to someone back in the bow. "See you later," she says, hurrying off.

The couple join me at the railing. Her floral muumuu echoes her husband's shirt. One orange flower matches her hair, which is dyed orange and sprayed into the earflapped shape of a 1940s football helmet. It doesn't move in the sea breeze.

"Thought we'd take a look-see what this island's all about," says she.

"We almost never get off ships anymore," says her husband. "I mean, heh-heh, how many straw bags can you buy?"

"Oh, you." She gives him a quick elbow to the ribs.

"Been cruising for years," says he. "Alaska, the Nile, the Amazon down from Iquitos, Mississippi paddleboats. You name it. Lost count how many times we sailed these partiklar waters."

"Still," says she, "It doesn't hurt to get up off our duffs every now and again. This being a brand-new island and all."

"Yeah," he says, winking, "they made it last week."

"Oh, you." Another rib jab. Good thing he's padded. "If I don't pry him out of that chair, him and his cronies'd play bridge 'til the cows come home."

I smile through closed mouth and clenched teeth, inhaling fresh air as deep as I can, keeping my system quiet until I can get off. The husband mistakes my silence for interest.

"No one actually lives there, you know," he says. "It's all day labor. Cruise line ships 'em in in the morning, back out at night. Smart idea if you ask me. Buy an island, fix it up American so's you don't have to worry that the food they set in front of you is some critter you'd pay to exterminate back home. And it's tricky figuring foreign money, how many funny little coins equal one good old American dollar. Not that any of them shopkeepers ever turned down old Ben Franklin."

Inhale, exhale. Slow and easy. Smile for the nice people.

"There's just too many foreigners," she says. "And all that terrible poverty." I assume she means on the other islands where real people live. "That's another reason I don't get off the ships anymore. Makes me cry just to see it. Especially the little ones."

I could almost swim the rest of the way. Just a few minutes more....
The man pulls out a cigar. Great. That'll help air quality.

"All real civilized." He flicks an old Zippo lighter set to the intensity of a blowtorch and touches the flame to the end of the cigar. The tobacco catches like tinder. "Don't know why folks didn't think up these islands years ago," he says, puffing away.

They did. Called them Nassau and Jamaica and St. Thomas and St. Maarten. And then came the tourists.

I LAND

I HANG BACK, letting the paying guests disembark first. Near the stern, Sean O'Brian and two of his crew bring boxes from below and load them onto dollies. "Hi," I say.

"Ah, mornin', darlin'." He pushes his Greek cap back on his head. "You win, you know."

"Win?"

"Sure, if you didn't have bad luck you'd have no luck a'tall. Terrible, terrible thing, what happened yesterday."

"Word does get around."

"I try to keep my ear to the ground. You're all right, then?"

"A little shook up."

"Well, this island's just the thing to heal what ails ya."

His men drop two metal crates the size of small caskets onto the dolly. "What's that?" I ask.

"What isn't it? We've got everythin' from sun lotion to towels. This island is like our ship. If I don't stock it, you don't got it."

The tender's horn sounds. "We'd best be getting off," he says. "Unless you're wantin' to take the ride back."

SPORTS EQUIPMENT rental booths line the pier, listing prices, times, insurance disclaimers. I pass Pimm reading the rates at the bike rental booth. "Are you meeting someone?" she asks.

"A few of the other entertainers, although I'm not exactly sure where they are. What about you?"

"I thought I'd walk around, see if there's water on the other side of the island."

"Sounds like an important job."

"Would you like to join me?"

Yes, yes, yes. Being alone is not an appealing option just now. "I'm not sure how long my ankle will hold."

"I was thinking of renting a bike. We can rent a tandem. I'll do the work."

"You sure?"

"You'll be doing me a favor. I teach spinning classes at a gym back home but the bikes on board are usually taken. This'll help keep my biking muscles in shape."

The main bike path is a paved road following the shoreline. Occasional side paths lead up into the hills. I steer, making a show of pedaling, but Pimm's doing all the work. At first we stay to the flatter shore road. It's less taxing for her and we roll past a goodly piece of paradise.

I ask about her family. "My husband travels. Some kind of consulting thing that would just bore you to tears if I tried to explain. Our kids are visiting my mom. She lives in L.A. and I figure it's all right to let her spoil them a couple of weeks each year."

"Is your husband on the cruise?"

"Yep. But he's a real workaholic. His body may be in paradise, but his head's in his office. Those damned computers."

"Yeah," I say. "Can't live with them, can't cook 'em for dinner."

We stop for lemonade on the far side of the island. The cruise line, anticipating our every need, has sprinkled our path with drink stations, food stations, and trinket stations. Never know when you'll need an emergency necklace. The lemonade is tart and frosty. We drop the bike on the sand, slip out of our sandals, and walk to the water. "I could get used to this," she says. "No obligations, no running around doing a million errands."

"You'd miss your family."

She laughs. "Ever drive car pool for active kids?" We walk along the water's edge, warm waves lapping our feet. "I've sometimes thought, when all the kids are fighting and my husband is off on one of his trips, that I'd like to get arrested for something that would put me in jail for about three months."

"Jail?"

"Just a little time for myself. They'd feed me, clothe me, and I could read at night without having to stop every two minutes to break up World War III." She picks up stones, skips them expertly along the water. "I like how self-contained your life is on board."

"Working a cruise ship's like any other job," I say. "I've had more temp jobs than I can count. Every one of them looked easier or sexier or better than the last, for about the first ten minutes." I try skipping a stone. It hits and sinks. "Cruising's great if you're single. But it's no life for a couple with kids."

Sand shifts underfoot and I stumble. "Mind if we go back?" I ask. "Walking on soft sand looks good in tampon commercials but it's hell on sore ankles."

We're rounding a curve to our bike and come upon Mr. Garlic Breath, pant legs rolled, shirt off, suspenders crisscrossing his broad back, industrial-strength Russian shoes set on the sand with the socks rolled inside. He clasps his hands behind him, tilting his head up toward the sun. He's not so much standing in the ocean as he is planted. There's something almost military in his bearing. Lt. Davis says he was spotted near my cabin last night. I shudder. He turns as we pass behind him, regards us without expression as we reclaim our bike, then turns back to the sea. I'm glad Pimm's with me. Safety in numbers and all that.

The relentless sun has toasted our bike, the handlebars burn my fingers. "Let's head up in the hills," says Pimm. "Looks cooler."

"It's hilly," I warn.

"Sounds perfect."

I steer up a path that winds through dense jungle foliage. How much is planted, how much natural, is impossible to tell. We duck under leaves as big as golf umbrellas and pass ribbons of water flowing down jagged rocks.

"Get him!"

"Got him!"

"No you don't."

"Nobody move. Where is he?"

"There."

"Where?"

"There! There!"

"Where, for God's sake?"

"Under that plant."

"Don't move!"

Urgent male voices machine-gun from the dense jungle to our left. Pimm and I stop, listen.

"Where's the bag?"

"Here."

"Give it."

Pause. The sound of feet scuffing. "Got him!"

"Careful."

"Easy. Easy!"

"Watch the eggs."

"Got 'em."

"Let's go, let's go, let's go."

A red-faced Ichabod bursts out of the bush in front of us, two of his men close behind. He freezes when he sees us, the others crashing into him. Shades of The Three Stooges. One of the men tries to conceal a large burlap bag behind his back, another cradles a small cloth bag like a preemie baby.

"Ladies," says Ichabod, tipping his hat as he passes.

"Ladies," say the others, nodding, moving cautiously around our bike, then scurrying down the hill.

"What was that?" asks Pimm.

"I think they're into reptiles," I say. "They had a couple with them on deck last night. Maybe they're collecting more."

"Is that legal?"

"I have no idea."

"They sure looked guilty about something."

She pedals us up the path to the top of the island, a rocky outcropping where we can sit and catch our breath and look out over the same water we've been sailing. It looks a lot calmer from up here. To our left, beautiful flowers twine a tropical pool that overflows to create trickling falls. I recognize the sound of a recirculating pump from my dad's backyard fish pond. Even paradise needs help now and again.

The side we rode up was a gradual incline. This other side is a jut of craggy rock, a steep fall to the rocks below. We walk out onto the promontory and sit on the cool stone.

"It's a shame your husband didn't come ashore to see this," I say.

"Oh, he finds ways to amuse himself. I think he prefers indoor sports." She gazes out into the distance. Our ship bobs in water as blue as a robin's egg. "Do you have a boyfriend?" she asks.

"I'm working on it."

"Problems in paradise?"

"Commitment problems, I think."

"He's getting nervous?"

"It's me, not him. I don't understand how people know when it's the real thing."

"I knew," she says. "I was eighteen the first time I saw him. Boom! That was it. We Italians call it 'the thunderbolt.' It was powerful like that. There's never been anyone else for me."

"You're lucky."

"I thought so."

"Thought?"

She drifts off again, her gaze returning to the sea. The vista is classic postcard. A couple wander into the lower right hand corner, walking barefoot along the water, talking, laughing. It's Uncle Leo and Miss Susan Gayle. Please don't let them start holding hands. Please. It's not something I want to see.

"Did anyone ever take something of yours?" asks Pimm.

Seems an odd questions. "A leather coat," I say, "in high school. And you can't leave food lying around anywhere backstage."

"Bigger. Something at the core of you. Something so important your entire world imploded when it was stolen?"

Shoot. She's going to confide something personal. I recognize the lead-in. Normally I'd be thrilled. But I'm emotionally fragile at the moment, would rather keep our conversation light. She's waiting for an answer. I try to think. "My sister fell in love with my old boyfriend, but I was already through with him. I guess, maybe, my record player. I really loved that antique. Some gonif stole it from my dorm room. I put a curse on them. Somewhere out there is a thief with no toes and chronic gas."

Uncle Leo and Miss Home Wrecker wade into the water, picking shells from the surf. She sells seashells by the seashore, and maybe one or two other baubles. Their laughter echos up the cliff as they round a corner out of sight.

"I'm an army brat." Pimm's conversation sure jumps around. "Grew up all over the country. My dad had this thing about honesty. He'd give us a pass on a lot of stuff, but if he caught us lying all hell broke loose."

I'm starting to feel a tad uneasy. It's probably residual jitters from the demolition derby in my room combined with my concern for Uncle Leo. Something rakes along the sheer wall below as if trying to claw its way up. The sound tears open my spine. I feel my courage pour out. Cut. Print. That's a wrap. I want this scene over.

The tender's bell clangs in the distance. "That must be the warning bell," I say. "We'd better get back." I stand and stretch. Pimm stands in front of me, the cliff edge at my back. She's not moving.

"Trouble with being an army brat," she says, "is one day you walk into the real world and find out not everyone was raised like you. Some people, sometimes people who call you friend, sometimes people you've loved for years, can look you right in the eye and smile at the same time they're twisting a knife in your back."

"Boy," I say, no idea where she's going with this, "ain't that the truth?"

Far below, an old Jeep rumbles along the one-lane path, the metal crates bouncing around in back as Sean and his men bring supplies to the outstations. I wave, hoping he'll see me, let someone know I'm here. They pass without looking up. *Listen to your instincts,* says Roblings. So why am I thinking I need to let people know I'm up here, alone, with Pimm?

"Are you religious?" asks Pimm.

What's the right answer? "I was raised to live the Good Life."

"Looks like that's what you're doing, all right."

"No, it means to do good acts, kindnesses. To think good thoughts. To help, not hurt." I try to casually move around her toward the bike.

"That doesn't sound religious to me."

"My dad would ask you who's the more religious man, the one who prays three times a day, then goes home and beats his family, or the man who perhaps only occasionally attends services but lives each day of his life doing what he can to better the world and the life of those around him?"

"So your dad goes out and spreads happiness around?"

"More like bad puns. But, yes, I would say he tries."

"My husband's like that." She's smiling but something's chilled in her voice. "I'll have to remember to tell him some people call it religion." She takes a step toward me.

"Hold it!" I say. "There's not much room. Let me get out of your way."

I turn sideways trying to slip past as she takes another step. There's a loud grunt from under the cliff. A clawed hand reaches up over the top, grabs hold of a vine inches from my ankle.

"Wha—!" I twist around too suddenly. Red-hot pain knifes my ankle. My foot gives way under me. Pimm's eyes widen as I lose balance. My arms windmill wildly as I teeter back toward the precipice.

"Oh, God!" I yell.

She reaches out, clasps my arms with iron grip. Hesitates. Something flickers in her eyes, fear, anger, a decision. She yanks me back to safety. My heart bounces off my ribs, tries to escape through my throat.

A rock climber hurls his body up and over the cliff's edge. He lies panting, sweat streaming off his muscles. He sees us. Smiles wide. "Bitchin'," he says.

Another climber follows, up and over, flops spread-eagle on the rocks. "Wotta rush!"

The bell clangs again, seems to bring Pimm around. "I think you're right," she says. "We'd better go."

It's as if the whole near-tragedy never happened. As if I almost didn't bite the big one, shuffle off to Buffalo, go to that final audition in the sky. We turn the bike around, riding the rocky road back to the beach. I don't draw clear breath until we finally make it to the bike rental place. The line of returnees is long and sunburnt. The person working the line is having trouble finding the Cruise Cards left as deposits. "Let me take care of this," I tell Pimm. "No need for you to spend your precious vacation time standing in line."

She doesn't protest, seems to move almost trancelike out to the pier. I watch her board the tender, breathe a little easier as it sails. She seemed so normal. I still don't have a clue what happened but it doesn't take a Bubbe Dubbe to foretell that a long friendship is not in our future. I return the bike, then walk out onto the pier and join the group waiting for the next tender.

A couple of Ichabod's friends come up to me. "Want to see something beautiful?" asks one, reaching into a small cloth bag tied to his belt. He takes out a tarantula roughly the size and furriness of a professional wrestler's palm. As the sister of three brothers, I know my tarantulas, have had a couple dropped down my blouses or set on my pillows as I wake. I'm not afraid of them. They're really not dangerous and, if you've ever spent a rainy Saturday sitting around watching one shed, you know they can be mildly amusing. But, by the same token, they are not my favorite pet. Especially not this one, which could arm wrestle a couple of dogs I know.

And why, I ask you, of all the people milling about on this pier, do Ichabod's buddies feel the need to share with me? Is it, perhaps, Angela's lizard print bag slung about my body? Or do I have a neon sign flashing across my forehead that says *Dangerous/ Demented/Disenfranchised people welcome?* Do I? I'll have to check.

HINDSIGHT IS TWENTY-TWENTY

LT. DAVIS WILL BE right with you," says the security giant manning the office. "Have a seat."

I fidget. What exactly do I want to tell him? Yes, Pimm seemed strange. But was she really going to push me off the cliff? When my ankle gave way, didn't she reach out and save me? Still, the whole incident didn't *feel* right. So, what do I say? "There's a gal named Pimm something-or-other on board who seems a little—" No. "There's this passenger, Pimm, who's maybe a bit bipolar." Hardly. Let's face it, as someone who grew up in the bosom of the family Tiersky with its long lineage of raving eccentrics, I should be more tolerant of the strangeness of others. I'll just leave quietly.

An officer walks out of the lieutenant's office. The security guard nods at me. "You can go in, now."

I decide to forget about Pimm the Peculiar, pretend I just stopped by to say hi. "Knock, knock," I say, waiting at the door.

"Yo." Davis sits, feet on desk, humming tunelessly as he studies a paper in a folder.

"Don't mean to disturb you," I say.

"*This* disturbs me." He holds up the piece of paper. I reach for it. He pulls it away. "Before I let you see this, I expect you know from dating Roblings that anything I might care to confide in you stays right here in this room with us."

I cross my heart. "Confidentiality is number one in my 'So You Want to Date a Cop' manual."

"Figured it might be." He hands me the paper. The official *Minneapolis Medical Examiner* seal is stamped at the top. "It's the report on Angela Parker's death."

I read to where it says: "*Cause of death:* severe blunt trauma to the head." My legs go wobbly. I sink into a chair. "Angela was murdered?"

"For Angela to have died accidentally with that wound," he says, "she would have to fall off a very high diving board into a very empty pool."

This makes no sense. "Why would anyone..." Possibilities flood in. "Was she sexually assaulted? Is that—"

"No. She was killed by one powerful blow to the back of the head. I'm thinking she was most likely murdered somewhere else, then dumped in the bike hold. The storm had tossed bikes all over the place and we found a few on top of Angela. It looked like an accident. The ship's doc corroborated that."

I stare at the report. "How could a doctor miss murder?"

Lt. Davis rocks his chair. "Nice guy, the doc. Retired after forty-six years practicing family medicine in the same Wyoming town. Mostly he treats seasickness, sunburn, muscle pulls, minor cuts, and abrasions. He gets the occasional appendicitis, heart attack. What he doesn't get is murder." Davis worries a toothpick around his mouth. "I'm not making excuses, here, and I'm not passing the buck. But I'm thinking maybe if the sea wasn't so rough when they found Angela's body and Doc didn't have so many seasick passengers lined up outside his office he might have noticed things. And maybe if I wasn't in such a danged rush to off-load Angela's body in Nassau so her grieving family could fly her home, I would have taken more time at the scene. Hindsight, as they say, is twenty-twenty."

The toothpick snaps and he pulls the two pieces out of his mouth, adding them to an ashtray filled with other broken toothpicks. "The fact is, Angela was sweet and well liked, not an enemy in the world. There was never a reason to suspect foul play."

I choke up thinking of the beautiful girl I watched perform over and over on the videotapes. "If Jackie hadn't been murdered," I say, "no one would ever have known about Angela."

"Not if you hadn't found the body," he takes the report from my trembling hand, "which I'm sure you weren't meant to," and puts the paper into the folder. "By the way," he says, "you were right, Angela was pregnant. About three months."

I jump at the loud knock on the outer door. "In here," calls Davis.

"You wanted to see me, Lieutenant?" Reggie, all square-jawed and hair-gelled, enters in dress whites. Dudly Doright at Sea.

"Reggie, this is Morgan Taylor."

"We've met." His voice drips acid. "Interesting message you left on my door."

Message? The gouge? "You think I keyed your door?"

He's already turned his back. Arrogant. So damned arrogant. I don't remember what I say or how I find strength in my legs to get up and out.

I stop in a washroom and splash cold water on my face. What was Angela doing with a jerk like that? His kind of self-important arrogance—so comforting in brain surgeons and jet pilots—is nauseating in this married man whose pregnant girlfriend was murdered.

Oh, lord. Did he kill her? The room sways off-kilter. I grip the edge of the basin to steady myself. Did Reggie find out she was pregnant and kill her? No. Can't be. Not from the casual way Lt. Davis acted toward him. Reggie must have a bulletproof alibi for the day Angela died. And it's possible Angela never told him about the baby. I wet a paper towel, press cold water on the back of my neck. Will the news that Angela was murdered, that she was carrying Reggie's child, have any effect on him? I doubt it.

"Smarmy," Grandma Belle would call him. "Expects women to fall at his feet so he can step on them." I know women who are pushovers for this type. And, yes, okay, maybe in high school I fell for one. In my defense, I was young and stupid and didn't know what to watch out for. But, I'm a quick study, learned that particular lesson early and well. And I would have warned Angela about him, if she'd lived.

A crew works in my old cabin, scrubbing, disinfecting, painting. An incantation wouldn't hurt. I peek in. The inside is stripped down to nothing but the beds, desk, and chair. Sean comes down the hall. "Are you following me?" I ask.

"I was about to ask you the very same." He looks into the cabin. "Have they found the fool who did this?"

"Not that I know of."

"I hope they get him soon. Security lads have been crawling like mountain goats over everything into everywhere. Makin' my crew jittery as grooms. I'll be glad when this is over. Get our lives back to normal."

"Remember that Russian?" I ask. He looks puzzled. "The one you gave a tour to?"

"Ah, the Russian. Yes."

"Someone saw him down here before this happened."

He shrugs that off. "He seemed harmless enough. Just the curious sort. Course, I'm a lousy judge of character. Comes from having so much of my own." He winks and limps briskly down the passageway.

Elaine isn't in our cabin, which gives me space to move around, hanging and stowing the donated clothing. The same clothes fairies who gave me purple ruffles have also been kind. I pull out beige chinos and a white middy blouse. The colors are off—I'm strictly winter: red, black, aqua, khaki—but at least I won't look like an escapee from *Bozo's Circus*.

An hour before the first show, I'm locking up the cabin when our cabin steward stops me. "Some of your clothes they are ready," she says. "From your old cabin? Washed up oh so nice. You want I should bring them and leave them on your bed?"

"That'll be great." I wonder what survived the attack. The way my luck's running, I'll probably get back the things I hate.

WHAT? AND GIVE UP SHOW BUSINESS?

ON GUEST Talent Night, the entertainment staff wear the same outfits, sparkly green-and-blue shirts and stretch slacks. Somehow, in the rush to alter Angela's show costumes for me, Rosa and Rhea forgot to do this ensemble. It swims on me. I tuck and roll and tighten as best I can but I feel like Harpo Marx. It might be funny if only I could forget it was Angela who last put this on.

Kathy hands out assignments backstage. I'm one of the "cheerleaders" working the aisles, keeping things festive as the amateur entertainers do their thing. "We have some seriously talented passengers," says Kathy. "I've skimmed the cream off the top and put together a solid show: singers, dancers, musicians, and comics."

Kathy's looking way too happy. Methinks my buddy's in love. My promise to Lt. Davis not to tell anyone about Angela being murdered was easier to make than it will be to keep. I'm sure the whole crew will find out soon enough. But it feels like lying not to say something to Kathy. She puts an arm around me. "Hey, Hopalong, how's your ankle?"

"Better. I'm thinking I'll be able to do a show in a couple of days."

"I'd love that. But right now Dominic needs you more." I groan. "I know, I know. Just hang in a little longer. I may have a line on a Magician's Assistant who can come on for him the week after next. Meanwhile, I'm having a blast being onstage. It's been too long since I've performed."

"Might you be showing off for a certain English teacher?"

"Lawsey me, Lucy Mae," she says, finger to dimple, "whomsoever do you mean?"

She's definitely showing signs of her old enthusiastic self. Now I'm glad I made that promise to Davis. Telling Kathy that Angela was murdered would take the edge right off her happy. "Polsky's cute," I say. "Seems nice. Doesn't foam at the mouth. Best of all, the two of you have one heck of a 'how we met' story to tell your kids."

"He's also from Minneapolis," she says. "Snow. Sleet. Sub-zero."

"Builds character."

"Builds frostbite. I'd have to wear boots, gloves, long underwear."

"Yes, thank you, I would love to be your maid of honor as long as I get to wear a puffy-sleeved antebellum dress and painful pointy-toed high heels dyed to match that will set me back three months' pay and I'll only wear once." She jabs me with an elbow, in the nicest possible way.

I work one of the back doors, handing out programs to the first-seating passengers pouring into the theater. I keep a nervous watch for Pimm but don't see her. I also don't see Uncle Leo or his new "friend." The crowd, over a thousand strong, quiets as the overture begins. The curtains part and three twenty-something sisters jitterbug onstage belting out "The Boogie Woogie Bugle Boy from Company C." Theirs is that great close harmony that cheered our nation through World War II. They're followed by a medley of dancing couples, each allotted one minute to perform their specialty: jitterbug, mambo, swing, Charleston, finishing up with a seventy-year-old Cuban couple dancing an incredibly sensual tango. "Uncle Miltie," a retired octogenarian attorney, performs a comic routine stolen verbatim from the borscht belt. When he exceeds his allotted time, Elaine runs onstage dressed as Little Bo Peep wielding a giant shepherd's hook. She chases Uncle Miltie around trying to "hook" him off the stage. The audience loves it.

A piano player rolls an upright on stage. It's Uncle Leo. The sickly pallor when I first saw him in Nassau has browned to a robust tan. The newly exposed skin on top of his head glows sunburn red. He sits at the piano, plays a few jazz chords. I've never seen him play the piano in front of anyone but family. Stagehands roll a bar and stools, used as saloon props during Country Western Night, center stage. A passenger dressed as a bartender carries on a tray of glasses and a bottle of scotch. Uncle Leo keeps playing as the man sets up his bar.

Susan Gayle strolls on from the wings wearing a skin-tight metallic blue evening gown. She casually drags a white fox stole along the floor behind her. The audience buzzes. If she never does one more thing, she's already a hit. But, as Uncle Leo plays the intro, she sits on the bar stool and sings:

"It's quarter to three,
There's no one in the place, except you and me.
Set 'em up, Joe.
I got a little story you oughta know."

Hers is no casual talent. This is a woman who knows her way around a song. I, who have studied all the tricks of this particular trade, listen as mesmerized as the rest of the audience. Near the end, I squirm uncomfortably as she turns toward Uncle Leo and sings:

"We're drinking, my friend,
To the end of a brief episode.
Make it one for my baby,
And one more for the road."

And as she finishes to wild applause, dragging the fur offstage left while Uncle Leo rolls the upright offstage right, it hits me that it's a really good thing Aunt Bertha's not here. It's bad enough she's used to being the star of the family, the flash and the flirt. If she saw Susan Gayle coming on to Uncle Leo like this and Uncle Leo enjoying the heck out of it, she'd go ballistic.

I catch him in the wings after the second show. The beautiful Miss Gayle is nowhere around. "You were great," I say, giving him a huge hug.

"I just wanted to see what it's like from up here," he says, glowing. "I was so nervous. Look at me." He raises his arms. Huge circles of sweat stain his shirt. "Do you still get nervous?" he asks.

"Every time."

"I mean, I've spent my whole life as an observer. I thought I'd check out the other side."

"And?"

"It's nerve-wracking." The freight elevator rattles up and he helps the stagehands load the piano. The elevator rattles back down.

"You off to the disco?" I ask, poking my nose where it doesn't belong.

"Nope. Got a bag of black licorice and a great book waiting. I need to rest up for tomorrow. Never been to Puerto Rico."

"I saw you today," I say, nice and casual. *With that home-wrecker,*

I think but don't say. The wise part of me says to stop right here. The stupid part plunges ahead. "Did your friend enjoy the island?"

"Yes, Miss Nosey, she did indeed."

Caught! "I don't mean to pry."

"Sure you do, kiddo. It's all right. I'd do the same." He fakes a left jab to my jaw. "Don't let this get to you, Mimi. It's between Aunt Bertha and me. We both love you. That won't change. This has nothing to do with you."

He walks off into the sunset, carrying his shiny head high and proud. His exit line sounds a lot like the scripts my friends' parents read just before they divorced. It's what parents say to help kids keep from feeling guilty. Never works. My friends spent years trying to think of the one thing they could have done or been or said that would have saved everything. It's the kind of mental tumult that keeps psychologists employed and psychobabble therapists flooding the airwaves.

I cut through the casino on my way back to my cabin. Miss Susan Gayle sits at a blackjack table next to a James Bond type, her hand lightly brushing his as they place their bets. She's changed into a peach chiffon blouse with a low-cut crisscross bodice that gives 007 a perfect view of her mounded cleavage. Busy lady. Strolling the beach with Uncle Leo by day, torch singing after dinner, flirting with Bond into the night. I don't get it. Maybe I'm not supposed to.

On my way out, I check on the Elvis living in the diorama underfoot. He and the mermaid are still entwined. It's good to know some relationships are constant.

FINDERS KEEPERS

I NEED SLEEP, don't function well without it. After last night's hippopotamus fiasco, I have some serious catching up to do. I pass the
door to my old cabin, which has been propped open to air out the
smell of dead chicken and new paint. An overwhelming sense of dread
washes through me as I avert my eyes and hurry past. A few doors
down, I stop. My family has this thing about facing fears head-on.
Remounting the horse that threw you. Getting back on the same stage
where you bombed the night before. Eating Tanta Hanna's brisket two
Passovers in a row. If I don't go back and confront that cabin now, it
will haunt me the rest of my life.

I walk back, gathering spirits of dead ancestors around me like a
shield as I step into the denuded room. Fear plays tag along my nerves,
shoots erratic pulses to my heart. I dare to inhale. Paint. All other
odors have been exorcised. Spots of wet paint still glisten on the wall
next to Jackie's bed. Someone threw a sheet over her thick custom
mattress to protect it from paint splatters. I lean across the bed, touch
the place where the hatred was scrawled.

"Ouch!" Something sharp pricks my leg. I pull off the sheet, run
my fingers along the mattress edge, feel the tip of a pin. Kneeling, I
lift the mattress off the box spring. The mattress is made in two parts—
a twin-sized quilted pad that piggybacks a regular twin mattress. I
remember when this design first came out. Mom bought one for her
and Dad. It cost a fortune, which was bad enough, but the salesman
neglected to warn her that the corners of her old fitted sheets wouldn't
be deep enough to cover the mattress-pad combo. She had to buy new.
And, since Uncle Steven's Bed and Bath Discount Store tended to lag
ten years behind current fashion, Mom was forced to buy the new
sheets retail. Retail! It hurts to think about.

For some reason this mattress has been flipped over. The quilted
part, designed to be on top to cushion sleeping bodies, is wedged
between the mattress and box spring. The extra section, which is sewn

onto my parents' mattress, is attached to Jackie's with Velcro. I pull it off. Someone has cut a slit side-to-side across the center. Something hidden inside creates lumps and bumps. Laughter erupts in the hall, voices joking in Spanish. I jump up, shut and lock the door, pressing my ear to the door until the voices fade away.

I lay the pad out on the floor. Trembling, I slide my hand inside the opening and pull out four jewelry boxes. Each is wrapped in a pink receipt. My hands shake as I open the long box with the coffee stain. It is Jackie's ruby and emerald Christmas bracelet. I unfold the receipt. It was purchased in Miami from the Casa d'Oro for forty-five hundred dollars, cash. A pearl-and-diamond choker was purchased for two thousand dollars two weeks ago at the Casa d'Oro in Puerto Rico. The receipts list a chain of shops in Miami, Nassau, and Puerto Rico among others. One of the boxes is empty. I feel around inside the quilting, find the thing that stuck me—a diamond-and-pearl lapel pin. It must have fallen out of its box when the crew was cleaning the room.

Large manila envelopes are also hidden inside. I open one, slip out statements from a couple of Bahamian banks. The deposits, all different amounts, are made weekly, a few thousand dollars at a time. I've never, ever, had this much money in an account at one time. You'd think someone with this kind of money would be taking a cruise, not working on one.

I pry open the clasps of another envelope and shake out a collection of photos. A bunch of snapshots, rubber-banded together, are the kind a tourist might take to show the folks back home: the Port of Miami dock, straw sellers in Nassau, cranes loading containers onto the ship, even a shot of Dominic wheeling his Vanish Box off-ship.

The second batch is much more interesting. The grainy black and whites were taken with a high-power lens. They show Jackie in sexually explicit embraces with a variety of men: Jackie and men frolicking nude in a waterfall on the private island; Jackie and men screwing in quiet coves along the ocean; Jackie and men in secret and hidden and private places where no one would see them. No one, that is, except the photographer she hired to record the moment. All of the men's faces are clearly captured. I flip the photos. Each bears a name, address, and date. Most bear dollar amounts, which vary photo to photo.

What we have here, ladies and gents, is blackmail pure and simple. I have found the mother lode. Whoever trashed my cabin was looking for either the jewelry or the photos or both. No wonder Jackie worked cruises. They provided a never-ending source of cash cows. Move over, Mr. Rolex-Armani. Make room for an entire group of men who had motive for murder.

I've got to get this to Lt. Davis. I wrap everything in the paint-spattered sheet and take it to the security office. The giant I'd seen this afternoon is still on duty. He's looking tired and testy. "The lieutenant's gone to sleep," he says.

"This is important."

"So's his sleep. Lieutenant worked forty-eight hours straight. My orders are not to wake him unless he's on fire."

"Tell him he's on fire."

He cracks his knuckles one at a time. "Must be full moon. A passenger just came in here, said the same thing. Someone ripped off his cell phone. I don't call that a fire."

"This," I set the sheet of goodies on the desk, "is a fire."

I start unwrapping the sheet when it hits me that I don't know this guy. Any joker can put on a uniform. Wasn't my kleptomaniac cousin hired by Northbrook mall security? What's to say it wasn't this guy's eye behind the camera that took these photos? Who's to say he didn't line up the pigeons that feathered Jackie's coop? Yes, I'm overtired and yes, I don't suffer Napoléons like this gladly, no matter how big they are. There's a long list of reasons I'm not feeling particularly trusting at the moment. I re-wrap my bundle. I'm not showing this to anyone but Lt. Davis. He's a friend of Roblings. That, I trust. Until I can talk to Davis, Jackie's stash is safe enough in my room, under my mattress.

I pick up the bundle. "Okay. The second he wakes up, tell him I've got something important to show him." I leave my name and cabin number. At least Napoléon has the courtesy to write them down.

ELAINE SNORES SOFTLY, earplugs in, eye mask on. She's left on the lamp for me. The clothes from my old cabin that somehow survived desecration by feces, sacrificial chickens, nail polish, and shampoos, clothes that were not torn or slashed, bent/spindled/mutilated, lie neatly folded on my bed. Our cabin steward has organized piles according to type: underwear, skirts, blouses, dresses. Jackie's silky whatnots mix with my Carter's cottons. Melon-colored skirts and tops blend with my Danskins. And perched atop the dress pile is the aqua cotton dress with big bold butterflies, as magnificent as the first time I saw it five days ago, a lifetime ago.

I tuck Jackie's jewelry and photos under my mattress and dress for bed. A series of rapid-fire thoughts race through my exhausted mind.

—*Who was that thug I saw Jackie arguing with on the Port of Miami dock, him all broken-nosed, puffy-eyed, thick-lipped?*

—*Was he another of her blackmail victims?*

—*Is it possible he killed Jackie?*

—*Might my suspicions of Rolex-Armani have sent the cops looking in the wrong direction altogether?*

—*Is the person who killed Jackie the same person who killed Angela?*

—*Dare I "borrow" the deceased Miss Jackie's butterfly dress until such time as she might ask for it back?*

Only this last has a clear answer.

DAY SIX

THE MOTHER OF MAGIC AND MURDER

CHITA RIVERA BLASTS ME awake.

"I like it here in America. Okay by me in America."

"Oops, sorry." Elaine dials down the volume. "Can't come into San Juan without 'West Side Story.' Sleep okay?" I nod. She dances off to the bathroom, singing alto harmony. Perky is annoying first thing in the morning. I bury my head under the pillow trying to retrieve a dream, grab at the ends of it. It disintegrates. I'm going to sleep in. Laze around. I'm gonna—

Knock on the door. Dominic calls, "Morgan?" Another knock. "Morgan, you in there?"

"Yummmawannaummmb."

"We've got to rehearse for tonight."

"Righhhhhht."

"Meet you in the theater in half an hour?"

"Perfect."

My morning mind, which awakens snail-paced in microscopically small increments, has all the razor-sharpness of toasted marshmallows. This is an actorly trait. If I need to remember something before the crack of noon, I have to stick huge notes where I'll positively see them—on top of the closed toilet seat or in the middle of my makeup mirror. For early auditions, I have family or friends call to be sure I'm awake in case I sleep through my three clock alarms, which I've done. And I put my house and car keys on top of whatever thingamajig I'm supposed to take—music, sides for a play, audition monologue— so I don't leave anything behind. Last night, I left Jackie's dress hanging out to remind me that I have to go face Lt. Davis with the news I might have been a bit hasty fingering this Rolex-Armani character.

Elaine pokes her head out of the bathroom. "If you get a chance, don't miss the rain forest," she says. "It's really beautiful in a 'Jurassic Park' kind of way."

"I have rehearsal."

"Yeah, me, too. Kathy wants to go over 'Live and Latin.' It's not like she hasn't danced it with us a thousand times just for fun. Anyways, you should try and go there next week."

Next week? Right. We get to travel this route all over again. And all over again. Gerbils on a wheel.

I pull the covers back over my head and am seriously flirting with the idea of sliding back into sleep for just a second or two when Elaine's joyous rendition of "Officer Krupke" gets me up and out. I dress for rehearsal, then putter around, stalling until Elaine leaves. The second she's gone, I lock the door and pull Jackie's photos and jewelry boxes from under my mattress. Just touching her things makes me feel dirty. I stuff them into Angela's lizard bag and take them to security. Can't wait to get them out of my hands and into Davis'.

"He's out," says the new guard on the desk.

"Out!? He can't be. Didn't he get my message?"

"He sort of rushed out this morning." He wets a finger, shuffles through papers on his desk, uncovers a stack of messages. Mine is near the bottom.

"I have to see him," I say. "It's urgent."

"He's off-ship. He said something about going to the police station in town. I don't know if he's still there."

"Look," and I put my note on top, "I'll be in the theater rehearsing. If he comes back, tell him I need to see him immediately."

"Sure thing."

DOMINIC'S TIMING this morning sucks the big one. His body is here but his mind is one taco short of a combination plate. For a while he goes through the routines on auto-drive, which takes you only so far in the magic business. There comes that moment of truth when an illusion either works or fails. And this depends entirely on split-second timing. Dominic fumbles locks, snags fabrics, misses cues. He blames me.

"You're not concentrating," he says. Guilty. I have a few unpleasant things on my mind. And the theater air is arctic. It's hard to move quickly with frozen joints and numb skin. I work harder. "You've got the beat wrong," he says. "You're moving too slow."

We try again. And again. And again. It takes an hour but I'm finally hitting every mark exactly. Even this master of misdirection can't make it appear the fault is mine. Sweat glistens on his forehead. His skin's turned that waxy white of Jackie in the duffel.

"This isn't working," I say.

"If you'd only—"

"*I'm* not the problem."

He slumps against the table. Feathers fly up from the doves hidden below.

"Dominic?"

"I don't feel well," he says, sweating hard.

I pull scarves from the wand, blot droplets from his face, neck. Heat pours off him in waves. "You're burning up," I say.

"I'll be fine."

"Wouldn't bet on it. You go see the doc, I'll stow the gear."

"No, I'll—"

"You can barely stand. Do I have to personally lead you?" As if I could find the way.

He points with trembling hand. "The freight elevator is there, just beyond the wings. Be careful with the tripod stand when you—"

"I can do this blindfolded," I say, closing up shop. "My brother paid me extra to clean up after our act, which brought my pay to about two cents an hour."

This wins a faint smile. He nods in the direction of his menagerie. "The animals?" he asks.

"I'll take them to my cabin. You can pick them up after you see the doctor."

"But, the show—"

"I'll tell Kathy you're sick. She can't risk you infecting the rest of us. We'll figure something out."

He wobbles off. If he has the flu, as close as we've been working, I'm next in line. Oh frabjous joy. Can hardly wait to layer the flu on top of seasickness.

I push, pull, and wheel Dominic's equipment through the wings to the elevator as the troupe files in to rehearse tonight's "Live and Latin." The familiar work of breaking down a magic act transports me back to those glorious days of yesteryear when Margenon the Magnificent and his beautiful assistant Wanda performed magic most marvelous.

—"*What kind of name is Margenon?*"

—"*It's a stage name, Grandma Ruth.*"

—"*Your brother's name is Paul. After my father, of blessed memory.*"

—*"It's only for when we're performing. Margenon sounds more mysterious."*

—*"It sounds like a butter substitute. And Wanda? This by you is also mysterious?"*

—*"Ask Paul. He made it up."*

The unfamiliar terrifies Grandma Ruth, she breaks out in cold sweats, passes out. I stopped mentioning Margenon and Wanda.

Half an hour later I bring down the last load, tucking equipment in and around the other show props stored down here. The nearby engine room vibrates the floor underfoot. The space smells musty, old food smell, something chemical. Chemical toilet. That's the smell, that's what I remembered from camping with my family. The ship must use something similar. We kids hated that smell. Used to go in the woods. That stopped abruptly, as did our trip, when my sister wiped herself with a leaf of poison ivy. I retrieve the lizard bag from where I stowed it in the Vanish Box. The stench is fading but not forgotten. I still may have to rip out the lining.

I stop to hit a few chords on the upright piano Uncle Leo played in the talent show. It's funny how you don't pay attention to the quiet ones when squeaky wheels are around. I've known Uncle Leo all my life, but I've seen him mostly through Aunt Bertha's critical eyes. He was too quiet, too shy, lacked her ribald brand of raucous enthusiasm. That doesn't describe the man I saw up onstage. I reckon I don't really know my uncle at all.

The connecting door opens to the storage hold. Sean O'Brian brightens when he sees me. "Ah, darlin', that's a relief. I thought I was imaginin' music."

"This is getting spooky," I say, playing a run of spooky chords. "It's like our lives are running on parallel tracks."

"Well, now, down here is my world, so you can't be accusin' me of following you. And," he tilts his head at the piano, "it seems a strange place for you to be practicin'."

"I was just stowing Dominic's gear," I say. "I tend to get distracted."

"This dungeon could use a bit of music but I think you'd best be off. Cargo tends to shift around down here. Wouldn't want you hurt."

I sling the lizard bag across my body. Sean watches with interest as I remove the animals from their stage cages, zip the boa constrictor into a backpack, then cradle the rabbit in my left arm and the bird cage in my right. He waits as the elevator rattles back up to the theater.

Dancers stretch onstage. A few singers warm up together. Kathy's sticking a partially smoked cigarette back into the pack. "Down to three a day," she says.

"Packs?"

"Ho, ho. Serves me right for falling for a nonsmoker." She eyes the extinguished cigarette longingly.

"I hate to add to your load," I say, "but Dominic's sick."

"You're kidding, right?"

"Before you panic, I just happen to have a twenty-minute medley of female vocal impersonations that would fit perfectly between acts. I do a mean Streisand, Midler, and Minnelli, and on a good night I can out-Cher Cher."

"You sent me a copy of the tape, remember? That would be perfect. And I bet you just happen to have your music."

"Does a bear play cribbage in the forest? Your guys can do it cold. If you want, I can rehearse now."

"Can't. How about coming to the theater around five, run through it then?"

"Sure you don't need me now?"

"Go walk around town. San Juan is very romantic. Unfortunately, I'm here and Michael's there." She flops over, shaking out her arms and torso. "And, thanks. You're a lifesaver."

I tote my menagerie across the stage. Keith sits backward on a chair, chin resting on folded arms, staring out into the empty theater. It's as if Jackie's death has sucked the joy out of him. *She's not worthy*, I want to say. *She was a mean-spirited, game-playing tease.* If I showed him the blackmail photos I'm carrying, he'd know. But that might destroy him altogether. Grandma Belle says, "Sometimes the Lie is kinder." Unfortunately, the Lie only works if Truth doesn't come to call.

I TAKE THE STAIRS DOWN, cutting through the hall housing the Purser's Office, and security.

"He's still out," says the guard. "I promise, I'll give him your message."

Wherever he is, I know Davis is coming down hard on himself for letting Angela's murder slip by. It's ironic that back in Chicago, Roblings is walking that same self-flagellating road. His discovery of three or four separate serial killers working the South Side means reinvestigating all those murders he didn't think were connected. They both blame themselves but there are other forces at work. Misdirection is the mother of magic and murder.

I turn into my hallway. Dominic staggers ahead, bracing himself against a wall.

"Hey," I call.

He looks worse than before. His eyes are ringed red, the left eye swollen. A deep cut puffs his lower lip. The sour smell of sweat clings to his clothes. "Fell," he explains.

"What'd the doc say?"

"Didn't see him."

"But—"

"He wasn't in. Look, I just need sleep."

The rabbit squiggles like crazy. Dominic takes it from me, nuzzles its fur. I help settle him in his cabin, square away the livestock, then bring a cup of hot tea from the mess along with a few aspirins. "I'll check back," I say, shutting the door softly behind.

I shake off a pang of guilt. I could do more. I could give him cold compresses, help him into dry clothes, scrounge blankets to cover him, take the animals to my cabin, and care for them until he's better. I could do any number of thoughtful, helpful things, but I don't. Why do people assume women are natural caregivers? I'm not. Never have been. Not since I was little and my "dying" grandfather moved in with us, taking over my room, banishing me to dwell in the basement where the wild things lived. Grandpa "died" with us for twenty more years. I don't trust sickness. Don't cater to it. It's not my job.

I make a quick stop in the infirmary on my way out. The nurse peers at me over plastic half-glasses attached to her neck by a chain of small seashells. "I'm not sure when the doctor will be back," she says.

"Would you ask him to stop in and check on Dominic?"

"For?"

"You saw how sick he is."

"I've seen no staff at all today," she says. "And I've been on duty since seven."

"Well, would you ask? He's pretty bad."

And I'm out of there. Okay, so maybe Dominic stopped in the office while the nurse was in the loo, saw that the doc was out, and felt too sick to wait. Or, maybe he never stopped in the infirmary at all. And, if not, where was the magic maker all the time I was stowing his gear?

I am overwhelmed by a sudden need to get off-ship. I am prone to mild claustrophobia in small elevators and the occasional voice-over sound booth. Just now, I feel a nervous buzz as the walls of this world press in. I pat the lizard bag, slung safely across my body, as I walk down the gangway. I'll wear it until I can deliver it into Lt. Davis' hands.

Twenty minutes later I've seen everything Puerto Rican there is to see near the ship, which isn't much. You've got your water, you've got your basic old stone wall. But the air is fresh and the winds are good and I find courage to begin broadening my vistas. The mobs of people are a comfort. I stay aware of who's around me, behind, on the sides. Sort of the same way I walk back home.

Signs posted along the streets point to the major shopping areas. The faithful move in joyful procession toward the Promised Land. I fall in line. As long as I'm in town, it won't hurt to find this Casa d'Oro, maybe stop in and see if they remember Jackie. Who knows, perhaps they can tell me something about the men who bought her such lovely jewelry.

"Miss Nosey," Uncle Leo called me. That would be right.

WHAT'S THE POINT OF NO RETURN?

DON'T ASK ME WHY I expected to find Casa d'Oro among the enclave of San Juan's exclusive jewelry shops. These are the reputable places touted by the cruise line, where eighteen-carat gold really is and "diamonds" don't turn into glass when you have them appraised back in the States. These are, in short, the shops that attract great swarms of tourists, hardly places Jackie would take her more married gentlemen friends.

Unfortunately, now that the idea of tracing Jackie's movements has taken hold, I can't seem to shake it. The pearl and diamond choker was recently bought from the Casa d'Oro here in Puerto Rico. Someone might remember something. I flag a taxi, give him the address. He drives for ten minutes, leaving the crowded streets behind as he follows narrow roads up gentle hills. I'm feeling a little less brave as commerce gives way to neighborhood. We go entire blocks without seeing anyone. It makes sense that Jackie sought out-of-the-way places to take her gentlemen friends. But this place is so remote, there's little chance of accidentally running into anyone not guided by Sherpa. I'm rethinking this idea when he stops on a street of charming stone buildings shaded by arbors of huge trees. "This is it," he says.

The buildings look more like homes than shops. "Will you wait here for me?" I ask.

"How long?"

"Five, ten minutes?"

"You pay what you owe now," he says. "I'll wait, have a cigarette. If you're not back when I'm ready, I'm going."

I give him the money. As soon as I get out, a man flags him down from across the street. The cabbie takes off. So much for oral contracts.

—*Why are we doing this?*

—*Because she bought a necklace here and what can it hurt to just take a look at this place?*

—*Were we followed?*

I scan the deserted streets, listen for cars, footsteps, helicopters. All quiet on the paranoia front.

The real truth is I'm curious.

That's what killed the—

All my life, I've run into a certain kind of person, a Jackie kind of person, who knows how to manipulate the world to satisfy her needs. She's charming and ruthless, flattens anything in her path. I've gotten in the way a time or two and have the scars to prove it. She's amazing if she's bright. She's dangerous if she's not. Jackie learned the hard way she wasn't as bright as she thought.

So, yes, I'm curious. Here I am carrying a bag that holds a small piece of Jackie's life. She'd still be running her scams, raking in jewelry, squeezing new victims for blackmail money if someone hadn't killed her. What's the harm in just going in and taking a look?

Casa d'Oro is one of several shops occupying the ground floors of old apartment buildings that ring an enclosed courtyard. The courtyard's wrought-iron door is locked. I knock. No answer. A metal chain hangs above the door. I pull it and a bell echoes inside. Almost immediately, a uniformed guard appears and demands something in Spanish. I pull a Casa d'Oro jewelry box from my bag so he can see I am a bona fide client. The door swings open and I sweep in as if I know where I'm going.

The guard, an Uzi held casually at his side, watches as I stroll the courtyard. I surreptitiously search for Casa d'Oro while pretending to admire the mosaic fountain, the multitudes of flowers, the looming presence of giant urns. Flowers overhang terra-cotta planters that line the apartment balconies above. You could shoot an 1800s film in this courtyard, if you keep the satellite dishes out-of-frame.

I nearly miss the shop. No character. No style. Casa d'Oro is wedged between two equally anonymous storefronts. Darkened glass windowpanes act as mirrors, giving up nothing of the shop inside.

—Okay, you're here. What next?

—Improv.

I knock on the door and am buzzed into a room barely fifteen feet square. It smells of wet clay and incense. Sophia Loren's clone works behind the counter—pouty lips, high cheekbones, hourglass figure. She raises an eyebrow when I enter, not slowing her telephone conversation as she looks me up and down, deciding in milliseconds that I am not worth her time.

The counter, a long glass case displaying mediocre jewelry, shows nothing approaching the quality of the pieces I'm carrying. A couple seated at one end of the counter carefully inspect a tray of emeralds compartmentalized by size. The woman picks some out and sets them on a piece of gray felt. Hers are the soft-skinned, perfectly manicured hands of a woman who does not do dishes, change diapers, or otherwise function in the real nail-breaking world. Her companion reminds me of the wealthy young Turks I waited on at the Board of Trade restaurant. Casa d'Oro, it seems, is where the seriously rich go to buy jewelry. Jackie's kind of place.

Sophia glances up as I set my bag on the counter. "One moment," she says in Slavic-accented English, resuming her conversation. I study a display of gold charms. One resembles the design of the charm I found wedged in Dominic's Vanish Box.

A small man dressed like an undertaker emerges from the back and sets another tray in front of the couple. Rubies this time. He lifts his eyebrows slightly at me. "How may I help you?"

Good question. "What is that?" I ask. "That Oriental character?"

"Ah." He sets it on a black velvet display board. "It is a symbol for safe travel. Extremely popular among our Chinese clientele. Much like we might wear a St. Christopher's medal. It is of interest?"

"Actually," I take out the pearl and diamond choker and hand him the receipt, "I came here for this."

He frowns at the receipt, lifts the necklace out of the box. "Where is Jackie?"

He knows her! Knows this was her necklace, even though her name's not on the receipt. "She, ah, couldn't make it. Asked me to come."

He waves me down to the end of the counter away from the couple. "Wait here," he says, disappearing into the back.

A minute goes by. The woman on the phone talks nonstop. Another minute passes. I don't like this. Where'd he go? Does he think I stole the choker? Is he calling the police? My heart dances something jerky.

The shop door buzzes open and Mr. Garlic Breath walks in. He's followed me here! I clutch my bag, look for an escape door.

"Meeeessshhhhka!" shouts Sophia, rushing to him, throwing her arms around the place his neck would be if he had one. She covers his deadpan face with kisses, then slips her arm through his, whispering conspiratorially as they head out the door.

I breathe again. Garlic Breath aka Wilbur Tompkins aka Mishka has come here for her, not me. I don't think he even noticed me. And if he did, he didn't recognize me. You know how it is when you see someone out of context. I relax my death grip on the bag. I have to curb this overactive imagination of mine that—

Garlic Breath turns slowly as the door closes, his coal eyes boring hard into mine. The door clicks shut. This scene is starting to feel way too Alice down the rabbit hole.

The small man returns with a large quantity of money. He counts out eighteen hundred dollars. "Please sign," he says, pointing to the receipt I brought in with the necklace.

I check the amount. "You're short two hundred dollars," I say.

"Yes, yes," impatient now to have me, a déclassé nonbuyer, out of his shop. "I take ten percent, same as always." The couple call him over. "Wait," he tells me, going to tend to business.

The pile of cash smiles up from the counter. Jackie was a busy, busy girl. A besotted lover buys her jewelry one week, she returns it the next for cash. Just an old-fashioned sentimental gal. The money looks real tempting sitting out all naked like. But I can't leave the choker and receipt. Jackie was murdered, after all, and a hard-nosed cop like Lt. Davis might consider these items evidence.

The man comes back, frowns at the unsigned receipt. "Is there a problem?"

"Um, I'd better check with Jackie. She didn't tell me about your cut. I'll get back to you."

He scoops up the money. "You know," he says quietly, "if you're interested in the same deal, I get ten percent of the retail price of any sale, and all pieces must be returned to me within two weeks of purchase, in pristine condition."

"What about pieces bought at other Casa d'Oro shops? Can I return them here as well?"

"Yes, of course. It is all the same...family."

I pack up the necklace and escape into the courtyard. It is deserted except for the guard and his pet machine gun. Garlic Breath and Sophia have vanished. Have they ventured out to explore the streets of San Juan, or did they, perhaps, retire to one of the lace-curtained apartments above? All right, so maybe he didn't follow me to Casa d'Oro. Maybe, like Jackie, the Russian has a taste for expensive jewelry and exotic playmates. Maybe he cruises this way often, which is how he knows Sophia. And maybe he has nothing to do with Jackie's death.

But I'm beginning to feel a lot like Lt. Davis when it comes to matters of coincidence. I just don't trust them.

STREET WALKING

THE STREETS OF the old city swarm with shoppers. My ankle, nearly back to its sassy self, was fine walking down from Casa d'Oro but doesn't take kindly to the jut of uneven cobblestones underfoot. I am paying more attention to the ground than where I'm going and come within inches of bumping into Uncle Leo. He's window-shopping with Miss Susan Gayle very much on his arm. Luckily, they are totally engrossed in a display of old maps. I back away, ducking into a side street. I don't want Uncle Leo to think I'm following him.

—*Like you thought the Russian was following you.*

—*That is a totally different kipper of herring.*

The narrow backstreets twist and turn until I don't have a clue where I am. I keep hoping for sight of water but each new street leads into another just like it. Finally one of the streets opens into a square. An ancient church commands one side. Wrought-iron benches are set around a cobble walk framing the grassy center. Toddlers chase a ball on the grass under the watchful eyes of mothers and grandmothers. Ida Mills sits on a bench, her cane resting on her lap, watching the children play. I stop to say hello.

"I just saw that darling magician," she says, patting the bench next to her.

"Dominic?"

"Lovely man. It was so sweet of you to ask him to do that little show for me the other day. My husband used to do card tricks like that. Oh, my dear, the hours he practiced. Close magic is a special talent, don't you think?"

She tosses out bread crumbs from a bag. Birds flock immediately. Dominic is back in his cabin, too sick to lift his head off the pillow. She must be a little confused. At ninety-three, she's entitled. She probably saw him earlier on board and just mixed the time in her mind.

"Have you been enjoying the shows?" I ask.

"Oh, I haven't seen any as yet. Might I ask how much it costs?"

"How much what costs?"

"To see a show. This 'Live and Latin' sounds such fun. I thought I might treat myself."

"You think you have to pay for—"

A rubber ball bounces up and rolls under our bench. A laughing toddler runs after it, hesitates when he sees us. Ida prods the ball out with her cane and picks it up. With great ceremony, she holds it out to the child.

What a dear woman. I could cry. I've heard of first-time flyers who refused the meal because they thought they had to pay extra for it. It makes sense. Is popcorn included in the price of a movie ticket? Do legitimate theaters give free drinks? Why *should* a person assume food on an airplane or shows on a ship are included in the fare? Like Grandma Belle says, "You can't know something until you know it."

The child, emboldened by Ida's smile, inches closer, then grabs the ball and runs off laughing.

"You just come," I tell her, "enjoy the shows. There's no charge."

"You mean they're free?" I think she'll be upset but she starts laughing, laughing so hard the birds fly off. "Oh...please," she says, trying to catch her breath, "don't tell...anyone. How terribly, terribly foolish of me."

"No. Someone should have told you. Your travel agent, your cabin steward."

"But don't you see? Everyone assumed I knew. And I've been too proud to ask, until now, you being in the shows and all...." She wipes her eyes with a handkerchief.

"You're not angry?"

"Oh, my dear, there are so many true horrors in this world, I will not waste one single second over this." She squeezes my hand. "One of the things I've learned in my many years on this planet is that anger does more damage to the vessel in which it is stored than to the thing over which it is poured."

And I leave her to her birds and the children, feeling calmer than I have for days.

Polsky sits on the curb near the bank of phones at the dock. At first I think he's waiting to make a call but a couple of phones are open. When I get closer, I see he's crying.

"Michael?" I rest a hand on his back. "Michael?" He looks up, sobbing. "What's wrong?"

He's quiet a long time. "She was murdered," he says softly.

"Who?"

"Angela. I just called home."

"Angela Parker?" He nods. "You knew Angela?"

"We grew up together. Her brother, Tom, is my best friend. Angela was like a little sister." He digs the heels of his palms into his eyes, rubs hard. "Tom and I booked this cruise as a surprise, to come spend a week with her. Tom's been worried about her, said she seemed unhappy. I told him he was just an overprotective brother. Then we got the news that she'd died. He never believed it was an accident." He pulls in jagged breaths. "I just talked to him. The autopsy report came in. Looks like he was right."

I sit next to him, take him in my arms, rock him gently. He cries for a long time.

"Who's the guy?" he says finally.

"What guy?"

"She was pregnant."

I hedge. "You know I wasn't around then." Reggie may be obnoxious but that doesn't make him a murderer. I don't think it's smart to turn Polsky loose on him. Not while he's this agitated.

"Kathy told me Angela was going with some officer," he says.

A dim light begins to penetrate my dense. "You've been using us," I say, "to get information. All this time. That first morning you came up to me on the dock in Nassau, that was no accident. You knew I was one of the entertainers."

He nods. "I saw you leave the ship. Remembered you from the show the night before."

"And when you found out I didn't know Angela, couldn't give you any information about her life on the ship, you moved right over to Kathy. She's the head of Entertainment, the woman who hires and fires and acts as Mother Confessor. What could be better?"

"It's not like that," he says.

"It's exactly like that."

He buries his head in his hands. "Oh, God," he rocks back and forth, "oh, God. I didn't expect any of this. I'm only here because Tom begged me, after Angela died, to come on the cruise, just like we'd planned, see if I could find out what really happened."

"You had no right to use Kathy like that."

"I swear, I'm crazy about her."

"You've used her."

"You have to believe, I never meant to hurt anyone."

"I'm not the one you need to convince."

PHOTO OPPORTUNITY

LT. DAVIS IS BACK in his office. I set my bag on his desk.

"Lunch?" he asks.

"These were hidden in Jackie's mattress." I slide the candid photos out of the folder. The harsh overhead lights lend a certain biker magazine flavor.

Davis whistles. "She was a busy lady."

"You have no idea." I turn one over. He scans the dates and dollar amounts.

"Ah, the smell of blackmail in the mornin'."

"This may be why she was killed, why our room was ripped apart after she was dead. Someone could have been looking for these."

"Interesting idea."

"That's not all." I pull out the boxes of jewelry, describe my visit to Casa d'Oro.

He is not pleased. "And just what the Sam Hill are you doing playing cop? What if something happened?"

"Nothing hap—"

"Did you bother telling anyone where you were going?"

"No, I—"

"Listen to me, Morgan. Listen hard. We're dealing with two homicides here. Someone, maybe even two different someones, are out there playing for keeps. You could have wound up zipped in a duffel and no one would ever know."

A walkie-talkie crackles on his desk. "Lieutenant? They're pulling up now."

"Roger that." He jumps up. "You, come with me," he barks, running out the door. "I'm not done yelling."

I'm out of breath by the time Davis and two of his men reach the dock where Ichabod and his buddies are unloading a van. The wheelchair is unloaded and the "disabled" man is helped off. You'd never guess he could walk. The group looks nervous as Davis and his men move in.

"Gentlemen," says Davis.

"Hello," they say, trying to look nonchalant. Lousy actors all.

"May I?" Davis nods at one of the men's sports bag. The man glances at Ichabod, then hands it over. Davis sets it on the ground and unzips it. A turtle the size of a Chicago softball frantically works its flippers trying to climb up the sides. Davis opens another bag, exposing an iguana with a nose horn. "And that," says Davis, pointing to the large cooler still on the van. It is brought off and set in front of him.

Ichabod's solemn group shift foot to foot studying their shoes like little boys called to the principal's office. Davis lifts the lid. A large lizard is crammed inside the cooler, unable to move. Its black eyes stare up at us. Davis nods.

"Martin," he waves over one of his men, "call Manuel's office and tell him to get his people down here right away."

"Right."

Davis unzips the other bags. Lizards, snakes, things that go hsssss in the night. "You gentlemen really ought to check before buying wildlife off the street. Basket venders and rain forest tour guides don't always know what's legal to bring into the States. Now, I'm not the expert on rare and endangered species, but I've got a Mr. Manuel Ortega coming who keeps up on these things." One of the men looks about to faint. "He'll let you know if you can bring any of these in. I sort of doubt it. If you'll all be kind enough to wait here with my men until Manuel comes, I'd appreciate it."

Davis ushers me back on board, striding forcefully through the hallways. I trot to keep up. "Pack of amateurs," he mutters. "They're lucky I have a couple of homicides on my plate.... If they were smuggling cocaine, I'd have their sorry asses in jail in two seconds. But smuggle Peruvian turtles, rhino iguanas, island boas, exotic birds, and the worst they'll get are fines and a slap on the wrist. Burns my cork."

"There's money in that?"

"Three billion a year, give or take. Second only to drugs. Although, at the rate we're pulling Cubans and Haitians out of Florida waters, smuggling humans may just beat them all."

"What's going to happen to them?"

"My guess is Manuel will put them back on-ship. He's more interested in stopping the big dealers than a bunch of jerks adding to their own collections. Guys like that aren't worth the paperwork. But it will do them good to stew in their sweat awhile."

"You may want to check out the wheelchair," I say.

"We're ahead of you on that. You can cram a lot of birds and eggs and snakes into metal tubing. I know it doesn't look it, what with Angela being murdered and all, but not everything gets past me." He sits back at his desk, still cluttered with Jackie's photos and jewelry. "Now, where were we?"

"You were thanking me for bringing you all this wonderful information."

"I was chewing you out for putting your life at risk." He flips through the photos. "Thanks for expanding my list of suspects."

"I have another one," I say. "Jackie had a fight with a guy on the dock in Miami." He gives me a hard look. "Hey, I forgot all about it until last night when her butterfly dress came back from the cleaners. See, she was wearing—"

He holds up a hand. "Spare me. Is this joker on board?"

"No. He has a face like a punching bag, not something I'd forget."

Davis upends my goodie bag, shakes out the packet of small photos. "What are these?"

"Just some snapshots," I say.

He lays them out on the desk. "Something hidden in a dead woman's mattress isn't 'just some' anything."

He studies the photos as if they're pieces of a puzzle. I point to the Port of Miami shot of kibitzers watching a crane loading cargo. "This is where I saw Jackie arguing with the guy."

"Mmmnnnn." He pushes the photos around, picks up the one of Dominic. "Any idea why this?"

"Jackie was his assistant. Maybe it's a memento."

"I don't think Jackie was the memento type. What's this thing?"

"Vanish Box. He uses it when he does charity shows."

"He's a funny kid, comes off tough, but he really took it hard this morning, when I told him about Angela being murdered."

"You told him?"

"What, you think you're the only one I'm going to tell?"

"When?"

"Early. I wanted to set up appointments this afternoon to question everyone who was on the ship when she died. I caught Dominic on his way to rehearsal."

"He didn't say anything to me."

"And I'll bet you didn't say anything to him." He has a point. He puts the photo down. "Do me a favor," he says. "Don't go off-ship anymore today. I've got enough to worry about."

"Roger that." I stop at the door. "You know, Angela's brother always thought she was murdered. He sent a friend—"

"Michael Polsky. Nice guy. Came to see me the first day. I told him her death was an accident pure and simple."

"I just saw him. He called the family, knows she was murdered."

"Yeah." He hunches over the photos. "Yeah."

NOW YOU SEE HIM, NOW YOU DON'T

DOMINIC DOESN'T ANSWER. I've knocked twice. Nothing. The container of hot tea I'm bringing from the mess burns my hand. I knock again.

—*What if he's sleeping?*

—*What if he's dead?*

—*Where'd you get so dramatic?*

—*Look who's talking.*

"Dominic?" I knock harder. "Dominic?" His cabin steward pokes his head out of the cabin next door. "Whazzup?"

"Dominic was real sick this morning," I say. "Now he's not answering. Could you take a peek and see how he's doing?"

"Sure thing." He unlocks the door.

Dominic's not answering because Dominic's gone. So are the rabbit, the snake, and the doves. The tea I brought this morning sits untouched on the desk. A couple of dresser drawers hang open, odd bits of underwear and clothing dropped on the floor. It has the look of panic packing.

"He's usually not this messy," says his steward.

"When was the last time you saw him?"

"Not since early. Maybe he went to see the doctor."

"And he took the animals along because... ?" Neither of us has an answer for that.

AND THE WORD FOR "FEMALE CUCKOLD" IS...?

THE BACKSTAGE ELEVATOR rattles down to the storage area. *"I just saw that darling magician."* Ida told me, but did I listen? No. Because it made no sense. A man who can barely stand doesn't go traipsing off with his livestock. All I can think is, delirious with fever, Dominic staggered into town to perform one of his hospital charity shows. I can picture tomorrow's headlines:

> *San Juan Daily News:* Item:
> EPIDEMIC SAILS IN ON CRUISE SHIP:
> Disease-ravaged magician
> contaminates men, women, and
> children of all ages.

It's easy enough to check. If Dominic's doing a show, he'll have the Vanish Box with him.

It's dark down here. Faint light filters from the freight elevator's shaft, casting eerie shadows. I slide my feet along the floor, feel the wall for the switch. I ram my shin into a box. This space has more clutter than Grandma Ruth's attic. It also has zero ventilation. The smells—old sick, rancid food, strong chemical—gain strength in the dark.

The shadow of the Vanish Box looms large among the stored items. All right, so Dominic isn't doing a show in town. Then why take the animals? Why pack some clothes? A niggling thought starts to work its way in. No magician, especially one with this kind of financial investment, runs off without his equipment. Unless he's terrified of something. Or guilty of something. Or dead. What if Dominic's not in San Juan? What if...

The elevator behind me suddenly clanks and whirs, lumbering back up, stealing away my light. I find the switch, blink against the bright fluorescents. Has the Vanish Box been moved from where I left it this morning? I run my hand over its cool lacquer.

—I know what you're thinking

—It's only natural—after Angela and Jackie's murders...

The well-oiled bolts slide back noiselessly. I feel around inside for the spring release. Okay, I can do this. I force myself to hit the release. The hidden panel flips over. I jump back, braced for dead magician and assorted animals. No bodies fall out.

—You are so macabre.

—I prefer "dramatic."

The freight elevator bangs back down. Pimm staggers off. My early-warning system kicks in full force. Gone is the healthy animal who was strong enough to pedal us both around an island. This woman's eyes are bloodshot wild. Her ninety-proof breath could sterilize a wound. And something rabid has molested her nest of black hair.

She scans the room, spots me on the other side. "Hey, slut."

It's the vitriolic voice of the Nassau moped rider.

"What are you doing down here?" I ask.

"Came to hurt you the way you've hurt me."

"What are you talking about? I barely know you."

She weaves toward me through the detritus, bumping into boxes, stumbling over props. I back away, keep the distance between us. Serpentine. Serpentine.

Her upper lip curls into snarl. "You've been screwing my husband."

Roblings may have secrets, but I don't think a demented wife is one of them. His voice comes to me: Sometimes you have to out-crazy the crazies. I thrust up my arm like the Statue of Liberty and burst into an impassioned rendition of "Give me your tired, your poor, your huddled masses..."

She snarls, unfazed. "He's been sticking it in you, then coming home and sticking it in me. I would say that makes you and me pretty *fucking* close." Her hysterical laugh ends in a high screech, talons down a chalkboard.

I recite louder: "Give these, the homeless, tempest-tossed, to me."

"Pretty fucking close. That's funny, isn't it? Especially since you don't use condoms. Do you, whore? What's the matter? Against your religion?"

My singing's not distracting her. Tough audience.

A sudden explosion of sound rips through the room. Everything vibrates. Down the hall, the ship's engines fire up for departure.

"Look, lady," I shout, "Pimm, whatever, I don't know your husband."

"He knows you—biblically speaking—brought home a little gift from you—a little herpes. That's how I found out. One of us has been faithful in our marriage." That laugh again. It ices my nerves. "The stupid one. But I'm done being stupid. It took a detective about three seconds to find out who you were. I figure it's time for you and me to cut out the middle man."

"Oh, I don't think my agent would stand for th—"

"I'm going to fuck you directly." She lifts up the kind of cleaver butchers use to hack very large animals into very small pieces.

"Wait, wait, wait," I say. "Let's talk this—"

"What's the matter, Angela? Scared?"

"Angela? You think I'm Angela?"

My dense mental curtain rises. The scene comes clear. Reggie's wife stands center stage. I take a hard look, can almost make out the woman in his family photos, now ten years older, without theatrical makeup, cheap shampoo-in dye covering blond silk.

"Pimm, you have to listen to me. I am not Angela."

She staggers at me sweeping the cleaver in wide arcs. "If it walks like a whore, talks like a whore, acts like a whore—"

"Angela is dead."

She snorts. "Then why were you living in her cabin?"

"I was brought in to replace her."

"Oh, yeah?" Smiling as if she's caught me in a lie, "Then why are you wearing her name tag?"

"Mine isn't ready. The cruise line makes employees wear—"

"Liar, liar, pants on fire! I saw you. I saw you go into his cabin."

So, that's who keyed Reggie's door. "Angela is dead," I say. "Someone killed her."

"Not yet. But I mean to." Light glints off the blade. "The way you killed me. Pimm is dead. Long live Pimm." That maniacal laugh again.

Okay, so I'm getting the feeling we're not going to be doing lunch any time soon. We've circled the room, back to where we started. She's blocking the elevator. My only clear shot is the hall door halfway between us. She's strong, could beat me there, but the fact that she's drunk gives me an edge. The elevator cranks and whirs alive behind her. She spins around, startled. I'm out the door and into the hallway running as hard as I can.

GENTLEMEN, START YOUR ENGINES

THE NOISE OF the engines is deafening out here. Even I can't hear my screams. Worse, I've turned the wrong way. Two simple choices, left or right, and I picked the same dead end as before. Pimm explodes out of the storage room behind me, brandishing the cleaver as she shambles toward me. I yank open the door to the engine room, flinch at the jumbo jet roar.

"Help, help!" I'm out on the catwalk, running and screaming and waving my arms at crew working two decks below. Between the noise and their earplugs, there's no way they can hear. They're busy making preparations to get under way. No time for idle chitchat or to watch today's episode of "Leave It to Cleaver" wherein Reggie's wife hacks Angela's stand-in into itsy bitsy pieces.

Pimm stumbles through the door onto the catwalk. "Help," I yell down. "Help!" Paco crosses the engine room below. "Help!" Miracle of miracles, he looks up, smiles. He seems to be recovering nicely from the shock of Angela's death. Wonder how he'll feel about mine. "Help!" I wave frantically. He waves back, keeps walking. Exit stage right.

Pimm's gaining on me. I race along the catwalk, plunging through the doorway to the cargo hold. The cavernous room is deserted. No Sean, no Russian, no busy little crewmen wheeling boxes of supplies. My feet clank on the catwalk as I run to the stairs, race down, dive between rows of cargo as the door above bangs open.

"I know you're here, slut," screams Pimm. I peek out from between crates, see her weaving unsteadily. *Thwack*, she bangs the cleaver along the railing, *Thwack*, makes her careful way down the stairs. I duck back out of sight. *Thwack*. With each step, she clangs the blade against the metal handrail. *Thwack*. The sound zaps like electrodes. The good thing is—

—*Can't wait to hear this one...*

—*As long as she makes noise, I'll know where she is.*

I move on little cats' paws in and around the cargo. The red container cars with the Chinese symbol stand closest to the door leading to the bike hold. If I can get to the bike hold, I'm home free.

Thwack. She's down here, prowling, banging, taunting. "Come out, come out wherever you are."

I ease around the end of the container car. Metal ladder rungs lead from ground to roof. A duplicate car, set above this one, rests on two thick beams. The beams create a space between the cars. Big enough, I think, for me to squeeze into, small enough to keep me hidden.

Thwack. She's coming. I scramble up the ladder, stretch flat on my belly, and snake between the cars.

"Ollie, ollie ocean, freeeeee," she sings. *Thwack.*

Don't let me die, don't let me die, don't let me die. Not here. Not like this, like some human Oreo cookie, my cheek shmushed against the car below, the car above scraping my back.

Thwack. Metal blade reverberating on metal car. *Don't let me die, don't let me die, don't let me die.* Please, I promise to make more charitable donations, give up my bus seat to the elderly and pregnant, repay the IRS for waitressing tips I may have inadvertently forgotten.

Thwack. What if the container car above me crashes down on the one below? *Don't let me die, don't let me die, don't let me die.* This space lacks the vast expansiveness of an MRI machine. Air movement is nonexistent. Odors trapped here are a thousand times more foul than in the storage room. They seem to waft up from air vents cut into the roof below.

Thwack. Each strike cuts through me. *Thwack.* I have zero wiggle room. If she finds me.... *Don't let me die, don't let me die, don't let me die.* Not like this, not trapped like Bubbe Dubbe's Passover carp, kept alive in the bathtub until she was ready to make gefilte fish. *Thwack.* My heart rages against my ribs. I stop breathing.

She bangs along this car, hesitates for an eternity, then moves on to the next. My sweat joins the pungent mix. Unbearable. If she doesn't kill me, this stench will. I breathe through my mouth, trying not to think about the tonnage of railroad car pressing down from above.

"Hey! You there!" A man's voice! I strain to hear. The voice comes closer. "Get away from there."

"Where is she?" Pimm's voice.

"There's not a soul here but you and me."

"I followed that whore in here."

"Whore, is it? Ah, sure we have any number."

Sean's brogue is the sweetest sound in the universe. Thank You, thank You, thank You for gifts received. I nearly call out but she's wielding that cleaver, it might be dangerous to distract him. Best to let Sean handle her. An old salt who's tamed drunken sailors can certainly manage one demented woman.

"Would you mind describin' her," he says, "so I can help ya look?"

"Don't you humor me." *Thwack.*

"I assure you, I'm deadly serious, I am. And I'll thank you kindly to stop damagin' my cargo. Now, love, who exactly is it we're lookin' for?"

"Angela."

"A friend of yours, is she?"

"Don't patronize me!" *Thwack.*

"Listen, darlin', the only Angela I ever knew was an entertainer."

"That's the whore."

Silence. I wish I could see what's going on. "She's dead," Sean says.

"If she's so dead," her speech thick, "how come I followed her in here?"

"You're confused."

"You're trying to trick me. You're in this with her."

"Darlin'," his voice soothing, gentle, "I'm not in anything with anyone. But I can see you're upset. We need to—"

Something rams against the container car. Pimm shouts, curses. Sounds of a struggle.

"Let me go!" she screams. A clattering...the cleaver falling, skittering along the floor.

"Let me go! You're hurting me. Put me down. Stop it." And her voice, "Put me down," sobbing now between screams, "Please," trails off, "please," traveling far and wee until it's silenced completely by the shutting of a door.

PRECIOUS CARGO

THE ADRENALINE that poured steel into my backbone flows out in a rush. I lie drained and lifeless atop the container car. Minutes pass. I feel floaty, my mind drifting in euphoric slow motion.

More minutes. I toy with the idea of getting out of here, try moving my hands, feet. Too much effort.

I risk opening my eyes. Mistake! I'm entombed in this airless place. *Don't panic, don't panic, don't panic.*

I shut my eyes, concentrate on breathing—*calm in, fear out, calm in, fear out.* Slow, now, slow. My heart winds down and tucks itself in place. I imagine the sound of footsteps against the muted engine's roar. I imagine singsong voices drifting up from below. An eternity passes. I'm sure the coast is clear but there's no shame in being double/triple/quadruple safe. What harm waiting one more minute?

I've never seen rage like Pimm's, not even during rush hour on the Kennedy Expressway. Now I understand the raw fury that destroyed my—Angela's—cabin: "SLUT!!" "WHORE!!" It had nothing to do with someone searching for Jackie's blackmail photos. It had everything to do with Reggie's having "a little on the side," "a quickie," "a little roll in the hay." Sounds such fun. What harm after all? Enough, I reckon, to destroy the mother of his children. What was it Ida said? "Anger does more damage to the vessel in which it is stored..." Looks like it shattered Pimm all to hell. I personally think she should have taken the cleaver to Reggie. And, oh, that poor chicken, brutally sacrificed for nothing. Angela was already dead.

Already dead? Who killed her? Obviously not Pimm. Unless she killed her and forgot. No, I think murder is something you'd remember. I've got to get out of here. I wriggle backward, working my way out from between the cars. I risk opening my eyes again. Dim light shines up from vent holes. Why is there light inside a cargo car? I press my eye against one of the vents.

A sea of faces stare up at me. Men, women, children. Terrified faces. Chinese faces. None of us moves.

AN IRON HAND clamps my ankle, pulls me roughly. I claw wildly for something to hold on to as I'm yanked out from between the cars. My hand whacks against the top rung of the ladder and I grab hold, dangling off the end of the car like a monkey, hanging on for dear life. Garlic Breath stands a few rungs below, his face expressionless as he calmly reaches up and, one by one, pries open my fingers. I drop fast and hard, crack my head on the floor. It's a bad sound from inside. Blood-taste fills my mouth as the world turns black.

"You bleedin' fool," says Sean, I think to me.

"Shut the fook hup."

I open my eyelids a slit. Pimm's cleaver stares me in the eyeball. It's come to rest just out of reach under the container car wherein the smuggled Chinese live. And my family thought *their* crossing was rough. Give me your tired...

"What are you up to?" Sean's angry.

"I said, shut hup!"

I move my eyeballs, no easy trick, see Garlic Breath and Sean nose to nose. The Russian grips a gun at his side. Ugly gun, all hard-lined and gray metal. If form follows function, this baby's a killer. The cold floor feels good against my cheek. I wait for Sean to rescue me. I'd do it myself but I've had a rough day and I'm dizzy and my body doesn't seem interested in moving.

Sean clenches and unclenches his fists. Come on, Sean, put this moke away. Let's you and me celebrate our imminent departure from Puerto Rico.

"Brilliant!" says Sean. "You plan to kill everyone on board, do ya? Is that your brilliant plan?"

This dialogue's wrong. It sounds as if they know each other.

The Russian rams his fist against Sean's chest, sends him reeling. "I said for you should shut hup. She saw."

"Saw what, you worthless ape? Cargo. Look around. There's nothin' here to see but cargo."

"She vas spying, like other girl."

Other girl? What other girl?

"She was hiding," says Sean. "A crazy woman thought she was

someone else, chased her in here. This girl doesn't know any more than Angela did." Angela? "You don't have to kill her, too."

I'd like to second that.

"I am not open for discussion. I deliver you firearms, you deliver my cargo."

Oh, Sean. Are you tradin' weapons for humans, then? Not you of all people. Here's to the auld sod, please pass the bullets. And if we hit a pregnant woman on her way to buy bread—well, that's war, now, isn't it? Heavy sadness elbows next to my fear.

Someone's shot eightpenny nails into my head, jabbing pain in all directions. From my ant's-eye view, I watch Garlic Breath's shoes walk toward me. Step by step. They could use new half-soles and a good polishing. Sean's crepe soles follow. I'm probably late for rehearsal. Very unprofessional. I'll have Mommy write me a note: The Russian ate my gym suit. Pimm's cleaver shines a come-hither glint. Hey, I'm not that kind of girl. And what use would it be against the Russian's AK30000?

The men begin dancing. Their feet swirl and twirl and jump in exotic steps. It's so nice when friends get along. While they're dancing, I'll just scooch over and rest my hand on the cleaver.

Little by little...

They grunt while they dance. Bad form. You want to make it look effortless.

inch by inch...

They crash to the ground, grappling, Sean clasping Garlic Breath's wrist. For an instant, the barrel of the gun points directly at me, lines up exactly between my eyes. If he pulls the trigger now... Pain rips the place the bullet will go. Going to tear me a third eye, he is. Sean lunges, his steely arms forcing the barrel up and away. Thank you, thank you, thank you, my friend. You're not like the other terrorists.

slow and steady...

The two men tussle over and around. No style, no form. But, I must say, both highly enthusiastic.

...wins the race.

I close my fingers around the handle, feel the heft of the cleaver. The pounding in my head keeps time with the ringing in my ears.

Sean is on top of the Russian, bashing him with iron fists. The gun explodes. I scream. Both sounds ricochet off crates and walls. The two men freeze. Tableau surprise. Then, ever so slowly, Sean collapses, his head lolling to one side, eyes wide at the shock of it all. His body goes slack in the Russian's arms. I watch in horror as a red rose blossoms on his shirt, a bouquet pools on the floor around him.

No, no, no. Come on, Sean, get up. Please. I grip the cleaver tighter. Garlic Breath lies still, chest heaving. He's out of shape for this kind of murder. A defenseless pregnant girl was easy, a bitchy blackmailer no effort at all. But it's hard work killing someone like Sean, a passionate patriot conditioned by a lifetime of war.

I force myself to sit up, stand, clutching the cleaver to my chest. Garlic Breath looks over at me the way you'd look at something unpleasant on the bottom of your shoe. Sean's body lies across his arm, on top of the gun. His last act on this earth was to save my life.

—*Gone home to Ireland, have you, Sean?*

—*Oh, darlin', can't you see I've never left?*

The ship's warning horn sounds. We'll be under way soon. Garlic Breath shoves Sean's body off his arm, retrieves the gun. A drop of Sean's blood drips from the barrel. This man is going to kill me now.

He swings the gun in my direction. I raise the cleaver. My mama didn't raise no victims. I cock it back over my head like a football and hurl it at him with all the strength I have. It spins end over end in slow-mo. He steadies the gun with two hands, is pulling the trigger as the back of the cleaver hits his shoulder full force. The gun flies from his hand and scuttles across the floor, disappearing under a pallet piled high with crates. He looks around for the cleaver. This is my exit cue.

I run toward the door, grip the handle. He's on me, pulling me off, throwing me to the ground. I struggle to get up. He straddles me. I'm screaming now, clawing and kicking as he sits on my chest, pins my arms with his knees.

Can't move. I'm being crushed by a boulder. I keep screaming, try to shake him off. He's deadweight. I should be so lucky.

He bends forward, wraps his fingers around my neck. His expression never changes—strangling me, killing Sean, eating borscht, it's all the same to him. His thick thumbs press into my throat. Hey, this hurts. I can't breathe. I jerk my head, trying for clear breath. He's too strong. I feel consciousness slipping away.

Adrenaline pumps. My brothers never strangled me, but they sure pinned me this way enough times. I have one possible move. With my last strength, I swing my strong dancer's legs up and over Garlic Breath's head, hook them under his chin, yank him backward off of me.

Air. Fresh air. Horrible wheezing sounds come from me as I suck jagged breaths. He's tearing at my legs. I hold his head in a vise, squeezing hard as I can, not daring to let go.

The ship's horn sounds again. The engines roar louder, gearing up to set sail. His dead eyes snap alive, go wild with panic. Somewhere a door clangs. Somewhere a voice calls out. I try screaming but only squeaks come out. He punches my body, meaty fists ramming my groin, stomach, chest. I can't keep hold of him. He prizes open my legs, staggers to his feet.

For a terrifying moment, Garlic Breath looks down at me, then over at Sean's body awash in blood. The final warning horn blares. He may be dumb, but he's not altogether stupid. The instinct for survival is strong, even among Neanderthals. It's clear to us both that if he stays to kill me, he'll never make it off-ship. He glances at the container car. There are three billion more Chinese where these came from.

He lumbers out of the hold, his shoes stomping a trail with Sean's blood.

I'D LOVE TO GET YOU
ON A SLOW BOAT TO...

IT'S NEARLY MIDNIGHT by the time Roblings comes back from Davis' office and settles into the chaise next to me. The balcony of our immense stateroom—reserved, paid for, and abandoned by Mr. Rolex-Armani—looks out over the star-filled sky. Moonlight plays on the water as we steam back toward Miami.

"You could have at least told me you were going to solve the murders," he says. "It would have saved me the trip from Chicago."

"I know. I hate to see you suffer like this," I feed him a strawberry the size of my fist, "but the lieutenant didn't tell me he had asked for your help."

"I told him not to. Wasn't sure I could get away. Besides, I didn't want to cramp your style."

"You're my style."

"Yeah, I think so, too." He slips his hand in mine and we listen to the distant waves slap against the ship.

They've added a day to the cruise, extra time needed in Puerto Rico to take care of things. Once again I gave my description of Rolex-Armani, who they think is part of the smuggling ring. No one holds out much hope of finding him or Garlic Breath any time soon. The smuggling operation used to dock in Canada until that got too hot. There's no telling how long they've been operating in the Bahamas. Now, they'll just pack up shop and move somewhere else.

Sean's body will be flown back to Ireland. I told Lt. Davis about the metal cases Sean offloaded from our ship onto the private island. They were munitions cases, I realize now, arms given by the Russians as payment for smuggling the Chinese. The boxes were gone by the time the police checked. One thing I know as sure as I breathe, Sean never took a penny for himself in all this. I am a living testament to the strength of his character.

Pimm was freed from the brig, where Sean had stowed her after he'd wrestled the cleaver away. He'd had the kindness to put her in the padded cell, where she couldn't harm herself. Reggie's been given emergency leave to take her home. I watched as she left the ship. She was so heavily sedated she had to be supported on both sides to get down the gangway. I know she came at me with a cleaver, but I have to tell you it broke my heart to see her like that. The beautiful young actress so proudly displayed in Reggie's cabin is dead, my friends, killed by an arrogant husband. I don't think he'll like the creature I saw rising from her ashes.

But the worst moment for me was watching authorities lead away the Chinese illegals. Their clothing was no more than tattered rags. Some of them were so weak they had to be carried off on litters. Mothers clutched children, husbands embraced wives. I can't begin to imagine the horror of their journey.

"Where are you?" asks Roblings.

"I'm thinking that using cruise ships to smuggle illegals is a brilliant idea."

"No one ever accused these guys of being stupid, just ruthless."

"It's so sad. Such a long hard way to travel. If you could have seen how they were crammed together." Their terrified faces haunt me, the stench of rancid food, human waste. "A few more days and they would have made it."

"To what? Working as slave labor in sweatshops to repay the fifty-thousand-dollar smuggler's fee?"

"It's not right that people aren't free to live their lives."

"Bleeding heart liberal." He feeds me a grape.

"No, just the descendent of immigrants who also, by the way, started in sweatshops."

He refills my goblet with an amazing red wine hand-carried from his private cellar. We clink glasses.

"What will they do to Dominic?" I ask. When authorities picked him up at the airport, he admitted using his Vanish Box to carry bodies of dead and seriously ill Chinese off the ship each week.

"They'll detain him in Puerto Rico until they decide how much of an example they want to make of him."

"I wonder why he did it?"

"He said the smugglers threatened him. I don't doubt it. The Russian Mafia are seriously bad people."

"They killed Jackie?"

"Mnnnn." He accepts another strawberry, pauses to nibble my fingers. "She caught Dominic wheeling a body off-ship, forced him to tell her about the smuggling, then tried to blackmail the Russians."

"Big mistake."

"Huge. They had to kill her. But another death on board so soon after Angela's would have raised all kinds of red flags. The smugglers couldn't afford to have authorities snooping around the ship. They made it look like Jackie ran off with one of her rich admirers."

"And I loused it up by finding her body."

"You're a real spoilsport."

"Did Dominic know they killed her?"

"He swears he didn't. But he had his suspicions. When he found out Angela was also murdered, he panicked. Figured they'd kill him sooner or later."

We are lulled by the wine and the balmy night air. I run a finger down Roblings' much-broken nose, trace his delicious mouth and the small scar on his chin. "I have an uncle on board I'd like you to meet," I say. "Uncle Leo."

"Bertha and Leo." Roblings never forgets names or faces. "He and I spent an hour talking computer crime at your family picnic. He's the one with the camouflage hair."

"Not anymore. And Aunt Bertha's not with him. I think they're going through a rough patch."

He lifts his left eyebrow. "And you'd like me to find out?"

"You're so good at getting people to talk."

"Helps if I have a rubber hose. Besides, I'm not sure I want to share you with anyone. We don't have much time."

"Don't remind me."

Roblings trickles a finger along the shell of my ear. No fair, he knows what that does to me. When we dock in Miami, he'll head back to Chicago and I'll stay on to finish my contract and give Kathy some serious moral support. Polsky has told her everything and she's deciding how she feels about it, about him, about them. He somehow arranged to stay on our cruise for another week and is determined to try to make things right with her. I have a feeling I'll be going to a wedding in Minnesota. I only hope they wait until summer.

"Tell me again what's back home," I say.

"Five degrees below zero, thirty-five below with windchill."

"More."

"The worst ice storm in forty years, downed telephone lines, ice-coated tree branches crushing cars."

"More."

"And me." He takes my hand, kisses my fingertips one by one. "I'm back home."

"But not right now," I say. "You're mine for another whole day."

"At least."

"At least."

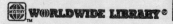

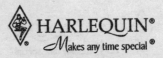

Elizabeth Gunn
SIX-POUND WALLEYE

A JAKE HINES MYSTERY

It's a gray, bone-chilling February in Rutherford, Minnesota, and bad moods are contagious. Things go from bad to worse when a schoolboy suddenly collapses while waiting for the bus and is pronounced DOA from a gunshot wound to the heart.

For detective Jake Hines, spring is still a very long way off. When a call about the shooting of a dog provides Jake and his team with the missing link, things start to heat up—and bring a killer's blood to the boiling point.

"Gunn's latest is a hard-to-put-down thriller—an excellent piece of craftsmanship."
–Publishers Weekly

Available July 2002 at your favorite retail outlet.